Jugnu

The Firefly

Ruchi Singh

ISBN 9798886067705

Books By Ruchi Singh

English

Novels

Romantic Suspense

The Bodyguard - Undercover Series # 1

Guardian Angel - Undercover Series # 2

Romance

Jugnu - The Firefly

Take 2 - Small Town Girl #1

My Love, A Liar - Small Town Girl #2

Bewitched

Short Stories

Women From Mars : Series Shorts

Temptation

Spark

Hearts & Hots - Series Shorts

Head Over Heels

You and Only You

Silent Love

A Promise is a Promise

Jugnu

(The Firefly)

by

Ruchi Singh

Published by Ruchi Singh 2017

All rights reserved.

Ruchi Singh asserts the moral right to be identified as the author of this book. 'Jugnu - The Firefly' is a work of fiction and any resemblance to actual event, real persons, living or dead is purely coincidental.

First Edition, Version 1.0 © Ruchi Singh 2017

18 March 2017

The sight was out of a movie when all of a sudden she turned the main lever and they were flooded with blinding light. Both Shankar and the kid clapped, elated, with what appeared to be a ritual.

She came down the ladder but stopped with a jerk mid-way, her descent hindered by something. They looked up to find the dupatta entangled in one of the nails. She tried to pull it but it was stuck.

Zayd took a step forward and stood on his toes to disentangle the garment. A whiff of something feminine assailed his senses and her breath fanned his neck. A muted desire fluttered inside him. He looked down; she was looking at him, exasperated and apologetic. Her eyes black, moist, looked a wee bit tired… and sad.

Something in that glance tugged a chord in his chest. His inhibitions and worries lost their relevance and faded away.

"Mamma, I wanth to shleep." The child tapped her arm.

She immediately dropped her eyelashes cutting off the silent communication.

Zayd noticed red vermilion, the sindoor, on her hair parting and moved back

To

My Parents

Foundation of my very existence and individuality

PROLOGUE

The sun dipped further below the horizon giving way to dusk when the little boy heard the roar. His head snapped up beyond the snow-laden canopy of trees, scanning the sky. The goats bleated in protest as his hand pulled at the leash, but were completely ignored since he had spotted the plane. An exuberant smile appeared on his face.

A plane's twinkling lights always reminded him of a *Jugnu*—a firefly, fascinating him to no end. He forgot the danger of remaining outside and stood gazing at the flight path. The air vibrated and the snow shuddered under his feet in resonance with the powerful thrust of the flying machine. How would it feel to be inside one of them, he thought? Powerful? Important?

He didn't know what kind it was, but he sure knew that it was a unique plane. After all, this was the first time he had spotted such a sleek one. How he wished he was in one of them, flying freely in the sky? Like a bird or like, his favorite, a firefly.

His father hollered from somewhere behind the thicket urging him to come back immediately. The thundering sound of the war-plane did not deter him so much as the thought of spending another night in the smelly, tiny bunker where seven members of his family stayed, not to count the two goats.

His mother had told him to bring the goats back in an hour. But when had he listened to her? He would never have any fun if he did everything his elders told him to do. Moreover, he wanted to savor his freedom for a couple of minutes more before getting into the bunker, where they would be holed up for the entire night and the next day too if the soldiers went onto a rampage.

Back in the village, their cottage stood crumbling under the fresh round of shells fired. When will this end? He wanted to play with the boys from the other side—his friends. They were the only ones he had known.

His father shouted again. The howling wind took the edge away from his threat but the message was clear. Taking a deep sigh, the boy tugged at the leashes and began walking towards the entrance of the bunker.

A moment later there was an ear-splitting sound, followed by a shattering explosion. His heart knocked against his ribs and his hand jerked back as he pivoted to look at its cause. The massive firefly spun on its own axis, spewing fire as a wing disappeared behind the mountain top. Amongst the sound of crumpling metal and a fiery spinning descent, he saw a speck of black jerk out clear, away from the orange fireball.

The next second a huge balloon blew out from that black-speck and dived behind the snow peaked mountains. There was another reverberating explosion and the plane was dissected into two halves. The twisted and mangled wreckage followed the path of the balloon leaving only a cloud of black-grey smoke in its place.

The sky cleared slowly and an eerie silence descended around him as if the whole thing was a figment of his imagination—an entire show pulled off just for his benefit.

Something stirred inside him, something dark and ominous. His heart thumped in his chest, and he raced back to the shelter.

***

ONE

Driving on the National Highway 22 Zayd couldn't shake off the echoes of his father's voice that made him feel like a failure once again. FM 94.3 playing his favorite songs on the car's audio system did nothing to distract his mind from their heated conversation yesterday.

And yet, he couldn't understand, what made him go to that house time and again.

Maybe he wanted to relive the happier memories. Or maybe, he wanted to meet his sisters. Their angelic faces swam in front of his eyes and the pain of losing something precious intensified.

Or perhaps, he hoped that Abbu—for once—would approve of his choices to bring his life back on track. But it would not happen. Not in this lifetime. He had to accept the harsh reality that he would never get a seal of approval from his father.

And all of it was because of that fated night four years ago, when he had ruined all his prospects of following Abbu's footsteps. What his father was not ready to accept that Zayd never wanted to follow the path he had carved out for him. Then, there was Abbu's wife.

Zayd's hand tightened on the steering wheel.

Vowing to enjoy his much-earned freedom, rather than dwell on the past, he pushed up the volume of the stereo. Beyoncé crooned 'Crazy in Love'—the lyrics hinted at not understanding one's inner self. He smirked at the song's timing. *Naanijaan*, his maternal grandmother, often said that he didn't understand himself. The context was different of course, but still…

Suddenly, from the corner of his eye, he saw something small scurrying across the road. Reflexes on automatic, he put his entire weight on the brake pedal. The tires screeched, his heart thudded. After dragging for about fifteen feet his brand new Scorpio came to a jarring halt, missing the object narrowly. The engine coughed, sputtered and switched off. His heart raced in the aftermath of the silence.

Shaking to his bones, Zayd got down, smelled acrid odor of burning rubber. A small child sat on the road, shocked and crying. He shouted at the villagers in the field, more from shock than anger. "Take care of your kids… you… you…" Cursing under his breath, he kicked the front tire. "Damn…"

A woman, covered from head to toe, came running, lifted the child and ran back towards the cluster of huts.

Glaring at the huts, Zayd climbed into the car but couldn't turn on the ignition. His trembling, moistened fingers slipped on the key. What if he had hit the child? Why did he stop? He should have run away. No. The police would have traced him and he would have been back to that hellhole again. The very thought of the prison cell had him sweating all the more. He placed his head on the steering wheel and counted his breaths.

Someone knocked on the window.

"*Bhai, sab theek hai?*" A villager stood looking concerned, and not furious.

Everything was okay. His heartbeat decelerated. There was nothing to worry about. The child was fine. No one was going to send him to jail again. He was out and safe. He nodded at the man in gratitude and switched on the ignition. The music filled the cabin, soothing his frayed nerves.

Following the signboard for Kasauli, Zayd turned left on the national highway and inhaled. The lush green, undulating sub-Himalayan range loomed at a distance like a giant moving kaleidoscope. Endless mountains merging with the picturesque valley took his breath away.

As the beauty of the panoramic view weaved its spell on him, the stress and anger dissipated and were replaced by wonder at the splendid spread of nature. The evening sunrays sieved by arrays of oak trees cast mellowed shadows on the road. Zayd took off his aviators, rolled down the windows and stuck his head out. The pine-fragrant, crisp air caressed his face and ruffled his hair, finally making him forget everything.

Dusk was merging into the night when he drove into the quaint Kasauli town. Though he had expected the cool weather and the divine silence, they still came as a pleasant surprise after the noisy Delhi roads. He knew he had made the right decision to come here and spend whatever time it would take to finish the next project. He switched on the headlights and let the peace seep into his soul.

It was already eight p.m. by the time Zayd had parked his SUV in the hotel parking where he had a room booked. He longed for a leisurely bath and dinner.

As he walked towards the reception, he looked back and admired the black beauty in the parking bay, gifted to him by his *naanijaan*, the only family member he was in touch with from the prison, the only person from whom he accepted anything.

Though Abbu's secretary had briefed him about his more than adequate financial status, he had not touched the money his father had transferred to his account after he was released. He had vowed not to depend on anyone anymore. Especially not Abbu.

Someone came out of the wide hotel doors interrupting his chain of thoughts. Entering the lobby, he moved towards the reception desk and gave his name.

"Zayd Abbas Rizvi."

The man at the reception opened a register.

Zayd felt the hair on the back of his neck rise at the receptionist's tone as he repeated Zayd's name under his breath.

"There is no booking in your name," the man frowned into the register. "No, we don't have a reservation under your name."

Perplexed, Zayd too peered at the register. "How is that possible? I had called and had specifically given today's date. Someone had confirmed as well... er... there it is," Zayd pointed at the open page then scowled. "How come someone else's name has been inserted in place of mine?"

"You must have called to cancel." The man behind the counter declared—a tad quickly.

The man's smug, confident tone irked Zayd. "Then why would I be standing here?"

"Someone on your behalf might have cancelled. We are a reputed hotel sir, we do not make such kind of mistakes."

"And I do?" Zayd couldn't help the incredulity creeping in his tone.

"I didn't say that."

"Don't play word games with me, Mr. Pant." Zayd read the badge pinned to the man's uniform. "I want to talk to the manager."

"Well… he is not in town."

"Who is the next in-charge?"

"I am. And all I can say is that maybe there has been a miscommunication. The room allotted to you earlier is now occupied and we are fully booked due to summer vacations." Pant tugged at his tie and ran his eyes over Zayd's clothes. "You can try some other hotel."

The contrast between the high handed and extremely cocky man and the sophisticated interiors of the hotel amazed Zayd. Did he think Zayd could not afford the room? Yes, his clothes were well worn and not up to the current fashion trends. But he sure didn't look like a charity case. It took all of his self-control to not lash out at the man. A twinge of déjà vu reminded him to keep his anger under control.

Zayd raked his hair with his fingers and ran his gaze over the lobby. He had been driving the whole day, fatigue and hunger made him snap, "Which one do you suggest?"

It was good that Pant shook his head imperceptibly and kept quiet. In any case Zayd didn't want to prolong the discussion that was pulling him towards a full blown anger episode. The doctor's number one advice 'to keep his anger at bay' was to move away from the scene, which according to Zayd's interpretation, meant to take the cowardly way out. But he had learned it the hard way that there wasn't much of a choice the moment his anger surfaced.

He picked up his laptop bag and stormed out of the lobby—so much for the hospitality of hill-towns. Even when the goof-up was at their end, there was no word of apology, even for the sake of formality. Perhaps—

"*Saab… saab…*"

Zayd turned to see a small man in a porter's uniform, running towards him from the far end of the building. Now what?

"*Saab*, I overheard your booking problem. I can take you to a *fandoo* comfortable place, with hot, delicious food." The man tilted his head all the way up at Zayd.

"And why do you think I should listen to you?" Zayd's suspicious Delhi nature came into play at the easy and eager invitation—more so because of the up-handed attitude of the staff back at the hotel. He walked towards the parking bay.

The man was taken aback at Zayd's harsh tone but pressed on nonetheless. "It's a neat guest house *saab*, with huge gardens both at the front and the back," he said, almost running to keep up with Zayd's long strides. "And the food is famous all over Kasauli. People order food for home parties."

"Really?"

"*Ji, saab.*" The man beamed showing his spotless set of dentures with one tooth missing.

Zayd felt the sincerity pouring out of the man, but would it be prudent to trust someone at a new place?

"You will get homemade ginger tea whenever you want," the man added to his sales pitch.

Zayd's stomach growled, as if on cue. He hadn't eaten since the lunch at Dharampur. It was almost nine, and Zayd couldn't resist the offer of the tea. And what could be worse than the prison?

"What's your stake in this?" Zayd unlocked the car and opened the door.

"My wife and son work there," the man said and stood at the rear door. "I sit at the back, *saab*?"

"No, come to the front." Zayd started the car. "Does this happen often? The reservation goof-up?"

"Hmm… *jaane dijiye.*" The man looked out of the window.

"What do you mean let it go?" Zayd turned the ignition off, and frowned at the man, crossing and uncrossing his fingers.

"No, nothing, *saab*…"

"I'll go with you only if you spit it out."

"They needed a room for Kanyal *saab* and yours was allotted to them. He is MLC here. They care little about… er… Muslims—customer or no customer."

He uttered the last few words almost in a whisper, but Zayd got the drift. Exhaling, he switched on the ignition and drove out of the hotel premises.

"What's your name?" Zayd asked.

"Ramprasad," he said and gave directions to the residence, informing Zayd about the guest house, its amenities, and the rates.

The establishment was almost on the outskirts of Kasauli, flanked by a public school and a semi-constructed building in a huge field. Bulldozers and other construction vehicles were parked haphazardly in the field, and the construction material lay dumped all around barring the entrance gate to the house.

Ramprasad jumped from the car and hurried to open the gate, beyond which Zayd could see a single story bungalow. It took expert maneuvering to take the right U-turn to enter. As he took in the surroundings, Zayd's expectations from the guest house came down another notch. In any case, this was just a stop-gap arrangement—only for a day or two—he reasoned. He would shift the moment he found a decent hotel.

But the scene was completely different as Zayd went past the iron gate.

*****

TWO

The paved driveway led to a sprawling, stone-facade bungalow with a sloping, red tiled roof and white trimmed windows. The pillared corridor around the house gave it a colonial touch. Zayd fell in love with the octagonal gazebo at the far end facing the valley. It was a classic structure with a white metal trellis boundary that was laden with pink and yellow bougainvillea, fit to relax on a lazy afternoon.

Ramprasad guided him to a parking space at the end of the driveway. A battered white Maruti 800 car was parked in the cleared space to the right. Zayd parked his Scorpio parallel to the stationary car, again unsure of the wisdom of staying at an unknown place.

Muttering something about the lateness of the hour, Ramprasad rang the bell located between the two identical front doors. The melodious jingle reverberated somewhere inside. Zayd wasn't sure which door would open.

The quiet house, shrouded in yellow lights, gave wings to his imagination. What if it was haunted? Zayd shook his head, dismissing the bizarre thought. He then glanced at the stout Ramprasad who looked nothing like an evil accomplice luring him to Satan's den.

As they waited, Zayd glanced around the premises. The labor behind the well-maintained garden running parallel to the driveway was evident from the thriving plants swaying with the gentle breeze. Dotted with cast iron tables and chairs, it looked inviting in the cool, summer night.

After a couple of minutes of total silence, they heard a click on the door to the right. It opened to reveal a twenty-something lady with a dusky, serene face, a small mole on her left cheek, and her hair loosely pulled back in a knot at the nape. In a pale lime-green salwar-suit with her *dupatta* trailing behind, she definitely looked like a candle-holding ghost. Zayd's imagination, inspired by Bollywood, took another quantum leap.

And the drama ended in the next moment. She was totally uninterested in Zayd. The alert, kohled eyes skimmed over him impassively, then rested on Ramprasad.

"*Saab* wants a room," Ramprasad said. "I have explained everything and the rates too."

Nodding once, she stepped back. Though intrigued as well as unnerved by the silence, Zayd couldn't take his eyes off her.

"I'll get the luggage," Ramprasad said. "The blue room, *didi*?"

She again gave an imperceptible nod and Ramprasad retreated. Trying to distract himself from staring at her, Zayd scanned the large room that looked like a dining hall with three tables, each with a four-chair arrangement. The room was sparkling clean with chairs piled neatly above the tables. There was another door in front, parallel to the one they had entered. Must be leading to the kitchen, he guessed.

The woman moved behind a small desk placed near the entrance and took out a register. A photo of a soldier hung behind her. '*Flight Lieutenant, Rohit Joshi, Mar, 1999*' He read the name below the photograph. Another Brahmin family.

Zayd sensed the lady's eyes on him. She was holding a pen towards him. After four years of dodging the eyes of guards and criminals, it was an effort to look straight at anyone's face.

He tried not to squirm as he met her eyes. "Before you take me on, I must tell you. I'm a Muslim," he blurted then dropped his eyes on the pen.

She nodded and slid the register on the table towards him.

A small teen-aged boy limped into the room. "We have put saab's luggage in fwont of the blue woom."

The lady handed the boy a set of keys.

Zayd tried not to frown at his speech and entered his details in the register. He placed three days' advance on the table. She didn't even glance at him as she took the money, counted it and gave him a receipt. Her actions were precise and efficient, and her silence elegant, like the old furniture in the room. Both, Ramprasad and the boy, seemed at ease with it.

"This way, *saab*." The boy led him out of the house to the back through the side pathway. He must be the son Ramprasad had mentioned. A whiff of night jasmine made Zayd inhale blissfully as they took a turn and reached the rooms at the back.

The three guest rooms, with independent doors and windows, opened in the pillared corridor overlooking the back gardens. Ramprasad stood with his luggage in front of the middle door.

Zayd entered to find a cozy, carpeted room with an attached bathroom. The tastefully furnished room had bedcovers and curtains in various shades of blue, justifying its name. He peeked through the curtains of the French windows next to the entrance door overlooking the back lawns. This side of the lawn was not as scenic as the front and faced the side of a hill. But the peaceful ambience suited him. No lurking strangers or looming concrete structures. So far so good. Now the only thing left to be seen, or rather tasted, was the food.

"We sewve only veg food, but you can have non-veg from Waghu's dhaba on the Lowew Mall woad," the boy said as if he had guessed Zayd's chain of thoughts.

"Hot watew anytime, I bwing dinnew?"

Poor guy not only suffered from polio but couldn't even pronounce 'r'. "What's your name?" Zayd asked feeling a kinship with the disabled boy. The only difference was that Zayd's infirmities were not apparent to the naked eye.

"Shankaw, some call me *langda*." He didn't look happy uttering the last bit about his introduction.

"Shankar, it is then. It'll be good if you can bring a cup of that ginger tea your father had mentioned, before dinner."

"Yes siw." He beamed, saluted as smartly as he could and hurried out limping.

Zayd took off his leather jacket and switched on the TV. The news was just the same on every channel on account of the Lok Sabha elections. He switched to MTV and pulled at his shoelaces.

He was taking off his socks when his hand jerked at the high-pitched scream.

*****

Throwing the sock down, Zayd rushed out of the door, and almost collided with Ramprasad, who had come running from the driveway. A couple was standing to the left of his room, the woman shaking and holding the man's hand in a deathly grip. By the number of glittering bangles on the woman's wrists, and the gold and black beads necklace, he guessed they were honeymooners.

"What happened, *Sa…ab*?" Ramprasad panted.

Zayd couldn't see anything out of place in the direction they were looking.

"There was a fig…ure in the wo…ods… there…" The woman pointed a shaking finger towards the rear fence. "Something white… floating." The man held her, murmuring something in a low tone.

Zayd scanned the area enveloped under the yellow streetlight again. The shadowy wide expanse of the backyard, in-line with his imagination earlier, looked creepy indeed. Gently swaying trees made the shadows move, but nothing looked out of place. Wrought iron furniture and benches were fixed firmly on the ground, while a jungle gym and swing stood innocently vacant in one corner. He stared in the dark but saw no one lurking in the shadows.

"What's the matter? What's wrong?"

Zayd turned at the soft, musical lilt with a thump in his heart. The lady, who had registered him, stood barefoot under the yellow light of the corridor. She looked divine as her long, straight hair shimmered like a curtain around her frowning, flushed face and thin frame. The white *dupatta* hung on one of her shoulders as if she had absentmindedly donned it while running towards the commotion. The most arresting feature was her eyes, full of compassion and empathy.

She spared half a glance—an apologetic one—at him, then stepped forward to hold the trembling woman's hands. Zayd felt like a king at the attention.

"There was something near the trees Ashimaji, like a human form. It shimmered, then glided to and fro. I screamed, and the next second it disappeared," the woman said.

"Oh, what could it be?" The lady too scanned the fence. All was quiet. "Don't worry, I'll check." She switched on the torch in her hand and marched off towards the darkest area of the huge backyard.

"*Didi*, you are barefoot…" Ramprasad ran after her.

"Oh, never mind. Must be a cat… or some animal."

Zayd turned to go inside but stopped when he heard Ramprasad mutter something about snakes. He pursed his lips at the melodramatic plump woman, still cowering in the arms of the burly man, then glanced at the slender one who was out looking for visions and imagined ghosts, barefoot. Frowning, he continued to stand outside in case they needed any help.

"*Saab*, gingew tea and homemade snacks. Dinnew in ten minutes." Shankar arrived with a covered tray.

"Your *didi* is out there looking for something." He kept an eye on the two near the fence.

"Don't wowy, she'll solve evewythin."

"Really?" He glanced at the teenager.

"Yes." Shankar smiled with pride. "She can do anythin. Please come."

Casting a fleeting glance towards the fence, Zayd turned and entered his room once again.

***

THREE

Even though the day had barely started, a headache the size of a tennis ball was already hammering at the base of Ashima's skull.

Rishabh had acted difficult today—unwilling to bathe, not ready to eat breakfast. Exasperated, she couldn't control herself and had raised her hand threatening him with a slap, which made matters worse. His lips wobbled and his eyes filled with innocent tears, making her feel guilty. Cuddly blackmailer!

She lost precious morning time to cajole him out of his sulk and send him off to school with Shankar. Then she had to come to the kitchen to start the preparation for the breakfast, because Radha, Shankar's mother, was running a high fever.

Ashima now stood in front of the stove making aloo parathas for the guests, wondering how she would meet the basic necessities this month. And what guests? Only three! She stuffed the potato filling in the dough with such force that it came out from the other side. Damn! She took a deep breath and repaired the damage.

The pathetic occupancy would barely pay for Rishabh's fees this month. She had three rooms. Last year they were all booked in the summer months. She didn't even have time to breathe. But this year she could boast full occupancy only for a few weeks. She'd have to run another advertisement in the papers. Another expense.

And now the woman was seeing apparitions. Ashima crossed her fingers and hoped that they complete their stay for the next seven days as planned without imagining any other phantom visit.

"*Bhabhi*, do you have a hundred rupee note? Have to buy a few notebooks." Pooja entered the kitchen, rummaging in her bottomless bag for something, ready for college.

"My purse, upper left drawer." Ashima glanced at her sister-in-law, wearing jeans and a sleeveless yellow *kurti*, looking every inch the new generation girl.

"Do you think you should go like this? Amma wouldn't like it." Ashima turned the *paratha* on the *tawa*. She could sense Pooja's glare aimed at her back.

"When am I going to wear this then? It has been rotting in my cupboard for the past six months, in a few months the winters will start."

"You can always wear it under the sweater." Biting her cheek, she glanced at Pooja's now glacial expression and grinned.

"Very funny," Pooja smirked.

"Take a stole with it. Or a scarf." Ashima put a plate with her breakfast in front of her.

"I'm n—" Pooja left the sentence mid-way and whistled softly.

Ashima, in the middle of frying the *paratha*, stopped to look at what had caught Pooja's attention. The late-night guest was jogging on the paved track around the house, wearing a much worn, faded tracksuit and shoes. It was surprising to see him up and about so early in the morning. Tourists, the ones so young, did not get up early on the first day of their holiday.

He had seemed a bit shy last night. What was his name? Zaheer? Zain? No. It started with Z, but she couldn't recall the name even though she had matched the information on the registration form with his driving license. What the heck! Was she getting old? Already?

"New guest?" Pooja asked.

"Yeah… came in yesterday, late night. Muslim." Ashima glanced at the man when he completed the round and passed the kitchen window again. He was quite thin for a person so tall. She had even noticed the dark circles around his eyes last night. Maybe he had come to recuperate after an illness. What if he didn't like *parathas*? Though she had porridge and other standard breakfast accompaniments, she'd offer a second dish, maybe grilled sandwiches.

The steaming skillet brought Ashima's attention back to work and worries. "You know what… Miss-Overactive-Imagination saw something in the backyard."

"Muslim! What a waste…" Pooja sighed, still preoccupied with the tall man who had disappeared from her sight.

Ashima smiled and remembered her own college days. Pooja was in that age where her mind was either occupied by her studies or the opposite sex. Something in Pooja's expression reminded her of Rohit, and a familiar anguish brought the headache to the fore.

"Okay, I'm off." Pooja picked up the tiffin and thrust it in her bag.

Ashima nodded blinking back the moisture in her eyes and picked up another ball of dough.

"What are you wearing, Pooja? Go, change," Amma commanded as Shankar wheeled her in the kitchen.

"Amma! I want to wear this, its summer." Pooja stamped her foot on the ground. "*Bhabhi!*" She wailed.

Ignoring Pooja's plea to intervene, Ashima switched off the stove after the last *paratha* was done and turned towards the sink to wash the dough off her hands. She didn't have the energy to get into an argument with Amma that morning.

"Pooja. Go. And. Change. Shankar, tell your mother to take that Ayurvedic medicine I gave her last month." Amma aligned her chair with the small table in the kitchen.

"Amma! I'll be late." Pooja was now on the verge of crying.

"I don't care, you shouldn't have worn it. Don't you have any sense? This is not Delhi, and you can't wear sleeveless things." Amma picked up a bowl and served herself some porridge. "I don't want any arguments."

Pooja stomped off to her room.

Everyone always gave in to Amma's wishes. It had always been the norm in the family, more so after the incident with Rohit. Later, when complications after her knee operation had forced her to be confined to the wheelchair, she had become all the more aggressive in her want for control.

"Who is the new guest?" she asked in her customary brusque tone.

"From Delhi. Zaheer or something with 'Z'… Yes, Rizvi is the last name," Ashima remembered.

Amma swiveled her chair banging against the kitchen cupboard. "Muslim! Why did you let the room to him?"

"We don't have a choice, Amma. As it is the season is bad. I don't know why this year has been so lean."

"Have you told him that we don't cook meat or chicken in our kitchen?"

"I told him," Shankar intervened.

"Shankar, wash the utensils in which he eats. Twice," she snapped. "Or better still, keep his plates, cups, and spoons separate from ours."

"Amma!" Ashima gasped.

Behind her, Shankar nodded like a toy whose head was attached on a spring.

"I want them separate," she insisted.

"This is not right, Amma. The guests practically live with us and if he comes to know, it will be bad for the reputation." Ashima tried to placate her. "I'll make sure we wash them properly. And he is here only for three days."

"Fine, do what you want, but till the time he is in the house I will eat in the steel ones."

Ashima hid her exasperation by turning to serve her the breakfast.

***

The remnants of last night's nightmare faded from Zayd's consciousness as he completed his customary run of five kilometers. Panting, he stood watching the sunrise on the other side of the guest house. The breath-taking view of the valley, inaccessible to man or machine, was a treat to his eyes. The town woke up, down in the valley. The goats grazed on the hill—tiny brown specks against the green expanse. Someone was bathing in the small stream that ran down the hill across the guest house. Smoke rose on top of the huts. It was therapeutic to watch everyone respond to the daily routine.

The magic of nature had worked even on him. He had slept for four straight hours in the first spell of his sleep, which had never been the case in the past years. But he couldn't escape his past even at a place as beautiful as this one. The ritualistic nightmare began in the early hours of the dawn and left him drained by the time he woke up. In the prison, he dreamt every night and woke up many a time during the night. Perhaps, by and by, the silence and beauty of this place might give him the much-needed respite from his nocturnal horrors, he hoped.

He scanned the premises. Broad daylight showed a different perspective of the landscape. A waist-high boundary wall ran along the complete perimeter and was further secured by a three feet high barbed wire, on which a variety of flowering creepers thrived. Ramprasad was right when he said it was outstanding. Zayd looked forward to breakfast and then beginning work on his unfinished manuscript. Later in the evening, he'd find a hotel that had this kind of view and food.

Back in the room he gave the order for breakfast over the intercom and switched on his laptop. He had decided to tackle the climactic scene first. He had been struggling with it for the past few months, but last night the scene had suddenly become crystal clear. It would be mind-blowing. Akshat would be ecstatic—for once Zayd would churn out the novel on time. Kasauli, it seemed, was the right choice to park himself for the three months he had planned to finish the novel and plan for another.

His hero was about to murder the heroine due to a misunderstanding and just then, someone trains a gun on the hero's head. The scene floated in front of his eyes and his fingers flew over the keyboard.

A child chattered and giggled, breaking into his thoughts. Zayd frowned. He closed his eyes and concentrated hard to pull the setting in his mind, but the boy's delightful shrieks penetrated his imaginary dark room. The hero, heroine, and the marksman faded along with the gun and finally, the room disappeared.

Zayd sat there for a few minutes silently cursing the interruption, then looked at the time. He had been writing non-stop for the past three hours. Rotating his neck to work out the kinks, he parted the lace curtain to look at the cause of the disruption. A little boy, in a blue school uniform, played barefoot on the jungle-gym with Shankar supervising the boy's monkey-like activities. Too energetic for Shankar to handle, he kept dodging him to go higher on the jungle-gym. His youngest sister was the boy's age when they were together during his last summer vacation at *naanijaan's*. Last month they had met after a five-year long gap. She had been a little shy with him but opened up when he mentioned cricket, her favorite sport.

All of a sudden, the boy jerked and almost lost his footing on the bar. Zayd jumped up from his chair, but the little devil caught hold of the side grips in the nick of time and gave a beguiling smile to Shankar. Zayd realized he was gripping the table and relaxed his hold. He got up, deciding it was time for a break.

The summer sun was pleasant even at this time of the day. The breeze ruffled the plants and the flowers planted around the garden. He stood leaning on one of the corridor pillars and followed the conversation.

"See, Chhankal. I go thish high." The boy was now perched on the highest bar, balancing with both legs and hands.

"Wishabh baba, come down. *Didi* will be vewy angwy."

"You no touch me, Chhankal. I can come dhown own."

"Rishabh!" The voice rang out from somewhere to Zayd's right.

To his amusement, the little rascal scurried down like a squirrel at the authoritative tone and held Shankar's hand, looking like a picture of complete innocence. The ghost-huntress appeared around the corner, this time in a pale yellow suit. To his disgust, he found himself checking her out, again.

"I told you, no playing before lunch," she said, wiggling a finger at the boy. The threat had no effect on the kid.

"I no playing, mamma. Chhankal wantheth to play."

"Really?" She picked him up and nuzzled her nose on his throat. Merry infectious laughter rang out in the backyard.

An unbidden smile sneaking on Zayd's lips surprised him. The muscles on his cheeks protested. When was the last time he had smiled? He didn't remember.

The woman hugged the child to her and hurried off, not noticing Zayd standing by the pillar. Shankar followed in her wake complaining about the kid.

The child spotted Zayd and peered over his mother's shoulder. He hid his face in the crook of her neck when Zayd winked at him. Her *dupatta* slid down her silky hair, reminding him of a poem by Keats.

Zayd watched them go and wondered whether he was the soldier's son. He recalled the name on the photo—Flight Lieutenant Joshi—and the year as per the date stamp on the photo was March, 1999, prior to the Kargil war, the year he was sent to the prison, the year Myra died.

Myra's name, as usual, brought on the familiar despair and sorrow. The bleak memories overshadowed the cheer induced by the kid and his antics. He took a deep breath and walked along the paved path. Strolling along the wall, he watched the butterflies dancing in tandem with the breeze, out of his reach but in line of his sight.

"*Saab*, lunch?" Shankar stood at a respectable distance with his hands behind his back.

"Do you have a dine-in room?"

"Yes, yes, dining woom, this side."

Shankar took him to the front room where the lady had registered him. During the day, it was transformed into an inviting sunny dining area, with four tables, each seating four people. Shankar pulled out the chair of a table on the far side of the room, adjacent to the large French window, which Zayd had failed to notice at night. The red-and-white checkered table cloth was spotless, and a red rose in a white miniature vase adorned the center.

Shankar brought a glass and a jug of water. Zayd was surprised by the professionalism with which he served the food. The meal was complete with salad, pickles and a choice of two varieties of desserts.

He should start gym work-outs soon to counter the delicious food. Tomorrow he'd visit the police station too. The very thought of anything related to prison had his heart thumping nervously. But he had delayed it enough. Any more delay and the whole Hyderabad would be up on his case—his lawyer, his father, Akshat. They all would call and give him long lectures on life's responsibilities and priorities.

Then he knew what would happen.

By and by, the town would come to know about his crime including the lady in pale salwar suits. Most probably he would be evicted—politely of course. She would wear a mask of civilized behavior and would ask him to find another place.

He had to find a hotel room soon. They helped one to remain anonymous.

***

FOUR

The Kasauli Police Station was a small, single story building with a sloping roof near the main market. The dusty exterior matched the unkempt interiors. Zayd clamped down the wave of nausea brought by unwanted memories as he entered the police station. He asked for the liaison officer, as per his papers. A constable pointed him to a small room inside. He found the inspector snoring on his seat with both his legs propped on the table and his mouth open.

Zayd knocked on the table.

The man showed no sign of hearing him and snorted while sleeping. The nameplate showed his name as C.P. Bisht.

Zayd tapped his knee with a hand and the inspector got up with a start, dropping the paper weight in his wake. The pen stand went flying on the other side and crashed on the floor. It contained everything but a pen.

"What's the problem? Don't you have any manners, barging in here just like that? Can't you see I'm resting? Was awake the whole night yesterday because of that drunkard!" He justified, straightening his shirt and tried to slide his feet into the shoes, which slipped further under the table. He cursed and struggled some more.

Once he settled down, he looked up and down, scanning Zayd. "City sticklers, pretending to be civilized and superior, and behaving like bloody villagers in a small town. Do you think we don't understand the meaning of all this? What's the problem?"

Zayd took a couple of deep, discreet breaths and held out his papers, hating himself for the way his hands shook. "I need to show these and register here."

The inspector snatched the letter from his hand. His eyes widened at the contents, as Zayd had expected. Bisht smiled, twirling his moustache between his fingers.

"Oh, so you are that Rizvi, okay… okay… yes, I had received the notice from Tihar."

Zayd wasn't surprised at the glee on the face of the inspector. In fact, it was quite a familiar experience.

"The warden had even called me from Delhi. Very good, hmm… so you have been to jail and that too for murder? Not one, but two! Two murders! *Wah*! Choudhary, oh, Choudhary! We have a hardened criminal amongst us. Sharmaji, Sharmaji, come and find that register."

The constable, who had met Zayd in the outer room, came running and stood there.

"Which register, saab?"

"The one which we have for noting the attendance of paroled people."

"But we don't have any such register!"

"Of course we have one, Sharmaji. *Naye ho naa*, ask Choudhary and bring it fast."

The constable scurried out of the room.

"So who did you kill? Was the girl a Hindu?" The inspector read Zayd's file.

Zayd kept quiet. There was no point in explaining that Myra was a Christian and also a foreigner. The harassment and scathing interrogation, which the inspector thought was his birth right, would follow in any case.

But this was nothing compared to what Zayd had endured in captivity. The moment they knew his religion—his and of the student who had died—through the prison grapevine, he had become an easy target. By the time his father intervened, it had been four days of hell. He was transferred to a separate cell. They never touched him again, but the taunts and jeering never ceased. The constant reminder, guilt, and losing Myra—the way he did—had drilled a black hole in his heart. His hands began to sweat and his breath became shallow. He tried to take a deep breath but the oppressive room seemed to be devoid of oxygen.

"*Chhupe rustam ho ji*, the girl also died… tch… tch, was she a Hindu? Was that the reason? Love-shove and all? *Bhagaa rahe the kya?*" Bisht looked up.

Bisht's coarse voice helped keep the anxiety at bay and Zayd breathed better. He wanted to sit, but hadn't been asked to sit. The constable was still not back with the register. He stared outside the lone window concentrating on his breath, trying to calm himself.

"*Kyun saale*, tongue got stuck or what. Look at me when I am talking to you. I don't want any trouble in my town."

Zayd looked at the inspector, trying to keep his revulsion and fear at bay. He desperately wanted a glass of water to wet his parched mouth.

"Aah, the silent type! You like staring, is it?" Bisht pushed up the spectacles sliding on his nose and flipped another page of the report. "Self-defense was it… bullshit! Where is your family from?"

Zayd sighed imperceptibly and ran his tongue over his lips. "Hyderabad." There was no harm in telling whatever was written in his official papers, but he hated talking about that time of his life.

"Didn't you think about your mother when you did things like that, going to the pub and killing people? *Aish hai ji! Baap ka maal udao aur phir zindagi bhar ka dard.*"

That comment brought a welcome wave of anger, which helped fight off the panic attack setting in, but that was even more worrying. Zayd tuned off the inspector's jabbering and studied the water filter. The doctor's advice number two 'to keep anger at bay'—divert your attention to an inanimate object. Blue and white in color, the purifier was a regular candle filter sitting on a stool in a corner. There were two steel glasses and a chipped ceramic cup balanced precariously on the edge of the stool.

"Father, what does he do?"

"Business." Zayd had been asked this question so many times that he spoke without thinking, the script ready for people like the inspector.

"What business? Do you think I'm illiterate? I can't understand?" The inspector raised his voice.

"Property."

"Oh! A big shot, huh!"

Zayd was spared an answer as the constable entered with a battered register. The inspector took his own time to flip through the pages while Zayd was kept standing.

"Here it is," the inspector searched for a pen in his pockets and eventually found it to enter Zayd's case details from the parole papers. "Okay, sign here." He finally extended the register towards Zayd, without offering the pen.

Zayd had a similar experience in Delhi and now he carried his own pen. He signed in one of the columns. The signature looked nothing like his as he scribbled his name with trembling fingers.

"So, when do I see you again?"

"In fifteen days."

"Right. Now listen, and listen hard. I don't want any disruption in my area, *bhai*. I'm warning you. Your recommendation from the warden is very good so I'm allowing you to go for fifteen days, otherwise I would have called you here every day."

Zayd turned to go.

"Oh ho! You are staying at the Joshi Guest House!"

With a hammering heart, Zayd looked back.

"Hmm… no hanky-panky there, mister. They are a highly respected family. If I see anything out of place, I will straight away put you in jail. Do you hear me? Joshi's son is a hero for us, an army man. Not like you, *bigdi huey aulaad*. Beating your chest on the might of your father's money!"

Zayd breathed easy when he realized the inspector again wanted to flaunt his power.

This attendance nightmare had to be lived for another three years, then he would be free to move around without disclosing his identity. Till then, he would save enough to buy a cottage or an apartment and write from there. Or he could travel from place to place according to his own convenience and whims.

Zayd came back to the guest house to find the little boy playing alone in front of his room. The moment he saw Zayd, he threw his plastic bat-ball on the ground and ran off.

***

At ten minutes to seven in the evening, the electricity failed.

Zayd scowled at the interruption and his laptop pinged, changing the battery light from 'green' to 'red'. Shucks! He had forgotten to connect to the power source when it had warned fifteen minutes back. He had been writing for the past four hours— non-stop. It was an ideal time for a short break. As he flexed his fingers and rotated his shoulders, Zayd heard a faint commotion outside. Shutting down the laptop, he made his way to the front of the bungalow.

The streetlights and other houses had electricity, but it was pitch dark in the guest house. There were two people with torches in the outhouse near the gate—at least he could see two light sources. Ramprasad and his family lived in two rooms of the outhouse and the larger one was a storage area.

"I wanth mom." The child's voice came from the right, sounding like he was on the verge of crying.

"No, Rishu. You know there are snakes around and we are barefoot," a girl said.

Zayd walked towards the two silhouettes. The boy was standing at the entrance of the house, holding the hand of a young girl in jeans and a kurta. They concentrated on the happening inside the store. The kid wailed suddenly calling for his mamma, trying to shake off her hand. The girl struggled to restrain him. The boy cried all the more under the girl's hold.

"Can I help?" Zayd asked the girl.

"I… I'm not sure. Bhabhi will be here soon. Rishu, don't!" The boy was pulling and wailing continuously.

"I can take him to the outhouse, shouldn't be a problem. We have met. Haven't we, young man?" Zayd sat on his haunches and extended his hands towards the toddler. Rishabh stopped crying and rubbed one eye with a fist. He curiously looked at Zayd for a moment, then extended a tear drenched hand.

Zayd stood up with the boy in his arms and walked towards the outhouse. The sight there was again something to behold. Shankar was holding a ladder, a wobbly wooden one, and his hostess was perched on the last rung, with one foot on the crates piled high along the ladder. She held the torch in her mouth and was doing something with the ceramic fuse holder.

She then blabbered. "I wink, I needh a pliew, Shankaw. Waitha minth…"

Zayd couldn't understand a single word.

"I bwing the pliew." Shankar, it seems had understood what she wanted, and disappeared behind the crates with the other torch.

The boy crackled, "Mamma you shpoke like Chhankal."

Zayd couldn't help but smile at the speech impairment going around. She was jolted by the kid's voice and the ladder wobbled. Zayd shot out his hand to steady it. Now he was totally committed with the kid in one hand and supporting the ladder with the other.

"Rishu, what are you doing here?" she said pointing the torch at them.

"I wanth mamma."

She muttered something under her breath.

Shankar appeared with a wire and a plier and handed it to her.

"Shankar, hold Rishu."

The child immediately went to his mate and Zayd held the ladder and the pile of crates, which wobbled as she worked.

The sight was out of a movie when all of a sudden she turned the main lever and they were flooded with blinding light. Both Shankar and the kid clapped, elated, with what appeared to be a ritual.

She came down the ladder, but stopped with a jerk mid-way, her descent hindered by something. They looked up to find the *dupatta* entangled in one of the nails. She tried to pull it but it was stuck.

Zayd took a step forward and stood on his toes to disentangle the garment. A whiff of something feminine assailed his senses and her breath fanned his neck. A muted desire fluttered inside him. He looked down at her. She was looking at him, exasperated and apologetic. Her eyes black, moist, looked a wee bit tired… and sad.

Something in that glance tugged a chord in his chest. His inhibitions and worries lost their relevance and faded away.

"Mamma, I wanth to shleep." The child tapped her arm.

She immediately dropped her eyelashes cutting off the silent communication.

Zayd noticed red vermilion, the sindoor, on her hair parting and moved back.

She stepped down the last step and followed Shankar out of the outhouse.

Glimpses of the various shades of her personality were raising Zayd's curiosity. She had been an elegant hostess yesterday, a courageous woman who hunted ghosts at night, and today he had seen her as a handy-woman repairing the electrical fuse.

He just sat in front of his laptop. His thoughts repeatedly went to her serene, mournful eyes instead of his plot. His muse had left him to follow Ms… Ms… He didn't remember her name. The first night the fat woman had called her by a name, but it eluded him. If she was the soldier's wife, then she would be Mrs. Joshi. But what was her first name? The servants called her *didi*, the boy called her mamma, and the young girl had called her *bhabhi*.

He rubbed his hands on his eyes, contemplating to go to the dining room for dinner, and probably bump into her again.

His phone rang.

"Hey Akshat! Yeah, the book is coming right up. Magnificently… yes… right on track… Don't worry. It'll earn the advance."

He turned while talking and saw Shankar standing at the door with a dinner tray in his hand.

'Damn…'

***

FIVE

The plain meadow stretched endlessly, with the wind ruffling his hair—reminding Zayd of his mother. She used to come and check on him before going for her numerous social events. If he was awake she would talk to him, discuss his school and friends. And if he was asleep, she would simply caress his hair and sometimes his cheek—he knew because he sensed her presence and would pretend to be asleep. No one else was allowed to touch his face or hair. He would sleep peacefully after she left, secure under her love and care. But tonight his only companion was the rich pine perfumed breeze, strolling along with him, whispering the lilting words.

Across the field he saw something glowing, and the wind changed its mood. It became warm and stilted, reluctant to move with him—somehow sensing the danger ahead, warning him. He couldn't stop. The sheer magnetism of the auburn orange glow pulled him towards it. As he neared the source of light, his eyes widened and heart galloped with the leaping flames. Someone whispered his name, and he saw Myra beyond the hot flames. A fire, raging to engulf anything, came between them.

Myra's hair was blowing with the turbulent winds. She saw him, smiled and opened her arms, but the fire didn't allow him to reach her. Her smile vanished and she cried for help. He became desperate. The fire would reach her anytime. He had to rescue her. The next moment, he saw his mother instead of Myra. His heart was ready to burst out of his chest. He frantically looked around for some source of water, but the meadow had turned into a hot, parched desert. Worried and helpless, he glanced at his mother, but she was nowhere to be seen and a woman in a pale green salwar suit stood in her place. Zayd's eyes snapped open.

He sat up straight, panting—dazed and disoriented. Realizing that he had gone to sleep at the table, he glanced at the time on the laptop screen. It was eleven p.m. This was the first time he had dreamt about his mother after Myra's death.

The nightmare left him tired and sad, reminding him of all that he had lost—his mother, Myra, and then the precious years of his life in the prison. His thoughts turned to his hostess, the manager of the guest house—capable, calm and full of sorrow. When and why did she creep into his subconsciousness?

The electricity played truant again jolting Zayd out of his reverie. He rubbed his hands on his face and parted the curtains with the tip of his pen. This time the street lights were also off. It meant it was not a disruption at the guest house, but a general power cut. He must have slept for two hours straight, the last saved time stamp on his file showed nine-o-three p.m. Sleep was out of the question now.

Maybe he would go for a run, and then settle down for an all-night writing spree. Ginger tea, of course, would not be available. He would buy an electric water heater the next time he went to the market, and some tea bags, and maybe sugar cubes. He was imagining savoring the rich aroma of ginger tea when he heard the gasp followed by a scream.

Zayd was out of the door in a flash and saw the couple.

The man pointed at something at the far end of the backyard. Zayd also saw something shift in white and raced after the silhouette. As he neared the fence, he saw a figure wearing a blowy overall kind of garb, but on the other side.

He scanned the barbed wire line. It was broken at various places. The electricity came on full, lighting the whole area and startling the intruder, who had begun walking towards the road. Taking advantage of the opportunity, Zayd jumped across the broken fence and sped towards the figure, determined to catch the ghost and beat him into a human.

The rustle of his feet on the dried grass alerted the intruder. The figure looked back, then ran. As Zayd reached at an arm's length from him, he lunged and grasped a corner of his hood. It slipped and came off. The man leapt up on the road where another man was waiting on a motorcycle with the engine gunning.

Zayd cursed under his breath as he watched them drive off, the hood dangling by his fingers. There was no time to note down the number of the motorbike.

Panting, Zayd turned back and found his hostess standing barefoot on the other side of the fence. He looked at her frowning, worried eyes and held out the makeshift hood—more of a dirty, ragged, piece of cloth.

"A souvenir from your ghost," he said and held out his hand.

Grimacing, she reached out and gingerly held the filthy white cloth between her thumb and fore finger. Examining the cloth, she turned back to the scared couple and tried to convince that they were a couple of miscreants and not any mysterious apparition. She pacified and sent them to their room, then turned towards Zayd.

The next moment, they heard the little boy crying. Mumbling incoherently, she ran back towards the private rooms for the family. He watched her until she went inside and locked the house.

Being on the opposite end of the property, none of the servants had heard the commotion.

***

Ashima was a little embarrassed taking the breakfast for the guest, but it was important. Normally she never spoke to the guests. Amma was very strict about this one rule when Ashima had started the guest house two years back. And Amma was right about maintaining her distance with strangers. But today was an exception. She had to thank him for last night.

She knocked on the door and waited. There was no response. She knocked a bit harder, but still nothing. She put her ear to the door and heard music blaring. No wonder he couldn't hear her knock.

She slowly opened the door. Clad only in his track pants, he was doing one-arm push-ups on the floor. As her eyes adjusted to the shadowed interiors after the bright sunshine outside, the tray rattled in her hand in disgust. Were those ugly worms wriggling on his arm! Try as she might she couldn't take off her gaze from the horrid sight. He stopped, and the worms became stationary. It was then that she realized they were tattoo marks. His complete left arm was tattooed and the rippling muscles made the design move.

He turned to exercise with the other arm but stopped as his gaze landed on her. His piercing green eyes, with long curly lashes, made her heart beat in a different rhythm.

He stood up in one lithe movement, a dull flush shadowing his face, and pulled on a sleeveless vest lying on the bed. His lips moved. She shook her head, indicating that she was unable to hear anything. He turned towards the laptop and reduced the volume.

"I'm sorry, I didn't hear you come," he said.

His voice came out a little hoarse, his tone a little gruff, as if he hadn't spoken to anyone in a long time. She mumbled, brushing off his apology, and looked for a place to keep the tray, which also gave her an excuse not to gaze at his sweating biceps. It was a mistake to come to the room. She should have called first or met him outside in the garden.

"Why did you come? Where's Shankar? I'd have waited for him. I'd have come to the dining room." Flustered, he swept off the papers and magazines on the table down on the floor to make space.

"It's okay." She put the tray on the table. "I wanted to thank you. I'm very grateful for your... for your support last night."

"I..." He coughed. "T'was not a problem. T'was nothing," He raked his fingers through his hair looking at anything but her. His biceps bulged.

Her heartbeat skipped again. It had never happened in the past. The close proximity with a stranger had unsettled her, she reasoned.

"Nevertheless, thanks a lot." Unwilling to embarrass him and herself further, Ashima hurriedly turned to leave. "Just keep the tray outside when you—"

"The fence is broken at places," he blurted, as if he wanted to prolong her stay.

"Huh?" She turned back.

"The fence, it should be repaired. Did you report the incident to the police?" He crossed his arms, then swiftly focused his gaze on the food.

"Last night's?"

"Yeah," he said now looking at something behind her.

"It was nothing major. Probably some young men playing a game of dare," she said. It was endearing to see that he was more embarrassed than her.

"Or they may be trying to scare off your guests. It has happened twice, right? Clearly they didn't have good intentions. Reporting will make a case against them." He brought his gaze to her face.

"Against whom?"

"Whosoever wants you to make a loss."

She sighed. He was right. But the two incidents had taken her by surprise and she had not been able to come to a conclusion. In her assessment, the news about the ghosts or the miscreants could harm the reputation of the guest house. She couldn't take the risk. The matter had to be thought through before taking any drastic step.

She exhaled again. "I'll think about it, Mr. Rizvi. I'm very thankful for your help, and am really very sorry you have been disturbed in our guest house, but be assured we will try our best for a pleasant stay going forward."

He looked at her intently for a second then nodded. "I'm sure. Thank you for your hospitality Ms... Ms... I'm sorry I didn't get your name."

His confident tone made her take a step back. That was quick. How dare he try to get familiar with her? Opportunistic cad!

"I'm Mrs. Joshi. Flight lieutenant Rohit Joshi's wife," she specified.

He tilted his head slightly, sliding his hands in the pockets of his track pants.

She turned on her heels and left.

Zayd watched her go, mentally smacking himself for mentioning the police. Who was he to counsel anyone on criminal offense? Shucks!

His mind went to the formal tone she had taken when he had asked her name. Annoyed, she had regally lifted her head and left the room. He smiled. This was the first time in two days that he had seen a spark in her.

Did he imagine that emphasis on 'Mrs' and 'wife'? Was she trying to convince him or herself that she was married? Warning him off, as women do when faced with unwarranted attention. Could he blame her? He was intrigued by her and did stare at her every time they met. Her straight hair was plaited today, but wisps of hair framed her serious, oval face—an interesting, arresting face. The small mole on her cheek fascinated him. The doctor advice number two definitely had some merit when applied even when he wasn't angry.

She had tried not to look at him after that one incredulous moment when she had spied his tattoos. Masking her disgust with a blink. Her eyes, bereft of a smile, did raise some very personal questions in his mind.

Zayd was at the end of his workout when he heard someone scuffling out in the corridor. The open window towards the corridor showed the two heavy weights moving out with their luggage, muttering phrases like 'bloody inconvenient', 'third class place', 'wrong decision'. They were leaving the guest house. Wimps!

Zayd decided to ignore them and concentrate on his breakfast instead. He uncovered one of the plates and the rich aroma of vegetable cutlets wafted up. His stomach gurgled on cue. He sat down to gain the calories he had burnt half an hour back.

***

The intercom rang as Ashima stormed into the kitchen. Shankar leapt up from the stool that he was perched on for cutting the vegetables and picked up the phone. He loved answering it. Ashima had taught him a few English sentences, which he could carry off with aplomb.

"Good mownin!"

He stood up after listening to the person at the other end.

"Yes, siw." He put the phone down in slow motion.

Ashima frowned at his uncharacteristic drooping expressions. "Who was that, Shankar? What did they want?"

"They want to leave."

"Who?"

"The lady who's always seeing ghosts, cowawd."

"Don't speak like that about a guest." Ashima chided him, but mentally chanted 'coward fatties' to let out some of her own frustration.

The couple had tentatively booked for another week, but she now had to settle with only one room occupied. The lack of customers at the guest house was surprising this season. She had built a reputation for providing a pleasant stay and a delectable menu. Nothing had changed except the revenue flow this year. It was as if the tourists' footfall in Kasauli had dried up suddenly, which she knew wasn't true. So why was only her business hit?

Sighing, she stood up to make the bill for room number one.

***

SIX

Zayd sat staring at the blank screen and couldn't visualize anything in his mind. No words appeared on the blank page.

A mere nightmare could never be the reason for his distraction. He had been tormented by the same one most of the nights with a few trivial changes in the scenery, timing, and the clothes that Myra wore. Every one of them ended with Myra on the pyre—alive—while he watched helplessly, unable to move.

The reason for his restlessness, however, was not Myra or the nightmare. It was the lady with the hopeless, clear black eyes—sad, blank and shimmering eyes. She kept intruding in his thoughts since the day she had gone looking for the ghosts, barefoot. He needed to block her from his thoughts. He needed to clear his mind of all the clutter—the nightmare, the happenings in the guest house, and more importantly his quiet hostess.

It was time to change the setting and take advantage of the freedom and fresh air. Confined in an eight by six cell, Zayd had been deprived of the basic things people took for granted for four long years. It was foolish to be cooped up in the room when he could enjoy the sunshine. He picked up his laptop and headed for the big outdoors.

The best spot was under the gazebo. He shifted the cane chair and sat facing the valley. The scene played out beautifully and he could sense a familiar feeling of déjà vu when the plot revealed itself scene after scene. His fingers flew on the keyboard on their own accord.

"Ashima!"

His head snapped up at the bellowing voice. Shankar ferried an old lady on a wheel chair to a sunny patch on the family's side of the garden. Then the object of his thoughts appeared at the doorway. The second door, which had remained closed when he had arrived, was the private entrance for the family.

"Bring the medicine box, Shankar. Aashi, were you able to find the Ayurvedic oil that Mrs. Kaul had mentioned?"

So her name was Ashima and Aashi was the short for it. Somehow, the short name suited her and complimented the petite persona. He heard senior Mrs. Joshi admonishing her on something trivial, that too in front of everyone. She stood and nodded at the right places, and the old woman cooled down.

"*Didi*, the office phone is ringing," a voice hailed her from inside the house, after she had fetched the oil. It was probably Shankar's mother. She ran inside. The buzz of activity continued all morning.

Though Zayd didn't pay attention to the cacophony or the family, he could follow everything going on. His ears became tuned to her footsteps, and he was unable to make any progress since the time he had heard her name.

After the courier guy left, Ashima was examining the contents of the parcel delivered when someone called from the gate. It was the vegetable hawker. She selected, bargained and bought the vegetables. After half an hour, the milkman arrived for his monthly payment. While she stood talking to the man, the mother-in-law called again.

Zayd also spotted her feeding the kid something from a bowl and later struggling with the homework on one of the tables in the corridor.

Every request, order, summon was for her but she never lost her patience or showed any sign of fatigue. She spoke in monosyllables, never more than necessary. He had not heard her laughing even once. Her voice cheered up a little only when she was interacting with the kid. Was it normal for someone to just run here and there, from one corner to another, doing everything alone and silently? Without any complaints, day in, day out. Where was the husband?

Something was not right.

When Shankar came with the gardener to seek her advice for one of the sunflower beds, Zayd had had enough. He left the garden seat for his room. It had been three days, and he decided he was definitely going hotel-hunting this evening.

He heard a click, and glanced around to find the little boy standing at the door. Zayd smiled and winked, but the kid ran off.

***

"What does he do all day, sitting with the laptop? People normally come here for sightseeing." Pooja remarked when she came back from college. "I have never seen him stepping out. What kind of a tourist is he?"

They were in the living room, which was adjacent to the guest dining area, but not open to the guests. The family had a separate entrance through this room to their private rooms.

"He doesn't even sleep late in the morning. Early-riser is… that one," Radha was mighty impressed with anyone who would wake up early and finish their chores.

"Really?" Pooja raised her eyebrows.

"Yes, I see him jogging every day when I wake up and come to the kitchen." Radha added.

"Strange."

"He wwites," Shankar added.

"Writes? What does he write?" Pooja's gaze bounced to the man outside.

"I don't know, I see him wwiting, like you do on computew." Shankar made rapid movements with all his fingers on the coffee table as if it was a keyboard and grinned.

Pooja chuckled.

"He is doing a course." Ashima said, glancing out beyond the white lace-curtained window and saw him bent on the laptop and typing fast. "It is on his registration form. A long-distance one, MFA something. Must be working on his assignments." She was a bit mollified with him after yesterday's breakfast debacle. He kept to himself and didn't seek her out actively, having his meals either in the room or out. Maybe she overreacted to his curiosity that morning.

All of a sudden it started drizzling. He closed the laptop and stuffed it under his shirt and ran for cover under the verandah, out of sight.

When Ashima came out looking for Rishabh's water bottle, she found him sitting on one of the cane sofas in the corridor, typing furiously, oblivious to the world. The first night he seemed like any other guest, but now she knew he was not a regular tourist. There was a certain loneliness about him. Radha had mentioned he woke up early but Ashima knew he didn't sleep well during the night too. She had kept tabs on him and had seen the lights on in the room late in the nights too.

Was he on some kind of study vacation? What about his family? And was there any story behind those tattoos? How could his mother allow him to have a whole arm full of tattoos? Like a weird gypsy or a druggy! She would never allow Rishabh a permanent one, not even a minuscule.

***

Zayd was immersed in his work when he heard the door creak. He glanced at the door, but saw nothing. Must be the wind. He put his fingers on the keyboard poised to convert his imagination to words when he sensed someone's presence in the room. The hair on his neck stood up and he twisted around.

He exhaled and smiled. "Hi."

The little boy, today in a blue-denim dungaree and t-shirt, looked at Zayd with those innocent eyes. All of a sudden he smiled and winked, or tried to wink, since both the eyes flickered, one less and the other more.

It took a moment for Zayd to understand what the kid was trying to do. Zayd grinned. "Aah! My wink intrigued you, did it?" He extended his hand. The boy took one step forward and placed a tiny hand on his palm.

"What's your name?"

"Lishabh."

"Hi Rishabh, I'm Zayd."

"Aaydh?"

"No. Zayd."

"Aaydh." The kid smiled with a knowing look as if asking Zayd to understand his predicament and take the pronunciation in his stride.

"Okay… Aaydh it is."

Zayd earned a dimpled smile again.

"So you want to learn how to wink, is it? Fine, I will show how to do it properly. Now you have to quickly close and open only one eye. Like this," Zayd instructed as he demonstrated with his left eye, and the boy again did it with both eyes. "No, no. You keep one eye open like this." He put one finger on his right lid and winked with the left.

The boy also did the same but both the eyes blinked again. Even the one below his finger. They struggled to get things right but every time both his eyes would close.

Zayd sighed. "Don't know how they teach so many things to so many children at school." he muttered and tried again. "Now what we need to do is, keep one eye open." He lightly placed his finger on the kid's eye. "And close the other eye."

The boy calmly followed his instructions and it happened. He giggled. Zayd grinned, both feeling proud of the accomplishment.

They practiced for four or five times with lots of laughing and giggling in between by the boy. At the end of it he managed to keep his other eye open—it just flickered as the other winked.

He left the room the moment he got the hang of it. Zayd watched him dart out towards the jungle-gym. Since Shankar was not with him, Zayd parked himself on one of the comfortable cane chairs arranged all around the corridor and monitored him. After half an hour, the child was missed and Ramprasad came to fetch him.

***

Ashima was putting away the leftovers in the fridge after lunch when someone knocked. Shankar opened the door, then someone took her name, and she almost dropped the bowl from her hand.

Her heart plummeted in her stomach at the sound of the hated voice. She had a colossal urge to run away to her bedroom, and pull the blanket over her head. But the voices in the living room forced her to face the reality.

"You should have called before coming," Shankar said.

"Don't act smart, *langde*, otherwise you will not be fit enough to even walk. You are a servant and remain a servant. Call your *didi*." The gruff voice commanded.

She had to deal with him. There was no one else who could handle this. It would not do to show the world, especially Hari Prasad Kanyal, her fear. She closed the refrigerator door with more force than required, rattling Rishabh's clay toys on the top.

Shankar came in, his nostrils flaring. "Kanyal has come." He lifted the belan from the utensils rack.

"What are you doing?"

"I'm with you." He slapped the *belan* on his palm.

"This isn't going to help, Shankar." Ashima took the wooden rolling pin out of his hand and placed it on the shelf.

Taking a deep breath, she entered the living room with Shankar close behind her. Kanyal—the local goon cum politician—stood slapping his teakwood cane against his thigh, looking at a painting on the wall. He was dressed in a plain white shirt and trousers with a Nehru coat over it, a typical attire favoured by politicians. If devoid of his perpetual lecherous glance and chewing tobacco, he could have been a handsome man in his forties. But no, he was all about leopard and its spots. He thought the lion-head cane he carried around enhanced his image.

She cleared her throat. He turned. How she hated his I-am-your-friend smile! Gutter slime!

"Aah... Ashima *ji, aap toh nazar hi nahin aati hein*! You didn't even respond to my phone call last week."

Keeping her face blank, she lifted her head a little. "We have nothing to say. Please call our lawyer for any further communication."

"Tch... tch... so formal." He took a step forward and whispered. "What if I wanted to meet you?"

She gritted her teeth and scowled back. Shankar took a step towards him, but stopped when she lifted a hand. "I'm sure your time is important, Mr. Kanyal."

His smile faltered at her curt tone, but he nodded. "Sure, but as you know, I've discussed this with Mrs. Joshi too. I think both of you should reconsider your decision."

"Our answer is not going to change with every passing day."

"What if I raise the price?"

"We are not selling this house, ever."

"How can I explain to you Ashimaji that it is in your family's benefit to take my offer and live peacefully? As it is, running a guest house is not a joke. Look at the situation, no occupancy or income and you look so tired and fatigued."

"Please do not concern yourself with my finances or health."

His pleasing, nauseous smile vanished. He slapped his cane on the table and took a step forward invading her body space. She gasped. It took all her will power and courage to not to step back at the belligerence.

"*Saab, aage nahin,*" Shankar said.

"Shut up, you vermin," he shouted, then added softly, his breath fanning her face, revolting her. "Do you realize your family is standing in the path of progress? My progress." He pointed a thumb to his chest. "I can wipe you all like this." He snapped his fingers in front of her face.

Shankar was going red in the face. Her own breathing had become erratic too. She hoped Kanyal didn't sense her fear and hear the vicious pounding of her pulse echoing in her throat and ears.

"Are you threatening us, Mr. Kanyal?" He was taken aback when she didn't cower back. She decided to take the benefit of his surprise. "I think you should leave."

"You will regret this, I am warning you!"

"I said, please leave!"

Shankar leapt forward and Kanyal hit him hard with his cane. Shankar fell down.

"Mamma?" Rishabh called from the other room.

Ashima moved to help Shankar, but Kanyal pulled her up. His grip on her arm made her gasp with pain. She yanked her arm away. The ceramic vase in the table crashed on the floor as her elbow crashed into it. Crying, Rishabh ran into the room to her.

"Excuse me!"

Everyone froze and turned towards the source of the harsh voice. Zayd Rizvi stood at the doorway, scowling at Kanyal. His gaze moved to Ashima and then fell on her arm where Kanyal had gripped her.

Kanyal left Ashima's arm as if he was holding a hot *tawa*. She picked up Rishabh and tried consoling him. Zayd's eyes flickered at Rishabh and his lips tightened into a thin line. His biceps flexed below the short sleeve of his t-shirt. Kanyal's eyes widened as his attention went to the tattoos.

"Mr.—" Ashima began.

"You have to take my offer or I... I..." Kanyal stopped as Zayd took a step inside the room.

Kanyal gave a sweeping glance around the room. "My lawyer will call your lawyer," he said casting a scathing look at Ashima and left in a huff. Zayd followed him out.

Ashima's heart was still pounding, but she too followed them to make sure that Kanyal was indeed out of the gate.

Hands in his jeans pocket, Zayd stood watching Kanyal get in his car and drive off. He had again come to her rescue. What would he think about the guest house? Yesterday evening, he had extended his stay for another week. Now, if he decided to leave she would have to refund the money.

"Mr. Rizvi, I'm sorry for the nuisance," she said stroking Rishabh's back, who was plastered to her with his arms tight around her neck.

He didn't respond and stood watching Kanyal's jeep leave.

"Mr. Rizvi?"

"Huh…" He looked blankly at her and then at Rishabh, who was hiccupping on her shoulder.

The faraway look in his eyes indicated he wasn't thinking about the guest house.

"Are you okay?" she asked. Though still thin, Ashima observed that he looked a shade better since the night he had come to stay.

"Yeah…" He nodded, still frowning.

"I'm sorry about this. Did you need anything?"

"What?" He raked his fingers through his hair.

"You came here, did you require anything from the kitchen or Shankar?"

"Yeah… Yes, a cup of tea, if it's not much of a problem."

"No, not at all. I'll ask Shankar to bring it to your room."

He nodded and left.

Ashima called out for Shankar, then pacified and reassured Rishabh. He was a little subdued and didn't want to leave her, but agreed to sit on the kitchen slab, playing with the utensils.

She poured some water in a pan for the tea.

Everything had been fine until last year when Kanyal had bought the land next to theirs. He was a small time property dealer. The trouble started when he won the elections this year. He began dreaming big and wanted to open a resort by buying their house for peanuts. He thought he would be able to intimidate them with his power and gang of thugs. But he had underestimated Ashima and her mother-in-law. They had thwarted all his efforts for the past six months with the help of their lawyer, a family friend.

Kanyal always spoke politely in public, but alone he had been insulting with discreet suggestions and innuendoes. But today's behavior had surpassed everything and broken all rules of decency, that too in front of a guest.

The tea boiled and spilled, making a hissing sound. She cursed at the additional work of cleaning the stove. Where was Shankar?

***

SEVEN

Satisfied with the day's writing progress, Zayd had thought he would try to sleep early today. But sleep eluded him as usual. The day's events played in his mind. He could barely control his anger when he thought of the little one crying and the man's grip on her arm. He was lucky that the man left on his own. None of the doctor's tricks had come to his mind in that moment.

The strange mix of fear and courage in her eyes haunted him. Was the husband posted at a place where families were not allowed? The salary must be really low for her to run the guest house.

He turned to find a comfortable spot on the bed which would lull him to sleep, but couldn't. Cursing his habit of thinking and speculating, he donned his tracksuit and moved out of the room. A breath of fresh air might help.

Zayd scanned the backyard fence to make sure no one lurked there, and if anyone did, he would catch him red-handed. It just hit him that he had enjoyed that night's adventure. If it was not so serious an issue, he would have laughed at the man prancing at night wearing the *burqa* kind of a garment.

Strolling on the path along the valley, he reached the far corner of the backyard to the small gate in the boundary wall, which was always locked. But tonight it was open.

His eyes took some time to get accustomed to the faint moonlight.

Through the gate, four steps down, there was a secluded green patch secured by a six-foot high, barbed wire fence giving unhindered scenic view of the valley and the villages below. Pink-purple bougainvillea threaded through the wire provided privacy. Not that there was any need since the slope was quite steep beyond the fence.

He spied a figure huddled on the high-back stone bench. Another ghost? But this time the ghost didn't look menacing. Instead, it looked dejected and disheartened. She sat there with her arms around her folded legs and her head resting on her knees. Her despondent posture pulled at his gut again. His logical instincts cautioned him not to intrude, but the familiar aching tug urged him not to leave her alone. He took a step forward.

Her head jerked when his foot crunched the leaves on the last step. In one fluid motion, she stood and whirled towards him.

"I'm sorry. I didn't mean to startle you." He raised his hands.

She relaxed. "It's okay, I was going inside." She picked up a remote-control like device from the bench, still strung and on defensive.

"Please don't go on my account. I couldn't sleep and was curious when I saw the gate open. Please sit, else I'll feel… er… bad," he added lamely, somehow wanting to assure her that he didn't have any sinister intentions.

Ashima hesitated but sat down, smoothening the *kurta* on her lap. "We normally keep it closed during the day. It's not safe for kids," she said.

Zayd nodded and sat on the other edge of the bench wide enough for three people. His glance fell on the bruise on her arm. "He hurt you!"

"Huh?" She followed his line of sight, then rubbed her arm and shifted on her side. "It's nothing."

He was in two minds about discussing the afternoon's debacle. Though it reeked of trouble, it was none of his business. She might consider his curiosity as an intrusion. Moreover, Baba had advised him to lay low for the rest of the parole period. The memories of prison again brought a wave of fear and anxiety but he managed to suppress the negative emotion.

They sat there, staring at the valley below and savouring the soothing breeze and the sound of crickets— nature at its best. The scent of Night Jasmine was the strongest here, but he still couldn't spot the plant.

"Can't we talk?" he said after a couple of minutes of staring at the twinkling lights in the village. An urge to talk to a living being who was not a fellow prisoner or a sneering guard took him by surprise. The need to interact with someone who wouldn't address him as a number or a criminal was something he hadn't come across in a while now.

"About what?" She again shifted a little and glanced at him.

If she moved a centimeter more he was sure she would fall. "Anything, the moon, the stars or about you?" He couldn't help but look at her. The silver moonlight fell on her face, reminding him of the night when he had thought of her as a ghost. Today she looked like a delicate waif, with her nude face and that mole.

"Me?" She frowned at him, then at her hands clasped on her lap. "What do you keep writing the whole day, Mr. Rizvi?"

He frowned at the change in subject and the forced emphasis on formality. "It's Zayd."

"What?"

"You can call me Zayd."

"Are you writing some kind of thesis?"

She was a tough one. A corner of his mind saluted her perseverance to keep the conversation away from her. "No, I am doing my MFA in Creative Writing. I write stories, articles… anything that catches my fancy."

"Why Kasauli?"

"Needed a change of scene. This place is so peaceful. Who was that man? The one who came in the afternoon. He appeared to be bad news." Zayd couldn't stop himself. She needed to be warned.

"Yeah…" She sighed and again brought the converation back on him. "Is your course a distance learning one?"

"Yeah…" he repeated her response. Two can play the game.

"Are you from Delhi?"

That got him thinking. He was born in Hyderabad and lived like a nomad at various boarding schools. What should he say? Yes, he was from Delhi because he had been living there for the last four years, although in a prison. Because he had never ever set his feet out of that place for the full four years, hence he belonged to the place. Because it was the longest he had been living in any place at one go. And Delhi was also his mother's hometown.

"I don't think it was that tough a question." Now she looked at him, straight into the eyes.

"Yes, I'm from Delhi. What about you?"

"Kasauli, where else?" She glanced at her hands on her lap.

She was lying, and it annoyed him. He didn't know why, but it did. He gave up. Small talk was never his forte. They sat there, each immersed in their own thoughts. Delhi reminded him of the happy summer holidays when his mother was alive—the sprawling lawns and long corridors where he would play hide and seek with the large family and a bevy of servants.

"I think I should be going." She stood up. "Please lock the gate when you leave."

He came out of his thoughts. She looked composed but faint lines of worry still marred her forehead. For a second it took him back to the day when her mother had received her medical test results. At that time he was too small to know, but the reports had confirmed that she had cancer. The familiar pain cut through his chest.

The tension in her eyes pulled at his heart—the way it did in the outhouse. He wanted to comfort and soothe her. His pulse went haywire and his gaze invariably went to her hair-parting. The faint red line reminded him—again—that she was a married woman, and out of bounds.

"Good night, Mr. Rizvi."

"Good night… er… Ashima." He didn't know which little devil made him call her by her first name, after the resolve to be on her good side. Perhaps it was her relentless thrust on formality or constant reference to him as mister. He didn't know, but it felt good.

Her eyelids flickered at his face. Then she pursed her lips, schooled her face like a warden and left with quick steps.

Boy, was she angry!

For the first time after coming out of the prison, an effortless smile appeared on his lips. It felt good to tease and annoy her. A heavy stone that had lodged in his chest on the day of his sentence in the court loosened a bit. Though he had been released two weeks back, he felt free only in that second.

Yeah, it felt good.

***

Zayd had explored Kasauli and had even befriended Raghu, the famous *dhaba* owner. He had surprised himself by extending the stay for the full week without even scouting for any other hotel. Not that there was any problem in the guest house, except for the lurking ghosts and unwanted visitors. The food lived up to Ramprasad's sales pitch. He smiled. He was smiling a lot these days. But he felt bored too.

It was not Kasauli that was bugging him. He knew exactly what… no, who was bothering him. It had been two days since that night on the stone bench and Ms. Nightingale was not to be seen thereafter. It appeared that she was making deliberate effort to avoid him.

Would addressing her by her first name be considered that grave an insult in present times? So much so that she had decided to go incognito. But why did he do that? She would have thought he was hitting on her. Hitting on a Hindu married woman. Unacceptable. He could picture his father shaking his head in disapproval.

Zayd needed some brisk exercise to stop obsessing about her and clear his mind. The plot wasn't falling in place either. Akshat would call up any time and throw a fit if he told him the real progress on the book. He tied up his sneakers and decided to go on the Gilbert Trail, a famous trekking path for tourists.

The town was small and still untouched by commercial vultures. The sloping tiled roofs and chimneys added to the colonial charm of the place—beautiful in bright red, green or blue colors.

The Christ Church down the road was the highlight of the town. It reminded him of an old Victorian English movie he had seen with his mother. This was weird. Usually he thought of his mother when he felt low, which was the case most of the time. Today he remembered a good memory with her, which was almost never the case since the time she had died. Too many firsts made him wonder. Was it the fresh mountain air or something else?

Walking back on the lower mall road he stopped at Raghu's. The *dhaba* was in a nook off the road, sheltered by a jutting rock from the mountain. A hut stood on the cleared ground up the slope from the road, which was the Raghu family's living quarters. The rickety wooden benches and long tables were scattered haphazardly in the small area. Only the cooking area had a thatched sloping roof. The rest of the place was like an open-air restaurant, inexpensive yet inviting. The beetle-chewing Raghu did business only in the evenings—serving snacks with tea, and later chicken curries and naan for dinner.

While going back, Zayd thought he saw someone familiar near a grove of pine trees a little inside the forest along the road. Pooja, the girl from the guest house, stood there talking to someone he couldn't see. The whole setup looked like a sleazy Bollywood movie scene. The man hid as if trying to hide his identity thereby exposing her. They were having some kind of an argument. Then she turned and walked away. The man didn't follow her.

***

EIGHT

Ashima cursed her decision to bring Rishabh with her to the market a third time. She was already tired lugging the grocery bags in both her hands and Rishabh clinging to one of her legs demanding to pick him up. And they were only half way to home.

As she cajoled Rishabh to walk a few steps, she threw a fleeting glance at Raghu's *dhaba* where Zayd Rizvi sat with his laptop and numerous empty tea cups in front. So this was where he had been spending his afternoons and evenings the past few days.

The stone bench facing the valley was her favorite spot for relaxing after a full day of work, but Ashima had avoided it for the past two nights. In fact, she had restricted her movements all over the house whenever he was around. She, in any case, didn't want to encourage private rendezvous with a guest, that too a man.

The way he had taken her name that night had raised her hackles again. She had walked away seething at his audacity and ignoring her heart's erratic beating—it was nothing but anger. How could he take her name like that? She had never given him any encouragement to act so familiar, always treating him like a guest. What was he playing at? Did he think she was an easy game in her husband's absence? Sade's 'Smooth Operator' began playing in her mind.

Or was she being too sensitive?

Watching him bent over his laptop, she couldn't help but wonder. Everything about him was a contradiction.

She had never seen him talking to anyone, but he was on good terms with Raghu and Shankar. He woke up early in the morning and exercised daily. She had never seen anyone so disciplined with respect to their fitness.

Later in the day, if he was in the house, he would be writing, and if he went out, the laptop bag was always with him. He even had a mobile phone, which was a luxury considering they had been launched recently. Though the laptop and mobile looked new, his clothes and shoes were ordinary and well worn. The disciplined, quiet nature clashed with the full arm tattoo and muscled body.

"Mamma, *godiiii*…" Rishabh wailed.

Ashima sighed and looked down. "*Beta*, how can I? I have so many things in my hands? Walk Rishu, you are a big boy now."

"No mamma! Pick me up pleash, I tiredh… hunh, hunh…" He sat crying on the dirty road, with no regard to the dust clinging on to him.

Ashima gritted her teeth and felt like giving him a hard one on the back side. She glared at him. "Get up Rishabh or I'll leave you here and then you will not have the chocolate I've bought for you. I'll give it to Pooja *bua*."

The threat backfired. He began wailing all the more loudly. She looked around and had no choice, but to carry one of the grocery bags on her shoulder and pick him up, but she knew she would get tired after ten steps. The second option was to leave one bag back in the shop and come for it later, but she needed everything for dinner tonight.

"What's the problem young man?"

She heard Zayd and turned. Her heart skipped in her rib-cage as her gaze landed on him talking to Rishabh. The two day stubble accentuated his striking face. He was most certainly fairer to even Pooja, who was considered highly blessed in the fairness department. The snug blue jeans and the black t-shirt stretching on his broad shoulders and biceps made him look taller than her earlier impression of him. Zayd's deep voice coaxing Rishu to stand up made her realize that she was checking him out unabashedly. She shook off her frivolous thoughts and concentrated on her son and the problem at hand.

"I thought you told me you were a soldier." Sitting on his haunches, he spoke to Rishabh and her son was responding without any tantrums.

She stared at the two of them and frowned. When did they get so friendly? Rishabh played in the backyard in the evenings. She would have a chat with Shankar about this.

"I aaamm…" Rishabh continued to cry and answer.

"But a soldier doesn't cry. Timid kids cry, not the brave ones."

The crying stopped immediately and he rubbed his hands on his eyes, dirt smeared all over his face. Ashima sighed, a bath had become an immediate necessity. Rishabh looked at the man, rapt in attention.

"Now get up like a brave soldier and lets do a left-right march."

"I want *godi*."

"He is tired. I shouldn't have brought him." Ashima intervened.

"Where's the car?"

"The battery is down."

"Ok fine, come on, up on my shoulders." Zayd spread his hands towards Rishabh.

"I want mamma *godiii*."

Zayd then held out his hands towards her for the bags.

"Please, I shouldn't be asking you to do this! You have your laptop bag too." She didn't want to be indebted to him, even for such a small task, but Rishu had left her with no choice.

"It's okay. I'm also going back home."

She tried not to show her surprise at the way he said home, and reluctantly handed one bag to him. He bent down and picked up the other too.

"Can I request you to go ahead?" she asked.

The eyebrows came together as he stared at her.

"I'm sorry, but we shouldn't be seen walking together," she clarified.

That deepened the scowl. "Why?"

"They tell tales and spread things around."

"Who?"

"Moral police of the town. Here everyone knows everyone."

His lips tightened.

"Please do try—"

He exhaled. "Fine, you go ahead. I'll bring these later."

"I need them for dinner."

"I'll bring them on time."

"Thanks."

***

From the dining room, Ashima watched him enter the gate in long strides carrying the bags effortlessly. Shankar met him in the driveway and took the load off him.

"Zayd *bhaiya* is asking fo cah keys." Shankar announced the moment he entered the kitchen with the grocery bags.

"Zayd *bhaiya*?" Ashima couldn't contain the incredulity creeping up in her tone.

"…is asking fo cah keys. To give it a jump stawt." Shankar had left the parking lights on when he was cleaning it from inside.

She frowned. "Tell him, he has done enough, thank you. I'll take care of it."

Shankar went out unhappy about his decision being dismissed.

This was bizarre. First he tried to get familiar with her and he was winning over her entire family one by one. He had made Radha his fan by rising early and exercising. What was so exciting about getting up with the sun? Rishabh too was listening to him on the Mall Road as if he was his long lost friend, and now Shankar!

When did he endear himself so much to her staff and son?

"*Didi*, there is a man standing in front of the pine tree near the gate and staring at the house. I had seen him day before yesterday too." Radha entered the kitchen to start the evening meal.

"A man?"

"Tall and bald, a little old."

"Okay, I'll check."

Ashima pretended to stroll along the driveway glancing nonchalantly at and around the gate, but couldn't find anyone remotely resembling Radha's description. She dismissed the whole thought when she saw no one even after the third round. Her staff was getting unnecessarily paranoid since the ghost scare.

She also needed to have a discussion with entire Ramprasad family and Rishabh about strangers.

Real soon.

***

The PTA meet in Rishabh's pre-school was a long one. First of all she had to drive the fifteen year old, refurbished, Maruti car for such a long distance, and on top of it she was required to meet all the teachers, including the sports coach. This was what you got for sending your child in a private school.

"All for show," she muttered, getting in the queue to meet the behavioral counselor.

"Your child is winking at everyone these days, Mrs. Joshi." The counselor opened the conversation.

"What?" Ashima gasped.

"Yes, he winks at the students, the teachers and everyone. And once he starts, he doesn't stop. Must have picked up the bad habit from one of the servants at home."

"None of my servants would do or teach him something like this Ms. Khanna. They simply don't have time. We'll just clarify this." Ashima frowned at Rishabh, who was playing with building blocks at a separate table, oblivious to the discussion over his supposedly disgusting habit.

"Rishabh."

He looked up.

"How do you wink?"

He winked at her in answer, smiled and went back to his block tower. Eyes widening, Ashima glanced at the woman, now sitting smug in her chair. The counselor expelled a long drawn breath.

"Who taught you to wink, Rishu?"

"Aaydh."

"Who?"

"Aaydh, my fren."

"Who is Aaydh?" She asked the counselor.

The lady shrugged and shook her head.

"Who is Aaydh, Rishu?"

"My fren," he replied, least bothered about his mother's mortification.

Ashima sighed and changed the track. "Where is Aaydh?"

"In the guesth loom."

Ashima connected the lisping name and stared at Rishabh, engrossed in building the highest tower.

This was followed by long monologues from the counselor about positive and negatives of her three year old winking and the responsibilities of a parent. The lady labored to justify her salary, with Ashima nodding and responding with monosyllables interspersed between the tirade. She was allowed to leave with Rishabh after a good twenty minutes.

She looked at her son's happy, cherubic face, munching his favorite chocolate bar, and forgot every pain and tension of her life. He pointed at a flower and smiled. They stood admiring the school's garden and the ducks swimming in the small pond.

"When did he become your friend, sweetheart?"

"Who?"

"Zayd."

"I play, he play in eveninths."

Zayd had been in the guest house for more than a week. So it has been going for some time now, Ashima thought. No wonder Rishabh was much at ease with him in the market. Ashima sighed at the now crouching Rishabh who was trying to attract the ducks' attention. It was after a while that they made their way to the car. Rishabh settled snugly in the car, enjoying the journey.

As she took the last turn towards the home, Rishabh sat up straight and pointed. "*Bua!*"

"Don't be silly, *bua* is in college."

"No bua, there…" Rishabh pointed one pudgy finger at someone far away.

Ashima brought the car to the curb and switched off. She looked in the direction Rishabh was pointing at and it was Pooja indeed, with another student. The way they were talking and smiling didn't bode well with Ashima. The young man looked harmless, but stood too close to Pooja. She should have been in college. What was she doing here with this man? Ashima switched on the ignition and drove with another worry germinating in her mind.

***

Raghu's *dhaba* had become Zayd's alternate working haunt. After a few days, Raghu had learnt about his taste for black tea and had a cup ready whenever he wanted. Sitting with his back to the road, no one disturbed him while he worked on his story. The killer had had the first taste of the kill and had managed to fool the police and detectives. His mood was euphoric and he wanted to celebrate.

A vehicle screeched and stopped, swirling the dust all around. Someone shouted and banged the door of the vehicle, but Zayd was too deep in the world of his story to register the commotion.

A heavy hand slapped on his shoulder. On pure reflex—borne out of four years of constantly being on guard in the prison—he gave a twist to the hand and pulled the man forward. The man went sprawling forward into the wild hedge with a thud and a muffled grunt.

Zayd pivoted, his fists raised, furious to take on anyone else who might be attacking. Breathing hard, he found himself face to face with a well-dressed man, the one who had threatened Ashima the other day. The man took a step back with a dumbfounded expression on his face.

"Why did you do that?" The man asked.

"*Haath kyun lagaya?*" Zayd clamped down the revulsion creeping in his bones. "He shouldn't have touched me." The nervous tick began on his jaw as he clenched it.

The side-kick on the ground got up and dusted off the debris clinging to his clothes and shouted, "What the—"

"Keep quiet. I want to talk." The man, his boss, raised his hand and looked at Zayd. "Who are you and when are you going back?"

"Going back? Where?"

"Back home."

"What's it to you?" Zayd narrowed his eyes and fisted his hands to stop the trembling.

"Who are you?" The boss repeated and straightened to his full height reaching up to Zayd's shoulder.

Zayd slid his hands in his pockets and kept a wary eye on both of them.

"I don't want you to stay in the guest house. If you want I can make arrangements for you at a three-star hotel, at the same price. Have lot of clout in this area. How many days are you thinking of staying?"

Zayd stared at him incredulously. Every minute the picture was getting clearer. They wanted to run her out of the business and force her to sell the house. He could bet that the ghosts were also his men.

The man exhaled when Zayd remained silent. "Don't take unnecessary *panga* with me. You don't know who I am."

Anger replaced the nervousness and anxiety. Zayd turned away from them, sat on the bench and began typing. He didn't know what he typed, his entire focus was on the two men standing at the back. If they made any move, he was ready for them no matter what the cost. But nothing happened. A moment later he heard the vehicle drive away.

"*Saab, yeh toh achha nahin hua*, not good," Raghu said shaking his head and righting an overturned bench. "These people are locals, dangerous."

"Who is he?" Zayd watched the jeep driving away.

"Kanyal… Hari Prasad Kanyal. He has just won the local election."

The name jogged the memory of his arrival in Kasauli at the hotel. He could also bet that the plot adjacent to the guest house belonged to Mr. Hari Prasad Kanyal.

"*Saab?*" Raghu was still frowning.

"Don't worry," he said for Raghu's sake, but he was worried.

He had promised himself that he would not interfere in anyone's affair, but this man was hell bent on making it personal.

***

NINE

"**Pooja** what's happening in your college these days?" Ashima broached the delicate subject when Pooja came to help her in the kitchen as per their daily routine. Amma insisted Pooja should help and thereby learn to handle kitchen chores with Ashima.

"Nothing special, just routine stuff." Pooja shrugged, cutting the dry fruits for the dessert.

"No boyfriends and all?"

Pooja's hand froze at her words for a moment, then continued shredding the cashew nut. "What *bhabhi*? Boyfriends? In Kasauli? You are not even allowed to think like that, Amma would kill me."

"Nevertheless, there must be someone whom you like and admire, even if it is from a distance." She desperately wanted Pooja to voluntarily confide in her. "I fell in and out of love so many times before your brother came along and you know…"

Pooja kept silent for a minute or two, then said, "You are from Delhi and from an army family, that's the reason you are even able to talk about it. I can't even dream of liking someone."

Ashima glanced at her and decided to drop the subject since it was time for dinner and she didn't have time to spare. She inspected the dinner fare one last time and called Radha to start making chapatis, but Pooja's evasive answers and the memory of her in the woods kept niggling her until it was time to speak to Zayd about the winking business.

God, she was so tired!

Ashima took out the baby alarm her parents had gifted her, and checked the battery. Positioning the transmitter near Rishabh, she took the receiver with her.

Two steps from the door, Ashima turned back and opened her almirah. Opening the safe, she took out her mangalsutra. After a moment of contemplation she wore it around her neck and left the room.

She was about to turn towards the guest rooms when she noticed a faint light coming from the gazebo. He sat in his favorite corner of the garden, pounding at the keyboard of his laptop. The high mast light was not enough, but he kept typing with that single minded focus she had noticed about him. Nothing disturbed him when he was on his writing spree and typed like professional typists, using all the fingers.

He sensed rather than heard her approach. His fingers stopped and back stiffened when she put her foot on the first of the three steps leading to its floor.

He stood up and turned, supporting the laptop in his hands. His notebook and pen slipped down on the floor.

"I'm really sorry to disturb you. But… er… I wanted to talk to you." She picked up the articles and found him looking at her with those dreamy eyes.

"Yeah sure."

There was a hint of eagerness in his tone. In fact he looked pleased to see her. For a moment she saw his gaze flicker towards her mole then look straight at her, waiting.

His interested green gaze, and the crazy way her heart reacted pierced her self-confidence. She forgot the problem she had come to discuss for a moment, and stood there wringing the *dupatta* in her hand. She stopped when she realized she was making her discomfort known. The receiver in her hand reminded her of the issue. "I wanted to talk to you about Rishabh."

"Shall we sit?" He gestured towards the chairs.

"No, er… it'll take only a few minutes." She dismissed his request with a wave of her hand. "It seems he has been playing with you in the evenings."

"Oh, it's not a problem. I like playing with him."

"No, it's not that…"

His whole body tensed and his eyes narrowed, appearing greener under the low illumination of the garden. He looked angry. That was surprising, since he was interacting with her kid without her permission. In fact, he should be the one on the back-foot.

"I mean, I'm fine with him playing with you. But…"

"But…?" He frowned.

"It seems you have taught him how to wink."

"Yeah, I did. Is that a problem?" Though his frown deepened, he now sounded a bit defensive.

"Yes. He seems to be practicing at school on the kids and teachers. There's a complaint."

He let out a small laugh. "A complaint? About a three year old winking? Are they running a *gurukul* or what?"

"I would request you—"

"Oh come on! He is a toddler. He should be having fun, and some mischief should be permitted." He waved his hand in the air, then added. "They should be allowed to be free and—"

"Well, if you ask me, I don't mind. But he is winking at any and everybody including the Principal, the peon, and the ducks."

He laughed out loud throwing his head back, the way she wanted to do in front of the counsellor, but couldn't.

She smiled, and a sliver of pride ran through her at her baby's vivaciousness and daring. Their eyes met, and she saw the same sentiments mirrored in his eyes too. The shared emotion kindled something between them as they stood staring at each other. The valley breeze whistled softly breaking the silence. Her breathing became shallow as if the entire oxygen had been sucked out of the arbor.

She dropped her gaze to her toes breaking the contact. "I have told him not to wink at everyone. But in future if you teach him anything naughty, just explain the do's and don'ts as well."

"That makes sense." He nodded relaxing at her words. "I thought you didn't want me to interact with him at all."

"Why?" She frowned. "Why would I want that?"

"It's just... just that... I mean—"

He glanced at the nearby bougainvillea bush, at a loss for words, which was surprising since he kept writing the whole day.

Then he shook his head and said. "Oh, forget it. I got it. I'll take care." He looked a little uneasy and glanced down. "Why don't you wear slippers?"

"Huh…" She looked at her feet.

"Ramprasad was saying something about snakes et al…"

She chuckled. "Oh, it's nothing. They are timid creatures by nature. Totally harmless."

"Still, you shouldn't take chances." He nodded then looked directly into her eyes. "Have you… by any chance… er… been avoiding me?"

"No, not at all." Her reply came fast, a little too quick for her liking. "Why would you think that?"

"No reason. Nothing… just wondered, that's it."

"Was there a problem? Is it your room or food?"

"No, should there be a reason? Can't we just share a few moments without any motive? Without any baggage of life?"

Baggage? What kind of baggage did he carry at such a young age? He was studying. He owned a vehicle, a laptop, a mobile phone. His parents must be rich to send him on a holiday. They must have set him free to do whatever he wanted, at least that was what the tattoos indicated. What kind of baggage could he be carrying?

"Please." He waved a hand towards the chairs again, gesturing her to sit.

She glanced back at the house, the lights in the rooms were off. If she sat down no one would be able to spot them. In any case she had the baby alarm for Rishabh. But what about him? Should she trust him? What if he misconstrued her?

"Who are you afraid of now? Is it the society again? Or is it me?" His gaze flickered towards her hair parting.

"No, it's nothing like that."

"Then what? I thought you were your own boss."

The fact that he was challenging her made her question his intentions. Her heart—beating too wildly for her liking—wasn't helping too. She scowled and fidgeted with the receiver of the baby alarm, unable to think of any excuse.

He sighed. "Never mind, I wanted to give you this."

She looked at him. He was holding the keys to the back garden gate. Was there a little inflection of disappointment in his voice? Or did she imagine it?

"You may sit in your 'just me' place, I'll not intrude."

His resigned tone made her feel guilty of not taking up on his offer. But she couldn't make amends—the moment was lost. She nodded and took the keys, surprised at his accurate assessment about the bench off the back garden. He was too perceptive.

"Good night," he said as she turned to go. "… Ashima," he added softly, almost like a whisper.

Her heart thudded again at his deep baritone taking her name with clear emphasis on each syllable, imprinting it on his tongue. It felt kind of warm. No. Intimate.

As she lay down on the bed, Ashima absentmindedly patted Rishabh who was fast asleep. Disturbed, he turned towards her breathing deeply with the thumb in his mouth. She gently pulled his thumb out. He squirmed a little at the absence of the warmth and comfort, then settled down.

Despite the whole day of running around, sleep eluded her like a sulky friend. An unaccustomed restlessness had engulfed her tonight.

Her mind kept rewinding the conversation with Zayd Rizvi in the arbor. They both had shared a moment of pride about Rishu—she as a mother and he as a teacher. She had never shared this kind of pride about her little one with anyone. Amma, suffering with rheumatoid pain and obsessing with Rohit's astrological charts, was least bothered about her grandson, and Pooja, barely out of her teens, never showed any maternal inclination towards him. But he had cared.

Her heart had uncharacteristically knocked against her ribs when she had looked into his eyes—the intense hazel with brown iris. She could count the specs in them if she wanted. No doubt he was a handsome man. And she had come across many men like him whom she had admired, then dismissed as soon as they were out of sight.

So why was she unable to do that now? For God's sake he was younger to her! And her own husband was no less handsome, then why should a stranger's presence loom like a shadow on her mind?

Dismissing the irrational sensations as one of those moments, she picked up Rohit's photo frame from the side table and traced his smiling lips. Tears filled her eyes as usual. *Where are you, my sweetheart? Please come* back to me. She sent out a silent prayer to the almighty and vowed to call Ved the next day. Hugging the frame to her chest, she slid into a restless sleep.

***

It was THE day—a day when the whole house would be shrouded in silent, unspoken grief. Amma, as usual, had ensconced herself near the small prayer area inside the house. She wouldn't even eat breakfast or lunch. Thankfully, it was a week day. Pooja and Rishabh went to their respective college and school and were spared the ordeal of negativity and pessimism.

Ashima made it a point to go to the temple as well as the church.

She entered the oldest church of Kasauli, lit a candle, then sat in one of the pews, gazing at the altar. Educated in a convent, the church's atmosphere was not new to her. She found solace in the serene silence of the huge, uncluttered hall. There were a couple of other people—at a distance—each one seeking privacy while communing with the Almighty.

This year Rohit's memories had not brought the torrent of tears they usually did. The hollow and bereft feeling was leaving her, making her nervous. She was losing touch with the hope which had propelled her to live and go on. The grief was giving way to acceptance of the catastrophe and hopelessness. Time had become an enemy rather than friend in her case.

She forced herself to recall his last birthday that they had celebrated alone, just the two of them. He found the ritual of cutting a cake ridiculous, but tolerated and indulged her whims. That night, teasing her mercilessly, he had smeared the cake all over her face, then made love to her like she was his queen. A tear trickled down from one of her eyes. The memory triggered another one and she lost track of time.

Someone slid in her row breaking her trance. Trying to be discreet, she wiped her tears and couldn't help but sniffle. After a couple of deep breaths, she glanced on her right and found Zayd sitting. Her mind surprised her by referring to him by his first name.

"What are you doing here?" she muttered when he didn't say anything.

"Searching for some answers."

"What answers?"

"Shouldn't you ask, what questions?"

She sighed. "Okay, what questions?"

"What are you doing here?"

She pursed her lips. "Was this the question for which you were looking for an answer?"

"No."

She exhaled and got up. He held her hand.

"I'm sorry. Please sit." He pulled at her hand.

She stared where his hand gripped hers and he released her in a microsecond. She sat down and crossed her arms.

"I'm sorry. You looked so forlorn, I was trying to distract you."

Surprisingly, he didn't utter a word after she nodded and accepted his apology. She was also not in the mood for small talk. They sat in companionable silence gazing at the cross on the altar. In fact, she was looking at the altar and the candles, and he was staring at a paper in his hand.

She brought her attention back to her meditation. The yellow glow from the candles and the lights from the stained glass somehow soothed her. Why was the intensity of the loss today not as piercing as it was last year? Was she also falling into her mother's pessimistic, defeatist state? No, she was not going to lose hope. Of course he would come. They would hear some news soon. She was doing all she could. God would hear her prayers soon.

Zayd exhaled beside her, shredding the paper and stuffing the pieces in his pocket. He would have looked like an overgrown boy but for his height and two-day stubble.

"What are you tearing?"

"Nothing, it's a poem I wrote a long time back, but it hasn't come out well."

"Why tear it, when you can improve it."

"Some things can't be mended. The patches will always be visible."

He was a strange mix of a wise man and a spoilt brat. Appearance wise he looked as if he had been pampered his whole life, but at times he said something that hinted at a wisdom beyond his age.

"How did you know that I was here? Did you follow me?" She scowled.

His glance went to each of her features, one by one, as if wondering about her opinion about him. "I was sitting outside the church when you entered. Out of curiosity I came inside. If you call this following then yes, I did follow you."

She dropped her aggressive stare at the innocent explanation. "Sorry."

"What's with everyone today?"

Someone in the first pew turned and looked at them.

"We shouldn't talk here."

He nodded and followed her out.

The church was mostly deserted but safe with only the staff living on the premises. She was friends with most of the residents of the holy place and enjoyed walking in the well-maintained gardens.

They settled on one of the concrete benches under the shade of trees.

"So?" he said when she just sat there staring at a squirrel enjoying the sunshine.

She had never narrated the exact circumstances about Rohit to anyone. Till date everyone had known through someone or the other. No one had directly asked her. She exhaled again. "Rohit, my husband, is 'missing in action' since the Kargil war." Her throat clogged on the last word. She blinked fast. She wouldn't cry in front of a stranger.

He opened his mouth, then closed it. After a few seconds he said, "I... I'm sorry... I don't know what to say, I thought... I—"

"It's okay. Today, it's the fourth year since the news—" A lone, traitorous tear escaped her eye and rolled down. She wiped it on her shoulder.

"Didn't they conduct any rescue missions?"

"They have. The wreckage of the plane is found. He ejected before it crashed, but they... we are unable to locate him or... They are suspecting he might have landed across the border." She didn't voice the other probabilities they had laid out and their conclusions. In fact the other possibilities were unthinkable. Unacceptable.

"What about the Pakistan army? If he is there then they should inform our Armed Forces. They have done it in other cases, haven't they?"

"Yes. So far there is no news about him. I have approached and written to all governing bodies. There's no news." Involuntarily, she turned to him and looked straight into his eyes. "No news is good news. Isn't it?" She wanted some kind of a reassurance today, even if it was from a stranger. She needed that ray of hope to cling to, even if Rohit was in some Pakistan prison, or in a village—recuperating or unable to move. There was a chance that she would see him alive and he would come back.

"Yes... yes, of course."

His surprised, hurried answer embarrassed her. She regretted asking the question. This was one battle she had to fight alone. No, not alone. Amma was also with her. This was the only belief which united them.

"Life's never fair."

The profound statement, conveyed with a melancholy detachment, reemphasized her reading of his personality. Maybe writers become wise fast, far beyond their biological age. She noticed his clenched jaw and the pulse throbbing under his ear. The other night he had mentioned something about carrying a baggage.

"Why are you here? I have never seen you praying?"

He glanced at her, slightly amused. "Are you keeping tabs on me?"

"I have noticed you never pray during the Azaan in the evenings."

He nodded. "You are right, I'm not a fan of rituals. But I'm seeking answers for a few questions, and am tired of asking Allah. He has never answered so I thought to ask someone else. But it seems, same is the case here as well. Gods just keep quiet and watch the drama."

She smirked. "Some say all answers are within us. We unnecessarily blame the Gods."

He stayed silent. Clasping his hands tightly he watched a squirrel, who had dared enough to come near his foot.

"Is everything all right with you?"

"Yeah…" he replied immediately, then added, "Yes, everything's okay."

"Do you plan to stay here for long?"

"Why, you are already fed up of me?" Though he didn't smile, his eyes showed he was jesting.

"No, just making mundane conversation."

"Mundane. Yes, that could help. It's a good escape mechanism."

The way he nodded like a wise old man, brought a reluctant smile on her lips. "I thought young men were as reckless as they come and do not have any emotional bones in their body."

"I'm not young or reckless and neither am I emotional." He frowned. "You know my age?"

"From the driving license you had given during the registration. And twenty-four is young."

"And I bet you are a grandmother," he muttered under his breath.

Ignoring him, she looked around and asked. "What was the question you were thinking of asking, in there?" She flicked her head towards the main church hall.

He snorted and combed his hair with both his hands looking at the towering pine trees. "There are no answers to any of my questions."

His evasive answers had begun to irritate her. "If there are no answers, then I think we should go."

"What's the hurry? Your only guest is here with you."

She looked at his now grinning face. "Is that what you have learnt to do? Be flippant whenever you lose control of your emotions?"

"It helps, doesn't it?"

"Yes, it does."

"Mundane and flippancy. What a combination." He patted the bench. "Relax, sit."

They sat and had a light hearted chat, talking of everything—the sun, weather, news, politics, film stars and cricket but nothing personal—steering clear of pessimistic thoughts. It was as if they both were bound by an unwritten code of not going into something which might bring back memories and cast a dark shadow on the sunny day.

"What happened? Am I not right?" he asked on a political aspect they were debating on.

"You are right… yes. I should be going. Rishabh will be home soon." She stood up. She didn't want to go, but school was about to get over. "Zayd, could you please foll—" She picked up her bag.

"Yeah… yeah… I'll come after half an hour."

"Ashima…"

"Hmm…"

"You said my name."

Her gaze bounced to his incredulous face. She exhaled. "Yeah… so? Is that a big deal?"

"That is what I was saying, no big deal. And you have pronounced 'z' exactly right, as I want people to pronounce."

She shook her head.

He laughed. The laughter rang out in the garden making Ashima smile. There had been a subtle shift in their association today—from acquaintances to friends—bound by something tragic. Yes, something bad had happened in his life. He was just not ready to disclose.

***

TEN

The next morning, Zayd positioned himself under the arbor with his laptop. He sat facing the bungalow. His gaze kept floating to the front doors for a glimpse of her.

Their conversation yesterday replayed in his mind. He didn't have the heart to tell her that Flight Lieutenant Joshi might not have survived in the mountains of Kargil. And that there was no likelihood of seeing him alive or even finding his body. As far as he had read about the war, if Joshi had been found, the Pakistan authorities would have informed in all the cases—demise or injury or if he had been taken as a prisoner. But if he was missing for four years, then there would be negligible chances of him being alive.

His reminiscence was broken by a shiny black sedan entering the gate. A uniformed driver opened the car door and a lady alighted. She scanned the garden, threw a fleeting glance at him and entered the house. The driver took out various packets of all shapes and sizes from the car and staggered behind her.

Zayd re-read what he had written on his screen and swore. Nothing made sense. He deleted the paragraph, thought through the scene and started again.

***

"*Bhabhi*, aunty is here." Pooja peeked into her bedroom.

"Who, mamma?" Ashima frowned. "Oh… no," she muttered.

Pooja giggled. "You will be the first daughter to have such kind of disdain for her parent's visit."

Ashima smiled and turned to face her mother as she entered her room. Her perfectly tied tissue saree looked completely out of place in Ashima's spartan, humble bedroom. Pooja slinked out of the way after a hurried '*namaste*'.

With her maternal grandfather and father both from the army, her mother was the epitome of elegance, poise. She lived and breathed army life. She had opposed Ashima's marriage to Rohit, who was from a middle class family. But Rohit had captured Ashima's heart the moment she had seen him during one of the various functions. Since then, her mother had not forgiven Ashima or Rohit or her in-laws.

"How are you *beta*?" Her mother glanced around, her lips in that permanent sneer whenever she entered their home. Pooja and everyone knew her too well, so they kept to their rooms whenever she visited. Ashima looked at her mother and couldn't understand how a woman—a caring parent and her best friend before marriage—would turn into her biggest foe when she needed her the most.

"I wanted to meet Rishabh, and talk to you." Behind her, the driver entered the room, his arms full of presents for her and Rishabh. She never brought anything for Amma or for Pooja. "These are for you and Rishabh," she explained unnecessarily.

"Thanks Mamma... I'm well, how are you? And Daddy?" Manners and etiquettes were to be observed at all times of the day, regardless of any situation or frame of mind as per her mother. "Would you like to have something? Water? Tea?"

"Tea is fine."

She made herself comfortable, as comfortable as she could in Ashima's tiny bedroom while Ashima instructed Radha to bring tea and snacks.

"What have you thought about your Daddy's proposal?" She began her torture the moment Ashima sat down beside her on the bed.

"Mamma…" She sighed. "We have had this discussion so many times, I'm tired of it."

"And I'm tired of you. What's the need to run this pathetic guest house? Just leave everything and come live with us. Rishabh can go to the wonderful AF school and you can start your business as you wanted to before the marriage."

"I'm happy here."

"Happy? Really?" She waved her hands around.

"Yes."

"You are such a—" She held her hand. "*Beta* please… sometimes think without being emotional. Sometimes you need to be a little selfish… for yourself… for your future."

"Mamma, please stop thinking about my future or me." Ashima closed her eyes and rubbed her forehead.

"Can't you understand what you feel for Rishabh I feel for you?"

"But you are forgetting Rishabh is three and I'm twenty-six. I'll never impose my wishes on him when he grows up."

"Be careful what you say… and pray he doesn't turn out as headstrong as you have." She blinked and held Ashima's hands. "I want you to have a life. I want you to smile and enjoy, I want you to have all the comforts and pleasures of life."

"That is what the difference is. It's what you want, it's not what I want. Mamma for the last time I'm not your little girl, I have a little boy of my own!" The silence after her words and the tears appearing in her mother's eyes made her realize she was shouting at her. She sighed. "Look mamma I'm sorry, but why can't you accept that I'm happy here? Rishabh is thriving, I have enough to send him to the best school."

"Enough. Is this enough? Do you remember your room back in Chandigarh? Look at you. When was the last time you went to a salon? When was the last time you went to a movie? Had a vacation? Look at my friend's daughters, they dress up, go for parties. They don't have to toil in front of the stove even when the bloody maid is absent. Was this the kind of life I had envisaged for you? I don't know what kind of punishment God is giving me, my only daughter, my only child… suffering so."

Ashima snorted. "I'm not suffering as you mean, mamma. Did you know Rimi's husband is having an affair and Esha's an alcoholic? There is life beyond parties and dressing up. I love Rohit and I'm happy to look after his family. He is my strength."

"But he is no more!"

Ashima gasped. She felt like she had been slapped. Tears pricked at the back of her eyes, but she blinked them back. Her mother was immediately contrite and tried to make amends by reaching out for her hand.

"He is alive," Ashima whispered, brushing her mother's hand aside. "How can you think like that? Of course he is coming back. He is a soldier, he has been taught to survive."

"Oh sweetheart, it has been four years… oh, I'm so sorry." She added the apology as she spied Ashima's widening, watery eyes.

"He'll come," Ashima whispered. "And that's enough for me to look after his family. Imagine their unhappiness and worries. I want them to be hale and hearty when he comes back. Moreover Amma had shown his *kundli* to another renowned astrologer. He has told us this period in his life is quite tough, but he has a long life."

Her mother sat up straight, her gaze steady on Ashima's face. Ashima willed herself not to squirm.

She exhaled. "You have always been a dreamer. And his mother is feeding your hope, and hers too, with this religious mumbo-jumbo. When will both of you accept the reality?" Her mother was never one for subtlety when it came to her own opinions.

"This is my reality. And it's Rishabh's legacy."

"Daddy was telling me, you have called Ved again."

The abrupt change of topic jarred Ashima. "Yes."

She exhaled. "You have already blown away your grandmother's inheritance and Rohit's insurance money in these pointless search missions. How are you going to fund this?"

"Don't worry I'm not going to ask you."

"Okay then, come and live with us while waiting for him."

"No, I'm not going to leave this house."

"Oh, you are impossible. What kind of magic have these people woven on you?" She stood, her bosom heaving with anger. "What if he—"

"Don't say anything you might regret, mother."

Her mother stood up and stormed out of the room.

***

Zayd saw the lady come out of the house with a handkerchief to her face. The driver said something to her and handed her a book she had forgotten inside the car. She held the book for a few seconds then threw it on a chair in the corridor, sat in the car and drove off.

After a while Rishabh sauntered outside, picked up the book and ran to him. It was not a book but a photo album titled '*Jugnu*'.

After a few minutes of chattering and pointing at his mother and father's photos, Rishabh lost interest and ran off leaving the album with Zayd.

Ideally he should have returned it, but the unusual title piqued his curiosity. Thinking that he would return it at an opportune time, he took it to his room.

***

Zayd turned over the pink and gold cover in the privacy of his room. A baby Ashima stared at him from the front page. He smiled.

Although arranged in chronological order, it was a random collection of photos with Ashima and Rohit featuring in almost all the pages. In the childhood photos, they were obviously separate. With every page they seemed to grow in front of his eyes. Zayd looked at Rohit's humble upbringing standing stark in contrast with Ashima's fairytale one.

The first few pages held her birthday photographs. Rohit didn't have any. Zayd could not help but smile at all the frocks, the cakes and the gift openings. The birthday pictures were interspersed with the vacation shots. As he flipped the pages and she grew older, her feminine grace and allure became all the more evident. While Rohit was quiet as a child, she was in constant motion—vivacious, a mischief maker. Everybody had an air of indulgent tolerance about her.

A few pages later there were photographs of a college annual event where she was crowned 'Miss College'. She was wearing a golden saree and laughing at the camera. She looked so lively and beautiful, with the same vivaciousness he had glimpsed the other day when she was bargaining with the hawker over the vegetable prices.

From the next album pages Rohit appeared beside her. Zayd suppressed an unreasonable twinge in the vicinity of his chest and turned the next page. Rohit appeared to have eyes only for Ashima. The camera had brilliantly caught his undisguised adoration and affection for her. She too reciprocated and basked in the attention.

In the engagement photographs, Rohit looked dashing and perfect for her. They were a handsome couple—totally in love—surrounded by the two families and friends. The lady he saw earlier in the day was in the photos beside her. Maybe she was her mother. There was a slight resemblance.

Later, in one of the photographs, Rohit and Ashima were toasting something with their friends. The place looked like a pub, Rohit was wearing a bomber jacket and she was in a halter dress. They were having shots. It was a picture straight out of a Yash Chopra movie, where everyone was rich, sophisticated and enjoying.

Then came a few photographs of their marriage. Next they were somewhere on a beach. Zayd guessed these must be pictures of their honeymoon. An unfamiliar green emotion ran through his body and he snapped the album close.

Why should he be resentful of her association with anyone? He wasn't even aware of her existence at the time. But he was envious of Rohit, of his proximity to her, of her love for him.

It was ridiculous. He rubbed his palms over his eyes and face and focused on the chrysanthemums flowering in the pots outside, thinking about the stark difference between her past and present.

It was not only her urban lifestyle. She looked different now. He could see the beauty and elegance but the cheerful demeanor had been replaced by quiet determination. Another major contrast was her financial status. It was evident from the clothes and accessories she wore in the photographs and now. He had even spotted a tear on one of her *dupattas* the other day.

He knew after providing the best quality service and food for the guests, the rest of the income from the guest house went towards the private search missions for Rohit.

Shankar had been chatty about the family's circumstances and that was how Zayd knew everything. Right from Flight Lieutenant Joshi missing in action to the Air Force presuming him to be dead, and Kanyal threatening to gain the property for a few wads of green thrown their way. He shook his head at the predators of the society. Always hounding the vulnerable prey.

Rishabh looked exactly like Rohit. Perhaps that was the reason that motivated her to manage everything and gave her the courage to handle her numerous problems. Zayd kept thinking about her life—happy, carefree, kind of perfect. And then, something happened that marred the happiness and turned everything upside down.

It was not fair.

His life was a ready example of such pre-ordained unfairness. Barring his childhood, the only time he had been really happy after his mother's death was when he had gone to college and met Myra. She had taken him under her wing the moment she had joined the college through the exchange program. They were an item. She was the one who had offered the solace he craved. He didn't know how, but she began arranging for the drugs in her room. During the hours under the influence of the drugs and the company of Myra, he was able to forget the grief and guilt of losing his mother.

Yes, guilt.

Somehow Zayd had had this notion that he hadn't been there for her when she needed him the most. If he had been with her and had taken care of her, Ammi would have survived.

Within two months of those horrible reports, confirming that Ammi suffered from cancer, Abbu had packed him off to a boarding school in Shimla. All of nine years old, he had protested vehemently but Abbu insisted on following the tradition. He could never forget the tears Ammi tried to hide when he was leaving. Within a year in the hostel, he had tried to run away twice, but Hyderabad was very far and his father had contacts everywhere. He was found by the time he had reached the next town at the local bus stand.

The event that had created the final rift between Abbu and him was when Abbu remarried within one month of Ammi's death. To a woman who only pretended to be their well-wisher. It was the ultimate betrayal to Ammi and her memories. Abbu's actions only added to Zayd's loss and hatred and he never went home after the funeral. All the school holidays were spent at naanijaan's house in Delhi.

Then Myra happened. She had filled the void with her constant stream of novel ideas and plans for fun. She always wanted to have adrenaline running in their blood. But after two blissful years, she too left him.

He could never forget the shadows in Myra's mother's eyes when she had come to meet him in the prison. Many a sleepless nights had been spent thinking about what he could have done differently in all of his twenty years. He had let down both, his mother and Myra. The dispiriting feeling never left him.

He sighed and rubbed his forehead. Thinking about the past didn't help, but the present constantly kept throwing the questions at him, leaving him restless and angry.

Who said life was fair?

And who the hell was *Jugnu*? Ashima or Rohit?

***

ELEVEN

Ashima was folding the clothes and making neat piles on the bed when Rishabh zoomed in with his toy scooty, twisted his tongue, rolled his mouth and made a piercing horrendous sound. She cringed at the noise but tolerated. He climbed on the bed and put his mouth on her ear and increased the frequency, causing him to spit in her ear.

"Oh, Rishabh, what are you doing!"

He ran away giggling and evading her. After a short while he came in, and again rolled his tongue between his lips and created that horrible sound. Her head began to throb. When he didn't stop after repeated warnings, she threw the romper she was folding and grabbed him. He fell into her lap giggling and squealing. He went on creating the sound in between the squirming and wrestling with Ashima to be free of her hold.

"Rishabh… Rishu… sit still… please."

When he didn't listen to her, Ashima then pretended to be angry and lay down on the bed facing the blank wall away from him. He giggled and continued the ruckus, but got bored from the lack of response from her. The bed creaked when he jumped from the side table onto the bed. When that also didn't get any response from her, he rained wet kisses all over her cheek.

"Why are you being so naughty, Rishu?"

"I naughty only with you."

"Oh really, and from where did you learn to make such a horrendous sound?"

"Aaydh."

"Who?" She couldn't believe it. Zayd again!

"My fren, Aaydh."

Of course, who else? "And what else did he teach you, m'dear?"

"Only in fronth of mamma."

The cheek of the man! Of course, only he could have taught Rishu to irritate her. A discreet smile sneaked on her lips despite the headache. She needed to have a discussion with him again.

Realizing he had done something naughty, Rishabh sat quietly in one corner of the bed clutching his teddy bear stuffed toy. Though she wanted to cuddle him, she maintained a serious face and the rest of the evening passed peacefully.

***

Zayd woke up sensing something was wrong, he thought he heard a noise, but it could have been just a dream. The prison had made him wary of all strange noises, no matter how innocent. He blinked and concentrated on the sounds outside the room. Nothing. He took a deep breath and lay down on the bed again.

The sound came again, like someone kicked an empty can and then he heard a gasp. Zayd sat up with a jerk and switched on the bedside lamp. It was six in the morning. The guest house was normally peaceful at this hour. Rishabh went to school at 7:15, which was the time he normally heard the doors being opened or the gates creaking. He could see a faint sunlight through the curtains. Silence reigned again. What was wrong?

He put on his slippers, took the torch and the cane—bought at the local market—and opened the door fractionally to peer out. Nothing was amiss on this side of the house. It was quiet and peaceful. The mild-yellow, unadulterated sun rays fell on the green leaves and the slight breeze rejuvenated the senses. Closing his eyes, he inhaled the fresh mountain air and exhaled. His eyes snapped open as someone shouted again.

He ran to the front of the house and saw Ramprasad, Shankar and Ashima standing facing the front door. All of them had identical incredulous expression on their face.

His attention then went to the scene behind them. The entire garden looked as if a hurricane had paid a visit. The plants were bereft of leaves or flowers, and only the stumps were left. The chairs were upturned. The gazebo was in the same sad state as the garden with all the creepers and plants cut by the garden scissors.

When he saw the three of them still staring at the front door, he turned and felt anger rising at the devastation. The front two doors were smeared with graffiti in red, with crude insults for the family and threats to life.

"What the heck!" he muttered between clenched teeth.

The entire front wall had been spattered with multi-colored paint. Ashima was now close to crying.

"Mamma?" Rishabh came out with just a towel around him.

"Oh Rishu, go inside, you'll catch a cold!" Ashima came to her senses and checked herself. Blinking fast, she ushered him inside before he could understand or notice the chaos.

"Who did this?" Zayd barked.

"Don't know *saab*, saw it when I opened my door. So much ruined, so much work needs to be done now." Ramprasad's wife had followed Rishabh out and was quietly sobbing.

"I kill them." This came from Shankar.

"No one is going to kill anyone." Zayd snapped and stared at Shankar. When he didn't get any reaction from the lad, he caught hold of Shankar's shoulders and shouted, "Do you understand? Do you hear me?" He shook him for all that was worth, until he noticed everyone had gone quiet and was staring at him.

His hands began to sweat and tremble, and he felt the life going out of his legs. Zayd turned around and rushed to his room conscious of everyone's gaze on him.

Ashima swallowed the bile rising in her throat at the devastation and Zayd's outburst. Radha's sobs brought her back to reality.

"Shankar, call the police. When they have examined this, we'll clean," she said stopping Shankar in his tracks when he made a move to follow Zayd.

"This is all done by Kanyal… he is behind this… he must have given the local lads some money to do this. They must have come in the middle of the night," Ramprasad said.

Ashima sighed.

A constable came after an hour and did the formality of looking around. Even though he wrote a complaint, it was evident that this was nothing more than a sham visit.

"I think you should take this as an evidence…" Ashima showed the constable the paint cans thrown carelessly outside the entry gate. "…and take the pictures of the damage done."

To her surprise and annoyance, he nodded more vigorously but did nothing. Occasionally shaking his head with false sympathy, the constable only strolled around, examining the premises. Pacifying her in between her litany of complaints, he left.

The attitude of the man in the uniform worried Ashima all the more. She would have to contact her lawyer about the incident. Thinking about the next steps and more work, she turned to find Zayd standing in the parking lot watching the constable leave. He looked composed and under control.

As Ramprasad began straightening the chairs and tables, Zayd stopped him and asked for some plastic bags and brought his camera. He took pictures of the ruined wall and the doors. He sealed the cans in the bags, and then began helping Ramprasad and Shankar clear the debris.

Something in his defeated stance stopped her from asking any questions. Was the earlier outburst an indication of the baggage he was talking about?

"What are you doing? You are a guest!" Ashima said when she saw Zayd painting the doors, later in the afternoon. He had brought the exact shades of paint. "Please don't embarrass us anymore."

"I need to do this," he said solemnly.

His resigned tone confused her all the more. She exhaled. "I'll bring another brush." He resumed painting, and maintained a healthy distance so that no small talk could be held—Ashima took to painting the door and Zayd worked on the wall. They did a double coat on both the doors and then the wall.

"Are you okay?" she asked after he sighed twice.

He nodded.

She looked at the time and gasped, they had been painting for solid three hours now. "Meet me near the bench after dinner," she said ignoring his silence, then went inside the house.

***

TWELVE

Ashima placed the baby alarm beside her on the bench and thought about the day. Zayd's attitude confused and worried her. He was more devastated by the incident than he should have been. What if he was coming down with something? He hadn't given any emergency number in the registration form. What would she do in case something happened to him?

The gate creaked behind her back. She exhaled, bracing herself for another battle of wills.

"Are you okay?" She began the moment he sat down.

"Yeah."

"Want to talk about it?"

"Give me a copy of the complaint you had filed when we had that 'ghost-visit'."

She frowned at the brusque tone. Why was he asking about that event?

"Aashi—"

"I don't have it."

"If you don't have a copy, give me the original and I'll get it copied."

"I mean I didn't file the complaint."

"What?" He frowned. "You didn't?"

"I didn't feel the need, since there was no harm done."

"No harm done? Have you gone mad? You've lost your guests and revenue. How can you be so naive?"

"I thought it to be a one off incident, by some hoodlums." She frowned. "The complaint would have caused more harm. This is a small town and everyone would have come to know."

"And what happens now? We again keep quiet and let them torch the house the next time. I told you it builds the history of their harassment. It is clear Kanyal wants to run you out of the business and eventually grab this property."

"Yes, he does."

"You have to build a case."

"By openly taking his name?"

"Yes."

"I can't afford to pursue a legal case against him."

"Aashi—"

"Please let it be. I don't want you to get unnecessarily involved in this. And if you feel unsafe, you can always leave."

He stared at her defiant face. He was angry. No, not angry, but livid, the way he had been when Kanyal had assaulted them. How could she tell him that everything required money, which she didn't have?

"Zayd?"

He dropped his gaze again to his shoes. A caterpillar was inching towards him but changed track as if sensing the heat of his anger.

"Don't even think about filing a complaint," she cautioned.

He pursed his lips, refusing to say anything.

"I know you clicked the photographs, but I didn't want to make a scene in front of everyone with Amma looking on."

"We have to make sure he knows we are not scared and are not going to bow down to him," he said.

"There is no 'we' and—"

"If you don't flex your muscle, people think you fear them."

"The news would spread in the whole town. Do you realize you may fan his ego if you complain? I mean in a negative way. People don't give a devil's shit about what you think or feel, whether you are in control or not."

He chuckled drily. "'Devil's shit' I like the phrase, I'm going to use it in one of my stories. Let me note that down. How do you come up with these phrases? They are totally in contrast with your demeanor." He made a play of searching for a notebook and pen in his pockets.

She exhaled trying not to show how angry and exasperated she was with him. "Why can't you have a normal, serious conversation with me?"

"Because, I can't think rationally when you are around me."

"What?" Heat rose on her face. His words jolted her attention towards his eyes. The color was now like fresh mint leaves.

"I can't think rational—."

"Oh, forget it." She brushed his words aside with a dismissive wave of her hand and took a few discreet breaths. Schooling her face to an expression that she hoped was what she used to discipline Rishabh, Ashima continued. "I want to thrash out this Kanyal business. You have to understand he is a local thug and a criminal, who hasn't been caught. He has a group of muscled, trigger-happy men. We shouldn't rub them the wrong way, just because he wants us to. He is trying to needle us… to manipulate us into doing something irrational."

"You said there is no 'we'…?"

She glowered at him again. "Why should it matter to you, what he does to us… me?"

"It shouldn't. But it does. I don't know the reason, but it does."

"Zayd!"

"It does." He shrugged. "And I can't help it. Believe me I have tried to remain a mute spectator, I have tried not to care, but I do."

"Then you should leave the guest house."

He grimaced and sat silently, shoving his hands in his jacket pocket, defiant and sulking.

"You have to understand the small town mentality. Right now other people back me up because our family commands respect. And it is that respect that shields me from Kanyal. He may threaten us, but wouldn't dare lift a finger in broad day light. If an outsider sided with me, it would lift that blanket of security."

Zayd sat staring at the lights faraway, unmoving. A pulse ticked at his jaw. Ashima knew he was struggling hard to keep his anger at bay.

"Zayd, I'm really touched with your concern… and I'm not refusing your help because of any personal reasons but due to the society. You of all people should understand how conservative our society is…" She tried to convince him from his perspective. "Does your mother wear a *burqa*?"

"Yes, sometimes she did."

"There, you have your ans—" She turned towards him. "Did? What do you mean did?"

"She died when I was ten."

"Oh… I'm sorry. Who else is there in your family?"

"Has the Air Force given you any update on Flight Lieutenant Joshi?"

Her breath hitched and she swallowed dry air. "Why do you take me as an imbecile? Whenever I ask something about your background… your family, why do you change the subject?"

"It's not like that. Who is *Jugnu*?"

"Huh?"

"*Jugnu*? Is he or she a person?"

"How… Why are you asking this question?"

He held up the album. "Your mother left this on one of the chairs the other day."

The beautiful golden memories threatened to drown her. She took the forgotten collection with a trembling hand. She had put it together after Rohit and she had been engaged, and had kept adding the photographs as and when the various events followed. It had been very difficult to get the photographs from Rohit's childhood, but he had indulged her. Tracing the letters on the cover with her finger, she flipped the pages at random, trying to keep the tears from flowing.

Should she tell Zayd about *Jugnu*? But they were her memories, and were precious. Would it lose its charm—the romance, the significance—by saying it out loud? Maybe it would. She didn't want to lose any part of Rohit. She wanted him back. Looking at the album made the invisible stone sitting on her chest heavier. She snapped it close.

"It's nothing important—"

The baby monitor beeped, startling them. She rushed back, instructing him to lock the gates.

Zayd sat watching the caterpillar frolic on the ground, his thoughts warring with each other.

She was holding herself back and asking him to leave—like he was a coward! Yes, he had behaved like a coward in the morning but that was just for a few hours. Wasn't he out when the constable had come? Didn't he fight his weakness and had come out and helped?

But to be fair to her, she didn't know the demons he had been fighting—demons of guilt and fear, born as a result of his anger. It was very late by the time he had understood that anger was an emotion that when allowed to go out of proportion, could rip lives apart. Myra's, her family, his. And Ashima was doing what she could to keep her family safe and the house running, that too single handedly. Who was he to question her judgement?

What if he registered the complaint under his name? Could he? Should he?

He didn't have any grounds. And it would be courting trouble unnecessarily, given his past. But if the issue was not handled properly it might snowball into something massive which she might not be able to handle. He couldn't be here forever supporting her.

Why not? He could stay here for as long as it took to resolve the issue. He had nowhere to go, and he didn't want Kanyal anywhere near her.

Why was he being so protective about her? He shouldn't go that way. She was a complication he couldn't afford in his already messy life. And what would happen when his past would catch up with him? It would, he knew. If not in this week, then in the next. How would she react then? How would she manage then?

Fuck!

Everything was so messed up.

***

Ashima heard the cling-clang of something happening faraway, but the afternoon sleep had glued her eyelids and she just couldn't open them, no matter how hard she tried. Rishabh shaking her shoulder didn't make any difference either.

She caught hold of his hands and hugged him to her chest, patting him. He squirmed, giggled and thought a wrestling match was on. Making that atrocious raspberry sound again, he began romping her stomach. It reminded her she hadn't taken up the issue with Zayd.

"Oh… Rishu, I'm trying to rest here."

He jumped on her stomach, swishing the air out of her lungs. She gasped and tried to hold him still. He giggled. She opened one eye and found him near her face, trying to lift the eyelid of the other eye. His finger poked her eye and she was wide awake with pain.

"Aah… Rishu!"

"Sholy."

The sound of cling-clang came again. She concentrated on the sound now that seemed to be coming from the backyard, with a few men talking and discussing something. The sleep vanished immediately. Frowning, she got up and settled Rishabh with some crayons and a coloring book.

Ashima picked up her stole and put on her slippers. The slippers reminded her of something. She slipped them off, and marched barefoot around the house. There they were—Zayd, Ramprasad and two more men. She recognized one of them as the local carpenter.

"Is there a problem?" she asked.

Zayd didn't even glance at her and continued his monologue with the men holding the razor wire. No one else answered because he spoke without any break.

"I could've taken care of this. You shouldn't have bothered," she said when he finished the list of instructions for the men. "Ramprasad, let them measure the breakage and let me know the estimate for repair."

"It's not required. I have bought the material and they will begin the work right away. The whole fence will be repaired before the sun sets."

Ashima frowned at him.

Zayd stood with his gaze locked with her, in open defiance. Then he glanced at her feet and scowled.

Ramprasad coughed. "*Didi… ho jayega…*"

She nodded to him and muttered between clenched teeth. "I think we need to have a discussion… in private."

He shrugged. "Sure."

The fact that he looked amused grated on her nerves as they moved towards the secluded corner of the corridor.

"Look," she began once she was sure they wouldn't be overheard. "I'm the one managing the affairs here, and I'm supposed to take care of this house. I don't want anyone—and I mean anyone—taking decisions for my property. You should have consulted with me."

"Ramprasad told me about the makeshift arrangement you did on your own last year, and injured yourself. This is not the US of A, where everything is DIY. Even I would not be able to handle the razor wire fence. It needs experts, which these guys are."

"Still you should have consulted me."

He sighed and raked his hair with his fingers. "Yeah… you are right."

"You need not concern yourself with all this."

"No, I shouldn't, but can't help it. All this reminds me of something very bad."

"What thing?"

He stood watching the men working. His face had turned into granite and his jaw had clamped up. Now he wouldn't say anything, she knew.

"How much do I owe you? You must be having some receipt." She brought her attention back on the issue at hand.

"Yes, of course." He searched for the receipt, first in his front jeans pocket, then the back pockets, but couldn't find it. He muttered something about the jacket and walked into his room.

She waited outside, watching the men work.

He came out without the jacket. "I am sorry but I'm not able to find it. It was just a small piece of paper. I'll give you the full account after these people are done."

Ashima glared at him rocking on his heels, rattling the flimsy excuse. He shrugged when she didn't say anything. She pursed her lips and turned towards the boundary fence.

"Phew…" he muttered, making sure she heard him.

By the end of the day, he ensured no one could enter the property from any side except the front gate. Devious man!

She made sure she paid for the labour, but didn't get the receipt for the material he had bought from Dharampur. It was infuriating. To make matters worse, she couldn't find time to discuss the matter with him and he was not to be found whenever she was free.

He didn't even come to the garden that night. She had planned to discuss the payment issue and hand him a lump sum amount for the fence work.

Next morning he informed her, via Shankar, that he would be staying for the next two months in Kasauli, and paid for full boarding and lodging in advance.

***

Ashima couldn't sleep that night. Zayd's hazel eyes kept haunting her. He tip-toed in her thoughts frequently these days. Every moment today he had occupied her mind. His green eyes with their brown specs, his voice when he was angry or when it went soft with sympathy at her situation. What was wrong with her? How could she think about another man besides Rohit?

She picked up Rohit's photograph from the side-table. Her darling, so full of life and zest, so brave. No one could match up to him. Absolutely no one.

She took in Rohit's features, but couldn't remember the feel of his lips over hers. The glass was cold against her fingers as she touched the crinkles in his eyes. She had always teased him that his eyes resembled Tom Cruise, her favorite. And he used to get jealous, never missing a chance to criticize the actor. She hugged the photo frame to her chest and exhaled.

It had been such a long time since he had gone missing. He hadn't even met Rishabh, didn't even know his son existed in the world.

She had discovered she was pregnant after his news had come. She had been in a vegetative state for almost three days, not eating or drinking anything, wishing she was dead. Then she had fainted. Her family physician had broken the news of her pregnancy.

The fact that she was carrying his child pulled her out of the grief and depression. She willed herself to eat, drink, exercise, and to live. It was then that she noticed Amma's grief and a totally lost Pooja. She made it her mission to support them—they were her family, her responsibility.

The pension from the Air Force was enough to sustain the family but not for bigger dreams like the best school for Rishabh or a lavish marriage for Pooja. The injection her mother-in-law required every month was also expensive. The ancestral house required maintenance now and then. It was then that she had decided to convert the huge house into a guest house.

Her late father-in-law had retired as the principal of the Central School and was highly regarded in the town due to his service. Most of the younger generation in the town had been his students. How would everyone perceive her if she befriended a virtual stranger, a man who was a Muslim? Even if she had an emancipated view in these matters, the society did not. Any association, however platonic, would be frowned upon.

She drifted into an uneasy sleep, convincing herself about maintaining her distance and lecturing herself about ethics and moral values.

***

THIRTEEN

A car entered the driveway early in the morning when Ashima was pruning the daffodils. A young man in blue jeans and a white shirt alighted and walked towards her.

"Good morning." He took off his shades. "Akshat Mehra. I'm looking for Zayd Rizvi. I believe he stays here."

"Yes, of course. I'll see if he is in. Would you be comfortable here or would you like to wait inside?"

"Thanks, outside is better."

She nodded and called Shankar to see if Zayd was in, and to inform him about the visitor. Normally she would have called up from the intercom, but she was curious about the man. It helped with the marketing and spreading the word about the guest house.

"I'm Ashima Joshi, the manager here. Are you from Delhi?"

"Yeah… I'm his agent."

"Agent?" That sounded sinister. She had heard about agents only in the spy movies or in relation with someone shady.

"Yeah. For his novels."

"Novels?"

Akshat smiled. "Oh sorry, he wouldn't have mentioned it. Wait a sec…" He went to his car and brought back a couple of books. "This one is his latest novel, and this one here, won the award." He handed her the two novels.

Ashima looked at the author's name—Z Abbas—with no other details or photograph in the back or front. From the cover and the titles she could make out they were thrillers. A wave of betrayal washed over her. Why didn't he tell her that he was an established writer? Come to think of it, he had never confided anything about himself. Nothing on the day in the church or during the nightly discussions or in the past few days when he had acted so proprietarily. Whenever she had asked him anything personal, he had changed the topic or evaded the question.

"Akshat?" The object of her thoughts stood beside them.

"Hey! You rascal, what are you doing holed up in this beautiful place? Always on a vacation, aren't you?" Akshat hugged Zayd hard and slapped his back heartily like a long lost friend. "I missed you."

"Cut it out Akshat, it has been only a few weeks since we last met." Zayd held him at an arm's length, uneasy with the physical proximity.

"You haven't told anyone here that you are a celebrity." Least bothered with the cold welcome, Akshat continued the one-sided chatter. "I've got some news for you. But first of all, you need to autograph these. I have gifted them to Ashimaji on your behalf."

Zayd glanced at her and held out his hand. She pursed her lips and handed them without meeting his eyes. Akshat furnished a pen and Zayd signed the books, writing 'best wishes' with his signature.

Celebrity? Every day he threw a new surprise at her. Why didn't he ever mention such a big accomplishment?

God knows he had had ample opportunities. Men of his age should be bubbling over to share their success. Ashima felt Akshat glance at her, but she was busy glaring at Zayd. He had said she mattered to him and had still hidden such an important aspect of his life.

Handing back the books, Zayd held her glance, making her angrier. She looked at the signatures. He was not using his full name. What else was he hiding?

"There were a few things I wanted to discuss with you," Akshat spoke without missing a beat.

Zayd nodded and took him to his room.

She asked Shankar to arrange tea with snacks and take it to Zayd's room.

Later, Akshat called up to inform her that he would stay in the guest house for the night, and not to bother with dinner for both of them. She was free for the evening. After putting Rishabh to sleep, she began reading one of the novels and couldn't put it down. He had an amazing knack of creating suspense and weaving a flowing narration. Reading it, she lost track of time.

***

"Okay, can we talk about her now?" They were on their second peg of desi alcohol at Raghu's dhaba, after finalizing the contract for his next book.

Akshat was Zayd's best friend's elder brother and instrumental in launching his career. The support that Akshat had provided him during his trial and the prison stint was priceless. There was nothing he didn't know. And there was nothing Zayd could hide from him. He

137

couldn't. Sooner or later Akshat always had his way with Zayd.

"What about her?"

"Deny that you are not attracted to her." Akshat pressed on.

He rolled his eyes. "What do you want, Akshat?"

"You were so worried about her reaction to your celebrity status, and she was damn angry with you for hiding it."

"She is married." He took a sip.

"Married?" Akshat frowned.

"Your observation skills are pathetic. And she has a child as well."

"Oh, and where is the husband?"

"MIA, Kargil War."

"Oh, that's sad. It has been four years. Nevertheless, why were you so concerned about her reaction?"

"I wasn't."

"I might not be observant, but I sure know you are bothered about her opinion. You didn't tell her about you being a published author and she didn't like it."

Zayd sat gazing at the tumbler in his hand. There were water marks all over the outer surface area. At least it was made of glass and cleaner than the aluminum ones in the prison.

"Zayd?"

"Yes, I am bothered," he snapped. "If that's what you want to hear, so be it. But it's something which even I can't fathom. Does that satisfy you?"

"Don't go that way Zayd. Come to Delhi. Get a girlfriend who doesn't have a complicated past."

"You didn't add 'of your religion' as others do. But I heard it."

"Yes dammit!" Akshat banged the glass down, causing Raghu to glance at them. "Of your religion too. There, I have said it. What's wrong with it? It'll be less problematic. Aren't you fed up of the complications in your life? For once, can't you play safe?"

"I'm playing safe. I'm not making a play for her," Zayd said.

How could he? She had always kept that line maintained in the form of that streak of red vermilion in her hair-parting. He was sure her husband was dead but his ghost lurked around them whenever they were together.

"I don't want you to be lonely or brood," Akshat said staring at his glass.

"I don't brood. If I had brooded, you wouldn't have been sitting here, grinning ear to ear, dreaming about the money I'm going to earn for you." Zayd smiled and called Raghu for a refill.

Akshat opened his mouth.

"Drop it, Akshat please." He couldn't sustain his smile and stared at the orange glowing hearth on which Raghu was expertly making the naans.

Akshat looked at his face and sighed. "Okay fine, subject dropped. Are you okay?"

Zayd nodded.

"Panic attacks?"

"A few, nothing I couldn't handle. I'm sleeping better too." He smiled masking the turmoil going inside his mind about Ashima's reactions this morning.

Akshat nodded happily at the last bit of information and stopped pestering him for the rest of the evening.

***

"Is this the place?" Akshat switched off the engine and sat looking at the single story, depleted building the next morning.

"Hmm…" Zayd looked up from the papers he was checking. Akshat's SUV looked totally out of place amongst the battered police vehicle and other two wheelers parked outside the Kasauli Police Station.

"Let's get this done, then we'll sit at the *dhaba* and talk about the launch schedule and your non-existent love life."

"We'll not." Zayd got down and marched towards the station.

"Come on, don't be a spoil sport." Akshat had to run to catch up with him.

The procedure that was supposed to take not more than ten minutes took two hours. The inspector made them wait without any reason. He chatted with a man sitting in front, then had tea. After finishing two cups, he went for a bio-break, then called a man who had come later. It was clear to everyone that this was a battle of wills and ego.

Zayd, used to all of this, didn't pay any attention to the delay and kept jotting down notes on the notepad he had brought with him. Akshat's mood changed—from an agitated shaking of his legs to muttering the choicest expletives to finally moving out of the dusty rooms and standing beside his car.

"How do you tolerate them?" he asked when Zayd joined him.

"I had told you not to come, but you insisted on defending and adding to my clean image."

Akshat grimaced, before tightening his jaw.

Zayd smiled, "It's okay, I have enough time on my hands. And doctors have done a good job on me. Their tricks do help. That's the reason I take my notebook around, so that I can write. Waiting is easier to handle that way, and it irks them too."

As they drove off, they failed to notice the two men staring at them from another car parked on the opposite side of the road.

***

Though Ashima had been kept busy with Amma's quarterly medical checkup and her daily work, she wondered about Zayd's career the whole day. Both Akshat and he had gone out immediately after breakfast, and there was no sign of them during the dinner too.

She switched on the home computer and searched for his books and name over the internet. There was nothing much on the publisher's website. The media releases about his book mentioned the storyline or the narration style, but there was no personal information about the author, Z Abbas. Why such secrecy about his name and profession? And why did he use only his middle name?

Ashima picked up his second book lying on the chest of drawers and read the blurb. Why didn't he tell her about them? Normal people would like the readers to know more about their books so that they sell. Some would even brag exaggeratedly about them, but he had been completely silent, in fact he had hidden the truth that he was a professional writer. Why?

She couldn't sleep with the unanswered questions floating in her mind. She picked up the baby alarm. Her nightly sessions had always helped clear her mind. But what if he came too? Not that it mattered to her. She didn't need anyone's friendship. On a whim, she donned the *mangalsutra* around her neck. It niggled that she was being too sensitive but she ignored the feeling.

Ashima peered over the gate, but he wasn't there. With Akshat around, she didn't expect him to be there, and still a part of her missed him. The Night Jasmine was in full bloom, shrouding her with its fragrance as she sat on the bench.

There had always been something amiss. The various details she knew about him were like pieces of a jigsaw puzzle that did not fit—like the tattooed arm and his boyish demeanor. Everything contradicted. His compassionate interaction with Rishabh and Shankar clashed with his anger towards Kanyal. The way he interacted with Akshat and his advice of building a case history against Kanyal made her wonder if something had happened in his past. He did tell her that he was seeking some answers from God, but didn't share anything about what his questions were. Should she be wary of him? But she had always felt safe with him.

Her head snapped up and her heart leapt to her throat as she sensed someone sit beside her.

"Careful," he said holding her arm to steady her.

She put a hand on her chest. "Gosh, you crept up on me like a ghost."

He chuckled. "I had imagined you as a ghost when I saw you for the first time."

His smile vanished when he spotted the mangalsutra.

"I thought you were with Mr. Mehra," she said.

"He left."

"Left? When?"

"In the afternoon. You can send his bills to me."

She gritted her teeth. "I'm least bothered about the bill, Zayd. Why do you keep flaunting your money?"

"Sorry." He began rotating his phone. "You are angry," he added when she didn't acknowledge his apology.

"Why did you lie to me?"

"I've never lied to you."

"Hiding things amounts to lying."

"I'll never lie to you. Ask away."

"If I don't know what to ask, how will I ask?" she taunted deliberately.

"Aashi… please."

She sighed. "You said you are doing a creative writing course, distance learning."

"It's not a lie, I'm doing it."

"You are an established writer. Why do you need a course?"

"I was fed up of people telling me that I'm just a graduate, so I thought should pursue a master's degree. When I began earning, I enrolled. And with just two books, one doesn't become an established author."

"Why do you use your abbreviated name as an author and not your full name?"

He chuckled and shook his head. "You are interrogating me as my grandmother would." When she glared at him, he quickly added. "I didn't want people to know my real identity."

"Why not?"

He stared at her, his gaze scrutinizing her each feature. Then he glanced at her neck, and his lips pursed. Sighing he shifted his gaze towards the distant village lights.

"Why didn't you want people to know your real identity?" Nothing would deter her today.

He grimaced. "Among other things… I don't want to be associated with my father."

"Why not?"

"Well… we, my father and I are not—what you can call—a regular father and son pair. We don't get along."

She kept silent, waiting for him to complete.

"My father is influential and rich. People and he have always scoffed whenever I did anything constructive. They think either it is his money or name behind my effort and success. So in this case, I thought I'll not take his name to further my cause. Hence, I kind of took a pen name. As you know Abbas is my middle name."

She sat there pondering over what he had said when all of a sudden he took a strand of her hair between his fingers. She shrank back and tucked the errant curl behind her ear.

"I had always wondered how they would feel." He dropped his hand. "Sorry. Are you still angry? I don't want you to be mad at me."

"When and why did you get those horrendous tattoos? That too covering a complete arm."

He folded his shirt sleeve and admired the random artwork, then smiled. "They are disgusting, aren't they? I loved them when I got them. It was a phase in my life when I was in college. Bad company, weird friends. All of us overconfident, pleasure seekers, lazy. We loved to surprise and disgust others, especially the elders."

"Anything else?"

He sat rotating his cell phone.

She stood up.

He exhaled and looked up, his soft green eyes pleading with her to understand. "I did drugs too, Aashi.

But don't hate me for that. I haven't touched anything for the past four years." He held her hand. "Aashi… you are still angry… please don't go like this."

"I'm not angry Zayd. It's late."

"There's something else too… I want—"

The leaves crunched behind them and he left her hand in a nano-second.

Pooja stood near the gate, scowling and glaring at them. "Amma is in pain and is asking for the new pain killer the doctor has prescribed." After delivering the message, she whirled back and fled.

Ashima followed her silently, uncomfortable with their interrupted conversation. He was about to tell her something else. Something important.

***

FOURTEEN

"**Ashima**…"

Ashima looked up to find Mr. Sharma, the editor of a small local magazine and her father-in-law's close friend, standing at the door.

"Yes, Sharmaji. Please come in."

"I will not stay, *beta*. I was just passing by and wanted to give this to your guest Mr. Rizvi. He had given a poem for our magazine two days back, a little late, but we managed to publish it in the current issue. This is his copy. Could you pass it on to him?" He handed the magazine to her and turned to leave. "By the way, great poem, straight from the heart…"

Refusing her offer for tea, he left. Ashima quickly flipped the pages looking for Zayd's name found the poem.

I am a Sinner

Come punish me o'world, for I am a sinner!

Come, revel in my sins,

Come rejoice in my guilt, for I am a sinner

I sinned for I was born,

where I was born

I sinned for I felt the pain,

as they dishonored her

Come rebuke, as you utter my name with a curl to your lips,

But allow me to question why was I born, where I was born

Come penalize, as you condemn I took a life,

But allow me to remember, as I still feel her last breath

Come, revel in my sins,

But swear you forget another

Come rejoice in my guilt,

But promise you forgive another

And answer a question of my own,

O' cruel world, how many times would I be chastised,

for that one sin?

For I get punished whenever I write my name

For I get punished whenever I dream her pyre

For I am a sinner…

Her legs couldn't support her by the time she finished reading and she sat heavily on the bed behind her. The line 'Come penalize, as you condemn I took a life' shifted something inside her mind, as her stomach squirmed. What could it mean? Could it be…? Had he killed someone? Was that the reason he had reacted the way he had with Shankar that day?

He was trying to tell her something the night Pooja had interrupted. Ashima had expected anything but this. Wait a minute! It wasn't necessary that the poem needed to be based on a true incident! It could be a random thought expressed in the poem. She read it again with an objective viewpoint and remained unconvinced.

"Mamma," Rishabh came running and lay down on her lap, rubbing his eyes. She pulled his hands away from his eyes. "I wanth choco."

It was time for dinner.

She snapped the magazine close.

***

"Mamma."

"What mamma! Where are the crayons Rishu?" Ashima was irritated. Her head was pounding due to the lack of sleep since the past two nights. Rishabh's homework was still not finished, and he had to be fed, bathed, and tucked into bed for it was a school night. "When did you use it the last time?"

He looked at the ceiling and tapped one finger on his temple. Ashima bit her lip watching him imitating an adult, her anger dissipating fast at the antic.

"Bua'sh loom," Mercifully, the answer revealed itself.

"Finish this off, I'll bring them." She tapped the 'match the objects' worksheet lying in front of him.

She looked for the crayons everywhere in Pooja's room, but they were not to be found. Thinking Pooja would have put it in one of the numerous drawers in her study table, Ashima opened one drawer after the other, but no success. She was about to give up after looking through a few drawers when she saw a pink paper jutting out of one of the drawers.

Curiosity, after seeing Pooja with a man outside her college, made her take out the paper, which was haphazardly thrust under the diaries and photographs.

It was pink and scented. It looked like a love letter, full of praise about Pooja, in a language as unsophisticated as a bright pink ribbon on a maid's sandals. Even if one overlooked the language, the grammatical errors and spelling mistakes made Ashima cringe.

Worried, she folded the paper and neatly put it back under the diaries and photos, closed the drawer and left the room. She had given ample opportunities to Pooja in the past days, but she had not confided or opened up. It was time to have a frank discussion before the situation went out of hand.

***

Next day Ashima cornered Pooja when Rishabh was playing on the jungle gym. They had finished their evening tea, and Pooja was reading something on the kitchen table. Ashima wanted to finish the discussion before Radha and Shankar came in for the dinner preparation. The sooner the better.

"Pooja, I want you to tell me about your friend. I mean the friend who is a boy." She sat beside her and asked. "Who's he?"

The book fell down from Pooja's hand. "He? My friend? What are you saying?"

"I saw you talking to someone on the trek near the church—the day I had gone for Rishabh's PTA. I had asked you indirectly, but you evaded. Did you bunk college that day? Then today I saw a note in one of your drawers. I'm worried. And such a badly written note by a student studying in your prestigious college!"

"I don't know what you are talking about! And why did you touch my desk?" She reached down to pick up the book, finding a perfect excuse to hide her face from Ashima.

"Pooja… I found it accidently."

"I can also say things about you, which you may not like."

"About me?" Her eyes widened.

"Yes. I know you meet that Rizvi in the garden. Every night. What's that? And you have the cheek to ask me about my whereabouts!"

"Pooja—" Ashima sighed. This was not going the way she had planned. "How can you think like this? This is not about me. Look, I just want to know who you are going around with—."

"You are going around with that Muslim when you are married to my brother. Is that true or not?"

Ashima pursed her lips and glared at the defiant girl. Pooja met her eyes and lifted her chin a bit. This was the first time Pooja was on the offensive. Ignoring her accusations, Ashima tried another track to draw her out. "Pooja, I know there is nothing wrong in what you are doing. Probably the guy is a good person, but there is no harm in us knowing him. If they are aware that the girl's family knows, they do not dare take any undue advantage."

"Has Rizvi taken advantage of you?"

"Pooja!" Ashima was beginning to get angry.

"Don't shout! You have lost all the respect I had for you. Where does he stand in front of my brother? Why do you give so much time and importance to him?"

"It's nothing. Why are you stuck on him?" She frowned.

"Why shouldn't I be? Have you stopped hoping that *bhaiya* will be back? That he is alive—" Her breath hitched.

Ashima sighed and reached for Pooja's hand, but she pulled away. "It's not like that, sweetie. How can I make you understand? It's nothing! We just have some mundane conversation probably for ten minutes or so. That's it." She put a hand to her forehead where a pulse had begun to throb. "But we are digressing. You see I'm in no danger from Zayd, but this man from your college could be anyone. At least tell me his name, where does he live, and who his parents are. I should know who you are friendly with, shouldn't I? Don't I know all your girlfriends?" she pleaded.

Unmoved, Pooja stood there peeling the layers of the onion, shredding it on the counter.

"Okay, fine. Don't tell me. But please do not go alone with him anywhere. Meet him in the college with people around you. There are so many incidents happening… you have read in the newspapers, haven't you?" Ashima held both her hands in a firm grip, even as Pooja resisted. "Please trust me Pooja. Have I ever done anything that is not in your interest?"

Pooja extricated her hand and left the kitchen. Ashima felt as if she had failed an exam.

Pooja had always sought her out for all her problems. She used to take pride in their relationship. How could Pooja think like that about her? Was that what she was doing—substituting Zayd for Rohit? No. Her mind rejected the thought, while her heart continued to pound. Zayd was just a friend. It was just courtesy that demanded they should have a conversation. It was just humanity that prompted him to help her out. It was totally platonic.

'Liar,' a voice whispered.

***

The next day Kanyal, Inspector Bisht and other respected members of the town dropped in requesting an impromptu meeting. No one had a clue what was to be discussed. Kanyal, living up to his persona, demanded Ashima should be present for the discussion.

Mentally preparing herself for a tense hour to defend her stance on not selling the house, Ashima stood behind Amma's chair and endured Kanyal's so called honestly-I-am-your-friend smiling face. She knew most of the people gathered in their living room—some were their family friends and some were just acquaintances.

"What's the name of that person?" Kanyal looked at Ashima.

She was taken back at Kanyal's question. Zayd's was the last of the topics in her mind when she had got the summons from Amma. She hid her surprise behind a frown and shrugged.

"I mean, that man living in the guest house. He is not what he poses to be." He looked at her, then glanced at

Amma and the others, then back at her, like a chameleon gauging the reaction of the passers-by on a road.

Ashima could hear the distant tinkling of bells, even as flashes of the tattooed hands, the rippling muscles, his anger with Kanyal, and those lines of the poem ran through her mind. Her heart began beating in an uneven rhythm.

"Please go ahead, Mr. Kanyal." Amma prodded him.

"Oh yes. So, as I was saying, that man is not what he pretends to be." When Ashima kept her expression blank, he looked at Amma. "I would insist you call him too. I don't want him to brainwash your minds later."

"Mr. Kanyal, please continue." Ashima interrupted. "We are not kids that anyone can influence us so easily." Ashima wanted to add 'including you', but didn't think it was prudent to mention at the time. He was positively chortling with the information he had, so it might be something authentic but damaging for Zayd. Still, it needed to be heard before she could respond.

"Shankar, check if he is here and call him," Amma said.

Shankar's loyalty to Zayd had him routed near the door. He too sensed that Kanyal's visit couldn't mean anything good for them or Zayd. He moved only when Amma shouted at him again.

"So, Mrs. Joshi, this man is living in your house under false pretense." Kanyal concentrated his attention on Amma, since Ashima, unimpressed with his declaration, stood studying her nails. "He has misled you. He is no simple, innocent looking tourist. Inspector, why don't you say something…"

"Yes… yes…" Inspector Bisht looked flabbergasted when included in the conversation and cleared his throat.

A shadow fell in the room and everyone turned to look at Zayd standing at the threshold.

"Oh… good… good… he is here… very good… very good." Kanyal beamed and looked even uglier, if it was even possible.

Ashima grimaced discreetly.

Zayd took a step inside and leaned on the door frame, crossing his arms. There was no spare chair in the room. After scanning the coterie of people seated in the room, he exhaled and looked at her. She smiled, perfunctorily acknowledging him, while simultaneously trying to strike a balance between the turmoil in her heart and his calm acceptance of the crowd assembled in the room. He wasn't surprised or alarmed when he saw Inspector Bisht or Kanyal. And that worried her.

"Please come… I was telling these good people of the town about you." Kanyal sat straight and glanced at Amma.

Today, her nails fascinated her a lot. Hiding the nervous reaction, Ashima held Amma's chair's handles.

"I'm not afraid of saying the truth and will do anything to keep this town safe." Kanyal began. "And we have proof too."

The grip on the handles of Amma's wheelchair tightened. She knew everyone's eyes were on her.

"This man here is a murderer."

There was a collective gasp from the group. A cold wave ran through her as Kanyal confirmed something that she had been suspecting all along after reading that poem. Her ears stopped functioning. Ashima looked at Zayd. He was looking at her, his expression serene and indifferent. She glanced at the gathering—some were alarmed and some were astounded, alternating between murmuring something among themselves and talking to Amma.

"He is a criminal, and has served a sentence... he is still serving. He is out on parole, and dare you deny this." Kanyal shook a finger at Zayd, whose gaze was fixed only on her. "You have served time in the prison and... not fit to be living amongst these good, innocent people."

There was an eerie silence after Kanyal's monologue. No one said anything. They all stared at Zayd. Ashima stared at the floor. How did Kanyal come to know? Was he running a reference check on Zayd? Or did he read the poem? Amma was looking at Zayd, expecting him to say something in his defense. Ashima desperately wanted him to deny everything.

"Is it true or not?" Kanyal persisted.

"It's true," Zayd said meeting his eyes.

Amma inhaled and looked at Kanyal, then back at Ashima, who couldn't meet her eyes. The myriad scenes about him—playing oh so gently with Rishabh, treating Shankar with utmost compassion, the respect he showed to Amma and Pooja, and his innate empathy with her, along with Akshat bragging about his awards and him being an upcoming author—floated in front of her eyes. Was that an act? No.

She wished she wasn't in the room, wished she had some time to sort out her confusion and react to this fact in a rational way. But if wishes could come true, then Rohit would have been with her and this meeting wouldn't have happened.

Kanyal's and the other voices went on and on in the background.

She looked at Zayd. He was looking at her. Even in that moment of revelation, she didn't fear him. His expression was as blank as Rishabh's toy slate, but his eyes spoke volumes. Asking her to trust him. Believe in him.

After that first wave of incredulous surprise, a quiet acceptance settled in her heart. She had never been wrong in reading a person. And Zayd had definitely never given her any dangerous vibes. Bringing her attention back to her nails, she reached a decision.

"Did you all know about that? Imagine, hiding such a heinous crime," Kanyal continued to revel in his commentary. "He has murdered two people, served four years in jail and now he is out on parole. And where does he come to live? In a guest house full of vulnerable women! Did anyone know about his history? Tell me. Say something Ashimaji, did you know?"

In that chaotic backdrop, where everyone had an opinion, and Kanyal adding spice to the burnt curry, the conclusion was crystal clear.

"Yes, I knew." Ashima was glad her voice was strong and did not waver.

***

FIFTEEN

For the first time in her life, Ashima experienced pin-drop silence. Numerous pairs of eyes snapped on her face. Zayd too straightened, staring at her. Her mind went to his poem and those lines.

O' cruel world, how many times should I be chastised?

for that one sin?

For I get punished whenever I write my name

For I get punished whenever I dream her pyre

Lifting her head, she met all their gazes squarely. "Yes, I knew. And I don't have a problem. Everyone should be allowed to repent and reform."

"Do you think he would reform? A Muslim and a murderer?" Inspector Bisht snickered, speaking as if Zayd was not in the room.

Ashima risked a glance at Zayd who, for the first time since entering the room, was showing some emotions. Bewildered, he stood there watching her.

"I would request you to not insult a guest in my house." She addressed Kanyal and Bisht. "You have come to convey whatever you knew and you have done that. Thank you for thinking about our welfare."

"How did you come to know about him?" Kanyal challenged.

"I have my sources." Ashima glared at him.

He tightened his lips and stared at her. She stared back. Amma sat in a trance, waiting for a clarification from Ashima.

"Mr. Rizvi, I'm really sorry about this and apologize on everyone's behalf. Thank you for giving us your time." Ashima spoke formally but her eyes pleaded him to leave the room.

Zayd nodded and left.

Ashima folded her hands and stared at Kanyal and the inspector. Kanyal pursed his lips and left, with Inspector Bisht following him out.

There was a clear cut divide amongst those left and their support. Kanyal had sown the seeds of mistrust. Close friends muttered something supportive to Amma before leaving, while the others left silently.

"Aashi, if you knew, why did you allow him to stay here?" asked Amma in her characteristic dominating tone when they were finally alone.

"He is from a good family in Delhi. Haven't you seen the way he conducts himself and behaves around us?"

"Come and sit in front of me. My neck has developed a crick looking up at you."

Wiping her moist hands on her hips, Ashima took a deep breath and sat on the sofa that was facing the wheelchair. Amma looked worried, and rightly so, but she hadn't interacted with Zayd to the extent Ashima had. "He is not a hardened criminal, like Kanyal and the inspector are making him out to be."

"No one has 'I am a murderer' written on their forehead. How could you have been so naïve? For all you know, he might have come here to kill us all!"

"He didn't come here, Ramprasad brought him."

Amma was silent for a moment, then said, "Ask him to leave."

"He's already paid for the next two months. Ved is coming soon. We need the money, Amma."

***

Zayd was baffled by Ashima's claim. Abbu had made sure none of the newspapers or the media channels carried information on the case even after the judgement was finalized. In fact, he had asked Zayd to change his name, which he had refused, deciding not to hide behind a fictitious name throughout his life. Zayd had no regrets for whatever he had done. When he had voiced the fact, Abbu had thrown an epic fit, ranting and shouting at him for a week.

How could she know about the case? She wasn't tech savvy. Maybe she knew a hacker. Maybe she had someone higher up in the police department who had access to the cases and did a reference check for her.

He had to talk to her, had to explain. Though he could after dinner, he wanted to seek her out that very minute. Pacing his room, he couldn't think, couldn't write, couldn't do anything except give in to his urge to present his case to her. For the first time, Zayd wanted to justify his role in the crime. By evening, he had had enough and stormed out of the room to seek her out.

Ashima never thought she would defend someone like Zayd ever in her life. Ideally she should be afraid of him, but the emotion eluded her as far as he was concerned. After ages she had felt safe with him around. The fact about his imprisonment had surprised her initially but after a few hours of silent contemplation, her instinct told her that there had to be a compelling story behind the whole sordid affair. And it would be nothing but an aberration.

She was sitting on the gazebo steps, instructing Shankar who was planting seeds in one of the flower beds when she saw him approaching her with determined strides. She asked Shankar to fetch two cups of coffee.

Zayd sat on the grass near her. "How did you know?" He began without any preamble.

"I didn't."

"You didn't?" The eyebrows went up.

She shook her head.

"But… but… why then…?"

She sighed. "I was taken aback when you admitted. But I remember you were trying to tell me something that night when Pooja had interrupted our conversation."

"I should have told you earlier, but then I never thought I would stay here for more than two-three days or maximum a week. Later, I didn't know how to broach—"

"You don't have to explain, Zayd."

"Aashi, you mean a lot to me."

"Zayd—"

"Your opinion matters. Later there was no opportune moment or time. And I didn't have the courage lest you—"

"Would you like to share it now?"

He sighed and nodded.

She smoothened the kurta on her lap, waiting for him to begin.

"I was in a pub in Delhi with my girlfriend. It was a favorite haunt of the students. It was late in the evening, but not late by the pub's standard. Her name is… was Myra. Three guys from our college were also there, typical upper caste, rich… bullies. I was no less… in terms of money or arrogance. Since the day we, Myra and I, had hooked up they had been picking on us. It all started when the waiter served me first—" He swallowed and looked down, his hands destroying the carpet grass she had nurtured for the last two years. "One of the guys objected and insulted me… my family… our religion. When I intervened, the other one knocked my glass off. Then I couldn't control myself…"

Ashima saw Shankar coming with a tray. She shook her head not wanting him to interrupt. Shankar, as usual understood her silent command and went back.

"Myra tried to pacify us all. But they insulted her too. It, the situation, went out of control so suddenly. One moment I was fighting with the guy, the next moment I saw Myra on the floor with blood all over her stomach. She had been shot. In my rage, I snatched something from the table and stabbed one of them. He fell down. The other two ran off." He paused, breathing heavily. "Myra died. There was no help, no time to take her to the hospital. There was nothing I could do."

His voice became hoarse by the end, with drops of sweat appearing on his forehead and nose. The incident clearly still bothered him. He took a deep breath and wiped the sweat on his t-shirt sleeve. "By the time I came to my senses and ambulance came I realized I had stabbed the other guy with a restaurant knife. He died on the way to the hospital. They made it out to be Hindu-Muslim issue, though Myra was a Christian. The gun they had used to kill Myra was theirs, with their fingerprints on it, and since Myra had also died, the murder charges on me were reduced to self-defense. I got a minimum seven years of imprisonment. But I made sure the other two were not spared. They are also serving a sentence. Longer."

Amma had taken a peek at them from the living room. She scowled, pursed her lips, but didn't interfere thankfully. Ashima glanced at him sitting in front of her, eyes downcast and mind replaying the distant, life-changing event. The wind played with his hair, ruffling them, making him seem very vulnerable. If his friend died four years back, then he would have been barely twenty. Watching his hair dancing on his worried forehead a wave of protectiveness ran through her. She desperately wanted to reassure him that everything would be all right.

Oblivious to everyone, he just kept plucking the grass as he continued narrating the incident. "I have done four years, and was released on parole last month. For the next three years, I'm supposed to stay in India and mark my attendance at the local police station wherever I stay."

"So you were accused of one murder, not two?"

"Yes, but if I had had a chance I would have killed all of them." His hands pulled on another grass blade and twisted it.

"I'm wondering, how did Kanyal come to know?"

"I have to report to the nearest police station for three years, the duration of the parole. He or his cronies must have spotted me there or Bisht might have told him."

"Oh… okay." Ashima sighed. She was right that it was an aberration—an act done when you have been pushed to the wall and were desperate for survival.

"She died because of me," he whispered and looked at her, the pain visible in his troubled eyes. Then, in a flash, he dropped his gaze.

"Why do you think that?" She asked when he remained impassive, twisting the blade of grass in his hands.

"I led her to that pub that night. If I had agreed to stay in the room as she was suggesting… if I had not let anger takeover my senses, she would have been alive."

"She was with you in college?"

He nodded. "She was an exchange student from Germany. So many dreams and so many plans. All shattered. Just because I couldn't control myself. Sheer waste. I wanted to go and meet her mother after my release, but they didn't allow me. A criminal doesn't get a visa."

Amma appeared again. Ashima exhaled and stood up. "I have to go, it's almost dinner time. Hope you will put this behind you."

"If you want me to leave, I will."

She studied him for a moment, then said. "If you want to leave, you can."

***

"Hey," Ashima greeted Ved, Rohit's best friend and her biggest supporter, and ushered him inside the living room. The moment they settled on the sofa, Shankar ran inside to get some refreshments even before Ashima could open her mouth. She turned to Ved. "I'm so glad you could come at such a short notice."

He nodded but didn't meet her eyes and looked down at his hand. "Anything for you Aashi. What's up?" He raised his head, but immediately looked down.

His attitude perplexed her. "Nothing, I… er… I just wanted you to plan another mission on that ridge, which is the only stretch left, as we had discussed the last time."

He didn't say anything and just kept fiddling with his bike keys.

She frowned at his weird behavior. "What's the matter, Ved?"

"You know Aashi… I'll do anything for Rohit and you… but… er…" He raised his troubled eyes to her and continued. "He ejected, we know that from the wreckage and his last transmission. I have combed the area myself and there's no clue. The plane debris found on our side without him means only one thing, that he landed on the other side. We can't go like this… it has been four years now—"

He was repeating what they had discussed so many times. He looked defeated and that scared her. She caught hold of his hands. "Ved, please don't desert me. You are his only friend who has stuck with me, my only hope, his only lifeline."

"Think a little rationally. The Air Force has taken a stance on it. We can't go there. And there is no cooperation from the other side."

"I'm not asking you to do anything illegal." Her brows furrowed.

"No, you aren't."

"Then?" She shook his hands. "Ved, you have stood by me these four years, just one more mission wouldn't do any harm. I can't keep idle, doing nothing when I know he is somewhere out there."

"The mission is not a problem, sweetheart. It's you I'm worried about. I know this will leave you bankrupt. It's expensive, even if I take only the cost of running the operation. You'd be left with no money, nothing for emergencies."

"You spoke to mamma!" He must have nodded, she didn't care. "Money will come, Ved. Time is my enemy. With the Air Force abandoning the search, I have to keep looking for him. I can't just leave him there all alone, can I?"

"If the Pakistani army had found him, they would have flaunted him as a prisoner of war… or… er…."

His hands shook as their thoughts converged to various negative scenarios, thinking about the news pieces on the atrocities on the captured soldiers or the thought that Rohit might be… But she managed to block those depressing scenarios, as always. They were unthinkable. That was the only way. "I have written to the Pakistan embassy a number of times. If I had been alone I would have gone there myself, but the circumstances and the protocol…" Her voice broke. She felt so helpless.

"Aashi… Please don't get me wrong," he said as if he hadn't listened to a word she had said. "You have to accept that… that he is… that the Air Force—"

"Ved—"

"In all these years he would have contacted us."

"What if he has lost his memory? What if he is unable to speak?"

Ved waved his hand in the air and opened his mouth to answer, but she beat him to it, "I don't want to hear anything. When I'm paying, you have no right to refuse. This time I am not paying the discounted rates. I'll pay the full amount including your com—"

"Don't insult me, Aashi. You know money is not in the equation at all. You said I am your only hope. And that is the problem. Every time I agree for a search trip I raise that hope. No." He shook his head, as she began to negate whatever he was saying. "Don't deny it. You raise not only the money but your hopes too. Then when I come back, I see the disappointment in your eyes, yours and Mrs. Joshi's. Then comes the pain that you try to hide from me, but I see it anyway. You try to mask that anguish behind a brave facade, whispering something about the next time. I can't stand that."

She swallowed her tears but the moisture still welled-up in her eyes.

"I can't stand that pain anymore," he whispered.

Ashima lifted her hand from his and nodded. "I understand. You have been a rock, my anchor. But one last time, Ved… you said there was one stretch left."

He sat there looking down, thinking hard. She knew she had convinced him because he was shaking his right leg. Ashima crossed her fingers. After a few agonizing minutes, Ved raised his head and said, "Fine, I'll do it. But promise me this will be the last time. You have to accept that… and… you know."

Clamping down the urge to argue, she agreed and expressed her thanks as profusely as she could. He went on his way after discussing the details for the excursion.

She knew what Ved had been trying to say. Everyone wanted her to accept that Rohit was no more and move on. What they didn't understand though was that the minuscule possibility of him being alive would never allow her to leave her soul mate all alone, at the mercy of unknown factors. He would have moved mountains if she was in trouble. So why shouldn't she do the same?

Her mother had alienated the only person who was siding with her. Never mind, Ashima thought, she would look for someone else in the field. Ved was not the only expert in this area.

***

SIXTEEN

It had been two days since Zayd's sins were made public. Nothing had changed in his routine at the guest house except that senior Mrs. Joshi made it a point to glare at him whenever she would spot him. The change in her attitude, from refusing to acknowledge his existence earlier to open hostility now, amused as well as saddened him.

That night Zayd settled on the bench and hoped Ashima would come. He wanted to have a normal, light conversation with her now that his life lay bare and open in front of her. And he wanted to know about the punk who had paid a visit on the motorbike.

He had noticed the Harley-Davidson entering the gate, disturbing the morning peace at the guest house. His curiosity piqued when the man went inside the living room without ringing the bell. The curiosity turned into hateful animosity when Ashima looked positively delighted to see him.

He had seethed when the guy hugged her again before leaving. She was wiping her eyes on her shoulder. Did he make her cry? Who was he, who was allowed to hug and console her? How could anyone take such liberties with her? Her straightforward words, 'If you want to leave, you can' had drilled holes in his heart, and now this man behaving so familiar with her added to his insane possessiveness for her.

The sound of her feet crunching the leaves was like a soothing balm on his fresh wounds.

"Hey." He glanced at her. The more than usual kohl in her eyes prompted him to glance at her again. The thick black line was hiding, or trying to hide, the puffed up, red eyes. She had been crying... a lot. "You look pathetic."

"Thanks." Rubbing her arms, she tugged her legs up, holding them with her arms, and put her chin on her knees. The breeze was chilling that night.

"What's the matter?"

No response.

"Who was the guy on the motorcycle yesterday?" She raised her eyebrows at the sudden change of topic. He hoped he didn't sound too interested. "That man who spoke to you in the afternoon and left without even having a cup of Shankar's famous tea."

"Oh, you mean Ved. He is a good friend of ours, and a trekking consultant. He takes trekking groups on various Himalayan routes."

"Seems like a close friend."

"Hmm..." She nodded, but didn't elaborate.

He detested the way she managed to smile affectionately hearing about the visitor, even if for two-seconds, gazing faraway.

She rubbed her arms again.

He took off his jacket and draped it over her. "No... no, I'm fine." She tried to take it off.

"Humor me..." He draped it around her, pulling the collar around her neck. It looked huge on her. "Why was he here? Was he just visiting?" He tried to broach the subject casually again. Though he had some inkling, like a masochist he wanted to hear it from her.

"He is… doing something for me."

"What is—"

"Do you know any trekking guide?"

"No, but I can ask someone. Why?"

"No, nothing." She shook her head.

It was clear from the way she pursed her lips that the subject was closed, so he chose to disclose that he had guessed. "Is he the one who conducted the private search missions for Rohit?"

Her gaze jerked up to him.

She didn't mask the surprise or the pain, nor did she ask him about his source of information. Nodding once, she looked away and swallowed her tears. A familiar helplessness engulfed him once again. "How many times?" he asked.

"Three."

"What about the Air Force?"

"They did their bit. I don't have any complaints."

"Are you thinking of another search trip?"

Ashima didn't want to answer. Her worry-index for Rohit always went up whenever she met Ved, and he prepared for the departure. Myriad scenarios plagued her mind. She imagined Rohit riding in on Ved's motorcycle, a little sun-burned and thin, but hale and hearty. Sometimes she thought he would come in an ambulance and the doctors would declare him to be out of danger. *'Nothing to be worried about Mrs. Joshi,'* they would say. Other times, she would imagine him having lost an arm or a leg, but otherwise he would be breathing and smiling at her, looking at Rishabh in wonder. She sighed and as always, blocked all the negative thoughts, and relived the happy-ever-after scenarios.

"Aashi—"

"I don't want to talk about it. Please." The words came out like a snub—harsh and rude.

He got up and stood near the fence, hands in his pockets.

She immediately regretted her outburst and sat wringing her hands. Her worry about Rohit and her affection for Zayd battled inside her head. She knew Zayd was trying to be helpful, but she didn't want to talk about Rohit. But she didn't want to hurt Zayd either. Everything had become so complicated.

"Zayd…"

"Yeah…"

"I… I'm…"

"Show me your palm." He turned back holding something in his hands that were cupped together.

At first she thought it to be a jasmine bloom but suppressed a shudder when he placed an insect on her outstretched palm. Suddenly, it glowed making her gasp in surprise. The firefly brought back memories of Rohit. Did Zayd do it on purpose? Had he guessed who *Jugnu* was?

Ashima looked at Zayd and all the thoughts flew out of her mind. A faint smile played on his lips, but his eyes were a little wary of her reaction. There was something soft in his gaze—a kind of an anticipation of a truce, to let bygones be bygones.

What should she do about him? It was wrong of her to encourage him like this. She had nothing to offer him accept worries and problems. He had had a complicated past and should not get entangled in her conflicted present. She dropped her gaze to her hands.

The firefly glowed on and off for a couple of times and then flew off. He too should go away from here. The other day Kanyal had gathered a handful of people. What if he instigated a mob against Zayd? There were some very staunch hardliners in this town.

"Zayd, I think you should go from here."

He chuckled and looked at her from the fence where he stood. "What brought that on?"

"You shouldn't stay here."

"Why?"

"It doesn't feel right."

"If you are thinking about Kanyal, then stop bothering. He can't do anything to me."

"Why not? Are you some kind of a bigger goon than him?"

"Maybe." He grinned.

"Huh…?" She frowned. "Are there any more hidden corpses in your closet that I'm not aware of?"

"What do you think?" he asked, teasing her again.

"Fine, don't tell me. Good night." She pulled off his jacket, threw it on the bench and left.

Zayd continued to stare at the fireflies playing hide and seek, the way Ashima was playing with him. If *Jugnu* was her name, then Rohit had named her aptly.

He thought he was trying to lighten her mood but ended up upsetting her even more. She was scared of the attraction between them and didn't want to acknowledge the emotion, the way she wasn't accepting that Rohit was no more. He combed his hair with his fingers in frustration and sat down to brood.

Jugnu…

Will she be his *Jugnu*? His beacon in the dark?

***

Zayd pounded furiously on the keyboard, the story flowing so seamlessly that he was finding it difficult to keep up with the barrage of words his mind churned out. After a tense word marathon of two solid hours, he went through the stuff he had written. Mentally patting himself on his productivity, he corrected the typing mistakes here and there. He saw that dusk had crept up on him casting mellowed shadows all over. It was time to switch on the lights.

He rolled his shoulders, working the kinks out of his tense muscles, and glanced outside. And there she was, in the garden, struggling with the wrought iron chair, again barefoot. Using an iron rod, she was prying the leg of the chair out of the cemented floor. He hoped she wasn't irritated with him anymore.

This was the first opportunity in days when he could watch her to his fill, without wondering if anyone spied on him. Slim through and through, she looked taller than she actually was, barely coming up to his shoulders. The faint dusk made her skin glow. She had lovely waist length hair. A few tendrils were slowly sneaking out of her neatly done plait. Heaving, sighing, she muttered something when the leg refused to budge despite her repeated efforts. He smiled and stood up.

"Hi! Need help?" His eyes took in the beads of sweat forming on her forehead and her nose.

"No. This leg is just stuck. I can do it." She flicked back a hair lock that was kissing her cheek.

"Where is Ramprasad? Can't he do this? This is not a job for you."

"I can't call him for anything, anytime. And anyway nobody is available. I have given the family an evening off. Everyone has gone to the temple. But, I can do… ouch!" She held her hand up, looking at a broken nail.

He pursed his lips. Stubborn, independent, fool. He caught the iron rod she was holding. She resisted. Her eyes met his, over a curl sticking across her face. The black, determined eyes shone as moonlight fell on her face. She looked like a princess in her light-colored clothes, her face devoid of any makeup, all brave and ready to take on anything. His heart raced. Keeping his eyes locked on her face, he gave a little tug to the rod and it slipped out of her hands. He stood up and picked up the hammer lying on the side.

"Stand back…"

"Don't break the floor more than required. I don't want to pay the mason."

"Got it." Two sharp jabs with the hammer on the iron rod, and the leg came out, freeing the chair.

Her face lit up as if someone had gifted her a solitaire, but she stifled her glee. "Oh, thanks. You made it look like a child's play." She moved to take the hammer and the rod from his hand, her face all serious.

He held the tools behind his back. "Why so serious? Are you still mad at me?"

She broke the eye contact. "No. Please give them back to me. I have to keep them near the shed."

"I'll keep them, but look at me."

"What is this Zayd, when will you grow up? Give them to me."

He tossed them behind, on the bare flower bed, and wiped his hands on the jeans. "What about my payment?"

"Your payment?" She frowned, stopping midway, looking utterly desirable with her mouth half open.

He took a step forward, put a hand on her nape and kissed her without giving her anytime to react. She stiffened like a coiled snake for a moment then pushed at his chest. He didn't want to leave the soft supple touch and the faint smell of a flower that he couldn't recognize. But then the kiss couldn't go on forever since she was struggling, now that the initial surprise was gone. He lifted his mouth from hers and his hand from her nape. The next second, he felt a hard smack on his cheek.

"How dare you?" Her lips curled, as her eyes went wide with anger and her chest heaved. "How could you?" Her hands fisted.

He staggered back a step, more from her reaction than the sting on his cheek. Her face had turned hot, from embarrassment or anger he didn't know. He had acted on pure impulse. He had simply given in to his desire and never thought about her response, but the slap was the last thing he had anticipated.

"I'm sorry… I… I just…" He waved his hand in the air and clenched his jaw. "It won't happen again."

He turned, picked up the hammer and the rod, and walked towards the shed.

***

SEVENTEEN

Ashima had turned into stone, her feet rooted to the spot as she watched him go. Her lips were still quivering with the weight of his lips and her hand was still stinging. Why did he do that? No one could have seen them, but why did he just grab her? And why did she react the way she did? His kiss, a blow to her resolve to maintain a distance, threw her equilibrium haywire. How could things become such a mess?

With a heavy heart, she dragged herself back to the house.

As night fell, though, Ashima realized she had overreacted. She didn't know what to do. How should she call him for dinner? Or would he want the dinner in his room? He did that when he didn't want his writing spree to be interrupted. There was no one who she could send to ask him. She stood in the middle of the kitchen, twisting the dishcloth in her hand, unable to find a solution to her dilemma. The clock showed five minutes to nine and he hadn't asked for dinner yet. Stupid male pride, she thought irritated with him as she threw the dishcloth across the kitchen slab and reached for the in-house phone. Just then the gate creaked. Putting the receiver down, Ashima peeked through the dining room window and saw Zayd driving out of the gate.

***

Ashima patted Rishabh absentmindedly, trying to put him to sleep. He squirmed when he realized her mind was wandering. She smiled at him and put her hand on his eyes. He settled pulling her *dupatta* over his face, his favorite thing to hold while sleeping. She sighed.

Two days had passed and Zayd hadn't come out of his room. He took all the meals in the room and didn't interact with Rishabh either. All the communication was through Shankar. Ashima didn't have the time or the privacy to explain her instinctive reaction. On second thoughts, it was good that this happened. Maybe he would go away after a few days, as she had wanted.

She remembered the look on Zayd's face when she had slapped him. He was clearly shocked. But she hadn't thought before reacting. She had just acted on impulse. No one had breached her body space in the past four years, after that last night when Rohit had left for the war. Wasn't it natural for her to be uncomfortable?

And now he was sulking. He was such a baby. No, he wasn't!

Her heart missed a beat again. No, definitely not a baby. Her heart lurched again as she thought of his brooding hazel eyes. She had been deluding herself. She had been consciously seeking him out these days. She wanted to see him smile, see how his eyes changed colors with his changing emotions, the way he looked at her with intrigue and reverence. Yes, reverence. She was not being smug when she thought that. He looked at her sometimes with awe and sometimes with amused indulgence, especially when she enquired about his food preference or comfort.

He was not used to people thinking about his welfare. He had always been laconic in his replies whenever she asked about his family. But she knew that he had three sisters. They should be doting on him. Or maybe they were estranged, she thought suddenly.

Why did the thought never cross her mind? He had told her that he didn't get along with his father. Did his father blame him for the unfortunate incident? How could he? He was so young, barely out of college. He had seen the girl die, borne the guilt of taking her out at that time of the night. He had spent four years in prison, and was now here.

With four years in prison amongst the hardened criminals, it was amazing he had turned out the way he had—positive and honorable. But she could sense his anger with the whole world. It all made sense now. His reluctance to talk about his past was not only because of that unfortunate event, but also because he didn't get any support from his family. Parents get angry with their offspring, but for how long? She looked at Rishabh's angelic face, sleeping peacefully. Could a parent be so harsh? She could never be harsh with Rishabh.

He must be so lonely. As it was, his writing profession didn't allow him to interact with people and he didn't have any support from his family too. Maybe he couldn't go home. Her heart went out to him. She had to make amends. She picked up the magazine with his poem as an excuse.

***

Ashima pushed the door to his room. It swung open to the faint glow from the high mast light that filtered through the lace curtains. She couldn't see him and scanned the room. Hands in his jeans' pockets, he stood by the window looking out. She couldn't fathom what was of such an interest to him. He stiffened as he sensed her presence, but didn't turn around.

"Someone came by to drop this magazine. Your poem is published in this issue."

No reply.

She put the baby alarm and the magazine on the coffee table and moved towards him. Still, he didn't turn. She stood quietly studying him. He watched the scene outside the window with a blank expression, but a pulse ticked on his jaw. She touched his arm, forcing him to glance at her. He drew a deep breath and stepped back.

"I'm sorry."

He again turned to stare out of the window.

"That's what you get when you grab a woman and kiss her, without any regards to the place or time. You were lucky that I roam around without my sandals."

He didn't say anything, but his lips twitched.

"I'm sorry, Zayd," she whispered. "It was just an unconscious reaction. No one has come so close to me since… since…" She hoped the darkened room hid the color rising on her cheeks.

"You don't have to apologize. I shouldn't have crossed the moral line you have placed between us."

"I have to. I'm really sorry… I overreacted. You—"

He looked straight into her eyes. "Don't be so concerned, Aashi, or you'll make me fall in love with you."

"Don't talk silly." She looked down trying to control the way her heart stumbled, frantically thinking of saying something light.

"What if I admit I'm half in love with you?" he continued.

"Frivolous thoughts should not be given any importance." She carried on, ignoring his senseless rambling, but they were doing something to her innards. Her heart was twisting in its place and her stomach churned, bringing a burning sensation up to her throat. "You are a very emotional—"

"What if one doesn't have any control over their emotions?"

"One should try meditation."

He laughed out loud.

"No seriously." She frowned when he continued to shake in mirth. "What's there to laugh? What did I say?"

He chuckled. "Spend a few hours with me, Aashi."

"Why, so that you can laugh at me?"

"So that I can laugh with you."

She snorted.

"Let's have a picnic when Rishabh is in school… for a couple of hours. I don't feel any of my life's strife when I'm around you. It's all peaceful, like a cool breeze, when you are with me."

She sighed, silently thanking God he had abandoned his 'love' nonsense. "You should not be a crime writer, you should be a poet. Ah, that reminds me. Your poem is published. Someone dropped in with your copy of the issue." She handed him the magazine. "It is very touching and emotional."

"I've written one for you." He placed the magazine on the table without even glancing at it.

"Have you? Show it to me."

"Never."

"Why not?"

"You might take offense." He looked straight into her eyes once again, as he uttered the last two words— conveying something unthinkable.

All of a sudden, he had matured from a harmless friend to a flirting Casanova. The warm flush rose on her cheeks again. Frowning, she glanced at her feet. The conversation was going out of hand. Didn't he have a neutral topic to talk about? And why was she not able to think of any? What the heck! He was flirting with her and that was his prerogative, but why was she behaving like his girlfriend?

She exhaled. "Since you are feeling fine, I think I'll go now."

He didn't say anything but watched her as she bade him good night and left the room.

***

Things were right the way they should be—looking up. He was friends with Ashima again. His world that had tilted precariously for a few days had righted itself. The situation was back to normal with him sitting at Raghu's,

183

and sipping the insipid, lukewarm tea and eating mouth-watering samosas. And writing.

Dusk was falling, giving way to a clear, starry night. He was plotting his next novel on his notepad, sitting with his back to the road for minimal distraction. Paper and pen was his preferred mode for chalking out the broad roadmap for the story. The one he had been writing had finally found its way to the editor's mail box.

A motorcyclist raced across the *dhaba*. After a few seconds, another motorcycle drove in. Engrossed in his laptop, Zayd dismissed the faint whiff of diesel assailing him with a shake of his head. Raghu, facing the road, suddenly shouted and both the motorcyclists accelerated away leaving a warm swoosh of air in their wake. Raghu sprung up and rushed towards the large water drum kept for washing.

It was then that Zayd realized that something was horribly wrong. He pivoted around on the bench and saw his jeep on fire. He leapt to pick up another vessel for water but there was none. The fire raged as it spread from the rear to the front seats. Raghu shouted at him to stand back, screaming something about the fuel tank exploding. Which it did, just a few seconds after Raghu had uttered the words. It looked like the tank was waiting for a cue from Raghu. The explosion threw them three feet back as the metal splinters rained all over. Raghu screamed in agony. Zayd's calf was on fire. Someone on his right howled and cursed. Everything was over in a few minutes.

People from the other shops raced towards them. Some helped to contain the fire and some offered to take them to the clinic. After the three of them were given immediate first aid at a nearby clinic, Raghu's helper, who had suffered the maximum burns, was taken to a hospital nearby.

As the smoke cleared, Zayd stood watching his jeep smolder and sputter, giving out occasional sparks as the fire died down. The fire was now contained to a few wisps of smoke, but the vehicle was ruined. Nothing could be done. The carcass of metal stood wasted.

Zayd had never owned a car and when *naanijaan* had sprung the surprise by handing him the keys, he was jubilant. It was a gift. Something special. A symbol of change. Change in his fortune and luck. And they had wiped out that symbol. And the hope that came with it. Hope that he could turn around his life for the better. Bastards.

Zayd called the police and dialed Akshat to help in contacting his insurance company. There was no sign of the police, though, as time ticked by. No one came from the police station even when Raghu went to call them.

Eventually, dawn was breaking, with the sky turning a light blue from the dark indigo of the night. Most of the twinkling stars had faded, but a few stubborn ones still remained even with the changing colors of the sky. The azure blue sky, however, failed to abate the fire that Kanyal had ignited in his heart. Yes, he knew it was Kanyal. Zayd wanted to find that scoundrel and beat him to death. Kanyal was goading him to make a wrong move. But he won't. He won't lose control, he won't go to pieces, and he won't let the issue go either. A complaint had to be lodged.

Zayd was wiser by four years and he had had the therapy. He would keep everything under control.

After a long lecture to himself, Zayd entered the police station that morning. Constable Sharma was the only one present and he had no clue about the incident.

As he was convincing Sharma to register an FIR, Inspector Bisht sauntered inside in his customary gait, slow and superior to all. "So, whom did you piss-off this time, hero?"

Zayd ignored him and continued addressing Sharma, "Please note down the details."

A confused Sharma sucked up to Bisht. "He wants to register an FIR."

"FIR? What for?" Bisht bellowed. "Criminals do not have any right to file an FIR." He made a big show of arranging his desk and sat down.

Zayd's jaw clenched.

"You must have instigated a fight with the local people. Otherwise I have never seen this kind of incident happening in my area. Was that your vehicle? Are you sure you haven't stolen it from somewhere?"

Zayd tried to stay silent, but could feel his pulse rising and the blood gushing to his brain.

"When are you leaving this town, Rizvi? I would suggest, you take the insurance money and leave this place for good. I'll help you get the insurance claim." He leaned towards Zayd. "Take an advice from someone older to you. Your type of lads are a dime a dozen out here. People here would tear you apart once they hear you are taking *panga* with someone like Kanyal, you being a Muslim. Moreover you are getting too friendly with our local hero's wife, people are thinking *hamari izzat par hath daala*. Not good… not good at all. Nope."

Zayd was now fuming and trembling. Inspector Bisht was oblivious of his rage. Taking his silence as acquiescence, he continued in low volume, "They will not spare her either. They will taunt her. She won't be able to leave the house, will not be able to show her face in the town. The family will have no support and will be ostracized. Do you hear me? Why do you want such a fate for them? Just go from here and everything will be all right. For her sake… if you get my drift…" He patted Zayd's chest.

Zayd stepped forward and hissed. "Now you listen—"

"Wishing for death in this town, *babu*?" Someone jeered behind them.

Hearing the much hated voice, Zayd spun towards the intruder.

Kanyal stood at the entrance of the police station. He strolled inside the room, whacking his cane against his thigh lightly. "*Kya babu, bahut garmi hai*? One complaint and you'll be back to Tihar," he smirked.

Towering over him, Zayd stared at the loathsome man, barely able to control himself. The sight of his burning vehicle loomed in his mind.

"*Beta*… what do you think, *bahut sayane ho*, with one murder? Only one?" Kanyal sneered, then leaned in and whispered. "We have silenced off so many, no one has been able to even smell the bodies. Do take care, Rizvi *saab*. Next time, it shouldn't be that you are in the car."

Zayd kept watching him with no expression. Instead of standing down, his silence goaded Kanyal all the more. "It's all because of that woman, right?" Kanyal took one more step towards him and whispered. "*Saali*, doesn't even talk to me. And allows you to stay with her."

Zayd felt blood gushing to his head at the insults. The dam broke. He forgot everything he had promised himself in the morning. Grinding his teeth, Zayd stepped towards Kanyal and held him by the scuffle of his shirt.

"Hey… what…" The inspector rushed towards him.

"*Saab*!" Sharma shouted, standing behind his desk. "*Saab*… no…"

Zayd panted and heard people saying something, but the words could not penetrate the violent humming of blood in his ears. Kanyal had begun wheezing. The inspector tried to pull his hands, but Zayd held on. Bisht didn't even have the presence of mind to use his cane or gun.

"Zayd *bhai*… what are you doing? Leave him… leave him…" Someone stood beside him and shouted. Someone tall. "Zayd *bhai*."

All of a sudden, he was pulled off Kanyal, who slid down on the floor, clutching his throat, gagging and gasping for breath. Blind in his anger, Zayd struggled against the man who continued to talk to him.

"Zayd *bhai*, control, *ek aur murder apne sar lena hai kya?*"

It was a few moments before it registered that the man was Abdul, his father's man Friday. He took deep breaths.

"Leave me, I'm okay." Jerking himself free from Abdul he caught hold of Kanyal's neck again—not in a death grip but firmly enough—and glued him to the wall, leaning in closer to him. Kanyal's eyes widened as they darted towards Zayd's left shoulder. From the way Kanyal reacted, Zayd was sure Abdul had stepped up behind him. Zayd saw a satisfying sliver of fear in his eyes. Abdul had that kind of effect on people.

"Listen carefully, *babu*," Zayd growled, mimicking him. "You don't know who you are entangling with. There is a big difference in doing something and getting something done. I have done it and I can do it again. Do you know how I murdered him? I plunged the knife in his intestines and twisted it. Can you even imagine how it must've felt? It was like cutting a cake." He loosened his hold a bit, then continued. "Just remember one more thing, I have no problem in going to jail again, but if I send you to hell, all this *aish* will be over. One last time, stay away."

He turned on his heels and stormed out of the police station.

"What the heck, Abdul? What are you doing here?" Zayd shouted as Abdul followed him out.

"*Saheb's* orders."

Zayd turned on him and grabbed him by the scruff of his neck. "Since when have you been shadowing me?"

Abdul kept silent, but met his eyes unflinchingly. It was not his fault. He was just following his father's orders. Zayd left him. "Get the fuck out of my way. Tell him, I don't need you or him, ever."

"*Bhai, itna gussa theek nahin.*"

"I'll be angrier if I see you lurking around me or the guest house."

Zayd couldn't sleep that night.

His lawyer and Baba had warned him. There might be repercussions now. Kanyal was scared. He might file a complaint and Zayd's parole might get cancelled. And then Ashima would be all alone. The thought sent chills down his spine. Leaving Ashima alone was more alarming than going to prison for another three years. He couldn't leave Ashima. No matter what.

To top it all, Abbu had again sent Abdul to monitor his activities. 'Keep an eye over the brat!' he would have said.

Fuck! As if he was a teenager. Abdul would report the incident back home, and Abbu would have another weapon in his arsenal to taunt him. *'You couldn't even take care of a gift, Zayd!'*

***

EIGHTEEN

"*Didi*, someone asking for Zayd siw." Shankar held the door to the living area open.

Now what?' Ashima looked at Shankar but he only shrugged.

It had been barely two days since Zayd's car was torched. The insurance agent had completed his inspection and the remains of the car were sent to the scrap dealer. Apart from this, she had no clue what had happened. Raghu had taken a secrecy vow as far as Zayd was concerned. And Zayd had clamped down, refusing to tell her anything except that everything was under control. She was so worried.

"Who is it Shankar? Did he give his name?"

"No. I didn't ask. He is a big fellow, biggew than Zayd siw."

"Who is the man standing outside?" Radha came in bringing fresh coriander leaves for dinner. "*Didi*, he's the same man who I have seen roaming about a couple of times."

Wiping her hands on a kitchen towel, Ashima came out. Shankar was right, he was a big man, in his mid-forties perhaps with his head completely shaven. Built like a bouncer she had noticed in one of Mumbai's pubs.

"Excuse me."

"Madam, myself Abdul. I wanta meet Zayd *bhai*." He bowed his head after greeting her, then targeted his gaze at something above her head.

Ashima had never met a man more courteous. "I think I saw him going out. Why don't you take a seat and wait for him?" She gestured towards the sofa in the corridor.

"*Ji… ji…*"

"Would you like to have something? Water or tea?"

"*Ji… ji…* tea… tea and water."

She instructed Shankar to do the needful and arranged some snacks to go along with the tea. The man looked tired and hungry.

He looked flabbergasted when she asked him if he had come to the house earlier too. He admitted that he was employed with Zayd's father. So Radha was right. He had been loitering around the house for quite some time.

She heard Zayd enter as the gate tingled. It was almost dinner time and the poor man Abdul had been waiting patiently reading the newspapers. Zayd shouted and she rushed to the dining room window. He shouted and ranted without taking a name, pacing the corridor, while Abdul stood with his hands clasped in front and his head bent down.

Ashima ran back to the kitchen when Zayd made a beeline towards the living area.

"Aashi, can this man live in the barn for tonight? He'll go back tomorrow," Zayd called approaching the kitchen.

She came out. "Yeah, sure."

"Thank you. Don't bother with his dinner. He'll manage on his own."

"Where will he go in the night? Let him eat here. What's the harm?"

"I don't want extra work for you because my father thinks I'm a little boy and need a nanny."

She smiled at the picture he had painted, and bit her cheek trying not to smile.

"Don't you dare." He glared.

She swallowed her smile and said, "It's not like I cook. A few extra rotis or some extra rice is not a problem. Anyway, you can pay me for his food. It'll be extra income."

That satisfied him and he went back the way he had come. Smiling, she turned to see Amma at the threshold with a frown on her face. Her lips tightened in a thin line and Ashima's smile faded immediately.

"Since when are you and him on a first name basis? And how did he come in the kitchen?"

"It's just that he was angry... I'm... it's just that... he has been staying with us for more than a month. With time—" Hating that she had to justify her actions, and struggled not to sound too familiar with Zayd.

Amma raised her hand. "No need to give excuses. I do not approve of whatever is happening these days, Ashima. I didn't expect this kind of behavior from you. You have forgotten all the values, the decorum fit for our family. Rohit's family!"

"Amma, it's normal behavior for her. Her upbringing doesn't see any wrong with it. She is modern, unlike you or me. Values and decorum have a different meaning for *bhabhi*." Pooja smirked.

"Pooja—" Ashima tried to intervene.

"Don't interfere when elders are talking, Pooja. Go to your room."

Pooja pursed her lips and stormed out of the kitchen.

Wheeling the chair all over the kitchen, Amma went on to lash out at Ashima, calling her *manhoos*, and proclaiming that Ashima had brought bad luck for her son and family. She recalled all the mishaps that had happened since the time Ashima had come into her son's life. She repeated even the most trivial of mistakes, exaggerating them as much as she could.

This was not the first time that Amma was insulting Ashima, that too in front of Radha and Shankar. Unshed tears of humiliation and anger made Ashima's eyes ache, but she heard her out, like she always did. Leaving the kitchen was not an option. It would have made Amma angrier and her tantrums would have continued the next day too.

Spent and tired with her rant after sometime, Amma wheeled her chair out of the kitchen.

Radha and Shankar, used to it all for years, continued to prepare dinner, talking softly whenever it was absolutely necessary. Ashima sat down on the kitchen stool and stared outside the window, until Radha asked her something.

At dinner, Ashima couldn't eat beyond two morsels. She threw whatever was on the plate in the dustbin and retired for a sleepless night.

***

Ashima's head was splitting by the time she put Rishabh to sleep. She desperately needed to unwind and gather a bit of strength from somewhere. The urge to meet to Zayd took her by surprise. Was she getting addicted to him? But she didn't want to face him tonight. And going by Amma's tongue-lashing, she shouldn't even think about him.

But then, why should she be the one sacrificing everything? Why should she forfeit the little peace and joy she got from somewhere? Wasn't she a living, breathing person who needed a little support, a little hope, so that she could go on and on for the family?

Was she supposed to be a slave for someone to dictate her ways to her just because they were unable to trust her? She hadn't done anything wrong. Then why should she be defensive? And she wasn't at an age where she needed someone's approval or consent.

She picked up the baby alarm, the keys and left the room.

"Hey," Zayd said as she sat beside him, folding her knees and resting her chin on them, her favorite posture. Her hair slipped on her face like a curtain shielding her from him. He tucked the errant curl behind her ear in one smooth motion. She pulled back and frowned.

"I don't like talking to your hair."

"What a funny thing to say!" She smiled. It took an effort to stretch her lips. His next words, however, proved that she wasn't able to fool him.

"You are upset. Did Mrs. Joshi say something? She appeared angry."

"No." Her hair slid down on her face again. Again, he tugged them behind her ear. Involuntarily, a tear escaped and fell. With a muffled sob, she hid her face between her knees.

"Aashi…" He touched her shoulder. "Please…"

She hiccupped and broke down. His sympathy penetrated the stoic wall of survival she had erected around her, a wall behind which she had held her grief, fear, helplessness, and the weight of her responsibilities. The wall had developed cracks by the acidic barbs of her own family, Ashima thought, as her sobs echoed in the small area.

"Aashi… please don't." Zayd put a hand on her shoulder and pulled her to him. She clutched the lapels of his jacket, crying in earnest and couldn't stop. He gathered her into his arms and planted a kiss on her hair, making her weep harder. He tightened the circle of his embrace and let her cry.

She pushed against his chest after a long time, when there were no tears left. "I'm sorry," she whispered, her voice hoarse.

He loosened his hold, and ran his gentle gaze all over her face. The steady, reassuring beating of his heart beneath her hand made him more real than ever. His eyes had turned moth-green, the color of wet moss. Awareness ran down her body like an electric current. To her chagrin, he planted a kiss on her forehead. She pushed him half-heartedly, and he let her go.

"Thank you." She wiped her tears with her hands.

"What for?"

"For being here. For your empathy. For everything."

"I don't know why you say such things. People all my life have told me that I'm selfish, self-centered, violent, and spoilt to the core."

She sniffled. "Who says that?"

"My entire khandaan."

"Who all are there in your family?"

"A lot of people. I have a big family. There is my father, my sisters, my aunts, and my uncles. My grandfather used to say every family has a bad seed and I'm that bad seed in my family. And my uncles were relieved that they were not on his radar." He chuckled. "I'm glad he died before my prison stint. I never wanted him to be proven right and say, 'I told you so'." Zayd grinned.

Ashima smiled a weak smile.

"You are worried about something else too. Want to tell me about it?"

"Kanyal… who else? He is my biggest worry."

"What about Pooja?"

Ashima's gaze flashed at him.

"I saw her with a man on the trail I sometimes follow. It was looking quite clandestine, with that guy's back towards any onlookers and hiding his face with a cap. If I'm with someone I care, I'll shield her instead of doing the other way round."

Ashima dropped her gaze to her hands. "Hmm… I'll ask her."

They sat watching the usual scene of the village immersed in twinkling lights. No words were required for the quiet support he gave her. He had been doing that since the time he had arrived. No one had ever helped her the way he had done. Right now also, he was looking out for Pooja. Why shouldn't she trust him? Why shouldn't she lead her life on her own terms?

"Zayd."

"Hmm…"

"You were saying something about trekking the other day."

"Would you like to go?"

"Yes," she replied after a long pause.

"That's great. We'll have a picnic by the river. It'll be fun."

"Do you think it's doable?"

"Oh yes, I'll leave early. You follow the main road, and I'll pick you up near the next milestone. I have found a nice trail, just at the outskirts of the town. So is it a date?"

One moment she was all confident about her independence, but the next second doubts assailed her mind. "Zayd, I really shouldn't. What if someone spots us? Tongues would start wagging—"

"Nothing will happen, trust me. I can even bring a *burqa*, if you are game. It's a handy garment."

She smiled and shook her head.

***

NINETEEN

They had fun, just as Zayd had predicted. Ashima had never seen the trail that was unadulterated by humans—unspoiled and simply beautiful, spanning the valley on the other side of the town.

Zayd had picked her up from the gate of the church, where she had parked her car. He drove the hired car away from the town for five kilometers and parked under a thick cluster of trees. There was a hamper with dry picnic lunch, complete with a floor mat, disposable plates, cups and spoons, arranged at a place where no one could see them from the road.

After polishing off the sandwiches, he tossed her an orange and challenged her for a spitting contest. Whosoever would spit the pip of the orange the farthest would be the winner. He demonstrated by spitting one at least three feet away.

The first one she tried fell on her feet. In the second attempt nothing came out of her mouth but the spit. When she realized she had swallowed the pip in the process, she burst into giggles. Clutching her belly, she collapsed on the mat. Grinning, he sat down beside her and watched her laugh.

His steady gaze unnerved and sobered her at the same time. "Zayd?" She tried to distract him. "There is absolute silence from Kanyal since the day your car was burnt down. I hope he is not plotting something more sinister… like murdering me… or you."

He chuckled. "No… I don't think so."

"Why? You sound very confident!"

"I told you I'm a bigger goon than him."

"Zayd, be serious." She chewed her lip.

"I have some vague idea."

She raised an eyebrow when he remained silent.

"It's the Abdul effect," he added.

"Huh…?"

"Kanyal met Abdul at the police station and Abdul must have told my father."

"Your father?"

"I told you my father has clout."

"All over India?"

"Yeah, something like that."

"He must really care for you to take such pains."

He laughed, then immediately changed the track of the conversation. "Aashi, I need your permission."

"Huh…?"

"You look adorable. May I kiss you? Promise me you'll not hit me."

"You are an idiot." She swatted at his arm and walked to the clearing beyond the trees. Pretending she was admiring the scenery, she took deep breaths to steady her traitor heart.

"I have something else for you." He was still sitting on the mat, watching her. Even with her back towards him, she could feel his heated gaze on her.

She turned.

"Close your eyes." He picked up his laptop bag and made a great show of taking something out of it.

She frowned. "What is it, Zayd? Show it to me."

"No, first close your eyes."

She exhaled and closed her eyes.

"Now."

She opened her eyes and her mouth fell open too. Sitting before her were two plastic wine glasses and a bottle of French red wine. "Zayd, are you crazy? I don't drink."

"Of course, you do. I know that you love wine."

"How do you know that?" She narrowed her eyes. "Oh, the album! And how did you manage to get this fabulous brand and the right glasses here in Kasauli?"

"I'm your genie today." He smiled, opening the bottle with great aplomb. He poured the fiery red liquid in the glasses and offered one to her. "To us," he cheered.

Ashima smiled and took the glass. He tinkled his glass with hers and took a sip, his gaze not leaving hers. She also sipped, unable to glance away from him. She knew she should, but couldn't. A bird flip flopped nearby, breaking the trance around them. Ashima dropped her gaze to the plate in front of her.

"You shouldn't have done this. I could get drunk."

"I'll take care of you, don't worry. You relax and enjoy." He put on a latest songs' playlist on his laptop.

For the first time in many years, Ashima relaxed with no thought of time or worry about the huge list of chores to be done. She was pleasantly high and felt light in the head, completely carefree. She let out a loud sigh and lay on the mat, her hands under her head. The clean white clouds in the blue sky played hide and seek above the canopy of trees. Zayd also lay down mimicking her pose and glanced at the view. The clouds sliced the sun-rays as they passed, displaying a kaleidoscope of colors.

"Baba used to love lying under the trees."

"Baba? Your father?"

"No. Baba was my anchor in the prison, my savior who shielded me from the others, the nasty ones. He was the one who kept me sane for four years in that madhouse."

"Where is he now?"

"He is serving life term for killing his family. But I don't think he killed them, somewhere something went wrong and he is paying the price."

"What about your father?"

He remained silent.

"Why are you so angry with your family?"

"I'm not angry with all of them. I love my sisters—half-sisters, actually. They are too cute… always waiting for me to visit them… sharing little bits of their life with me whenever we meet." He sighed. "I don't know how I can love them so much given that I hate their parents."

"Their parents?" She raised her eyebrows.

"My father and his wife. I mean his second wife."

"Hate is a very strong word."

He remained silent.

After piecing together everything he had told her, it was apparent that Zayd resented someone taking the place of his mother. "Maybe your father didn't have a choice. Some people need other people around them to survive, because sometimes the memories aren't enough."

"Aashi, please I've had a lot of sittings with my counselors, and the sessions are not fun."

"I'm not your counselor, I'm your friend. I think you should live in Delhi, and go out with your friends like Akshat, and have some fun—"

"Yes, grandmother—"

"One should always live in the present."

"There is one problem with this philosophy though. I don't have a present. The past is the only constant in my life. Whenever I try to be free, it spreads its black tentacles, and pulls me back, overpowering me."

She ignored his pessimistic ramblings. "You should be amongst friends your age. It is therapeutic to spend time having fun. At least meet a few eligible girls, go out on dates et al."

Zayd went on his elbow and peered at her face. "I'm doing that." His eyes took in her features one by one—her eyes, her hair then back on her face, her nose, the mole, her lips. Ashima stared at him as a sliver of awareness raced through her entire body and her heart beat accelerated again. The chirping of the birds and the rustling of the leaves faded with the increasing buzz in her head. Something snapped inside her brain. Her eyes widened, the lazy haze disappeared, and she sat up all of a sudden.

"Ouch..."

"Aah..."

Her head had banged against his chin.

"Why did you do that?" he said rubbing his chin.

"You shouldn't come too close to me, you'll get hurt."

***

Ashima decided to take a bath after coming back. She prepared for her bath, reflecting on the unusual four hours. Smiling at the thought of the complete bottle of wine they had consumed. No... no... she had consumed. Zayd had kept her glass topped up, making sure she had all the fun. And she did have fun—lots of it. After a long time, she had a day where she wasn't taking care of others; instead someone had thought about her and had taken care of her.

It was relaxing, sitting and talking about her childhood and college days. Zayd, as usual, had cut off any conversation that steered towards his childhood or family. She was having so much fun after such a long time that she didn't want to spoil the day by insisting that he bared his soul. But one day she would get everything out of his system so that he would be free of his past and could enjoy life.

Radha had given her an odd look when she had entered the gate, smiling like an idiot, even when the effect of wine had worn off. Zayd had gone to Raghu's dhaba, making her promise that she'd meet him on the bench at the night. Next time she would—

Her gaze fell on Rohit's photo, smiling at her. She came thudding back to earth. Rohit! She had not thought of him in so many days. All the thoughts of the day she had spent with Zayd instantly poofed from her mind. What had she been thinking?

Next time? One day? There won't be a next time… Zayd would complete his novel and go away, to another location for his new story, and would meet other people, some other girl or woman, and… She closed her eyes, as something sharp pierced her heart.

How could she think about another man when she loved Rohit? How could she betray him like this? Why was this acquaintance of a couple of months overshadowing her eternal love for her husband? Her husband, her sweetheart, so vibrant, so brave!

She took Rohit's photo and clutched it to her chest. What was wrong with her? Why was she so bothered about Zayd going away and meeting other people? Wouldn't it be blasphemy to even think about another man when Rohit could be alive somewhere? She had Rohit, his son—their son—with her. One day, Rohit would be back. What more did she need? She had had immense happiness with Rohit to last her a lifetime. She didn't need or want anything from anyone.

Her finger traced his smiling lips through the glass surface. Rohit, her heart whispered. Would she be able to hold his warm body again in her arms? Of course she would. She shook her head, jerking away the germ of uncertainty tiptoeing into her mind. He would be back soon. How she longed to have him with her. How she wished he hadn't gone to the bloody war.

A drop fell on the glass. Startled, she fingered her hair, only to find that it was not dripping. She was taken aback when she realized that her eyes were wet. Another tear dropped on the frame. Why? Why this sudden loneliness, this utter feeling of desolation? She wiped the tears that had fallen on the photo and placed her hand on his photo again. Why was this not enough today?

"*Didi*, lunch?" Radha called from the doorway.

Ashima quickly wiped her tears. "Ask Amma and Pooja and make something. I don't feel like eating. Mr. Rizvi won't be having dinner at home."

"I hope you are not coming down with something *Didi*? Shall I make *khichdi*? Rishabh also likes it. You can have some with curd. It will settle your stomach."

"Okay fine, leave it on the warmer."

Ashima lay down on the bed searching for that inner peace that had calmed her when she had heard that she was expecting Rishabh.

Rishabh, yes, she should concentrate on him. He was the beacon of her life, her life's purpose. She should not let her mind wander and dream of things that were not possible in this lifetime.

Forcing herself to greet Rishabh as he entered the house, she sat on the bed. Unknowingly, Rohit's photo slipped from her chest and crashed on the floor. She gasped, her eyes filling up again. With mixed feelings, she picked up the photo frame and saw that the glass had cracked from the lower corner and the crack ran in all direction like the rays of the sun.

The rest of the day went in a trance until the in-house intercom rang after Rishabh was fast asleep. With trembling hands, she picked up the receiver.

"Hey, I thought you had forgotten about me. I've been waiting for the past fifteen minutes." Zayd's voice was husky, full of affection.

"I'm not feeling up to it. Can we please skip this today?"

"What happened? Are you all right?"

Ashima could imagine him frowning in concern.

She gripped the receiver hard, reminding herself to keep her voice light and her tone casual. "Yeah… nothing to be alarmed about. Too much wine and sun, I suppose. I'm not used to relaxing, I guess." She forced a chuckle out of her throat.

"Okay grandmother, you are excused. Sleep tight, and we'll have a tête-à-tête about your health tomorrow during breakfast. Good night, Aashi." He disconnected the call.

Her heart skipped a beat at the way he took her name, but logical thoughts clashed with the emotion, causing her to frown and question the wisdom of today's excursion. She exhaled and resolved, once again, to put some distance between them.

She lay down on the bed, but sleep eluded her. Dry eyed, she stared at the shadows of the darkened room. A familiar gloom, which had become her constant companion after hearing about Rohit's disappearance, swirled around her like cold winter fog.

***

TWENTY

Zayd was sitting at Raghu's when he thought he saw someone he knew driving off on a motorbike. Even though the girl had wrapped a scarf around her face, she looked familiar. He was sure she was Pooja.

Zayd asked Raghu to take care of his laptop bag, borrowed his motorcycle and followed the couple.

The bike stopped and the man and the girl left it near the roadside as they walked with hurried steps into the side lane. Parking the motorcycle, Zayd also followed them. They moved steadily through the town's winding up and down lanes, where a vehicle couldn't go. The girl stopped after a few steps and protested about something. The man turned around, placating her as he pulled her forward.

Zayd hid behind a pillar jutting out from the haphazard buildings on the street but he couldn't hear the conversation clearly. The girl protested again. Zayd couldn't remain hidden any longer and came out. The man pulled her towards a two-storeyed brick house, even when she resisted. Her stole fell down and Zayd saw Pooja's panicked face.

"But Nikhil, this doesn't look like a place for dancing."

"Come on, don't be a spoilsport. My friends are dying to meet you. You have to trust me." The man's attention was diverted with Pooja protesting. He didn't notice Zayd walking casually towards them. Another man, wearing a denim jacket, came out from one of the houses on the other side of the street.

"What happened? Is she throwing tantrums? You have to show her who's in-charge," the guy in the denim jacket said, catching hold of her arm.

Pooja stood frozen at his tone.

"Let her go," Zayd said politely, bringing himself into the fray.

Both men whirled at his voice and Pooja gasped. To Zayd's relief, she took advantage of their surprise, wrenched free of them and ran to his side. He put himself between her and the men.

"Who are you?" The guy in the denim jacket screamed. "Get lost! Now!"

"Let us go. I have called the police," Zayd improvised about the call.

"Really, now you will tell me you have a mobile, *kadake*." The man Pooja had addressed as Nikhil pulled up his sleeve. The other one also walked towards them flanking the narrow street.

Zayd took a step back with Pooja stumbling since she was glued to his arm, crying and sniffling. He scanned up and down the street, gauging the danger they were in and the best way to escape with minimum damage. He had no inclination to have another meeting with Kasauli's police staff. "Listen to me carefully. We're going to walk from here, and you both go home like the good men of this town. And we will forget everything."

"Pooja—" Nikhil began.

"Get lost, you bastard!" Pooja shouted even as she began crying earnestly, clutching Zayd's sleeve.

Zayd was surprised as well as happy that she showed some spirit given the situation they were in and lifted his hand in peace. "You heard her. Now as I said we are going to turn and walk away. You two will go inside the house and everything will be fine."

Nikhil laughed. "You think this is a movie? *Kat le, saale.* Or be prepared to get bloody."

Zayd turned, propelling Pooja forward, but keeping his concentration on the two men behind him.

The air swooshed behind Zayd. He stepped to one side, pushing Pooja towards the wall and shielding her. As the man in the denim jacket stumbled past them, Zayd winced and clutched his forearm. Pooja gasped.

The man's head banged against one of opposite walls on the narrow street. He cried out, slipped and lay there stunned in the shallow gutter. Pain seared Zayd's arm as something sticky oozed out on his palm. The man had nicked him with a knife. Damn! He had never anticipated they would be armed. Taking advantage of the shocked man lying near his foot, Zayd stepped on his wrist. The knife fell and rolled off.

Zayd glanced back at Nikhil. He appeared more confident than his friend. Then his eyes flickered at something to Zayd's right and he took a step back. Abdul's tobacco-laced breath assailed Zayd's senses. For once Zayd was thankful for Abdul's silent support.

Abdul picked up the knife and came to stand in front of Zayd and Pooja. "Go," he commanded.

Zayd held Pooja's hand. "Come on let's go… fast."

They ran towards the main road. Out on the road he hired an auto for Pooja and followed her on Raghu's bike. He didn't bother about Abdul. He was more than capable of handling the two novice street hooligans. And it would serve him right for meddling in his affairs.

"Wipe your tears. Go on, I'll follow after a while." Zayd paid the auto at the gate.

"Your arm is bleeding," Pooja sniffled.

"It's nothing. Go inside. Just let me know what you tell your mother, so that I'll also say the same thing in case she or anyone asks."

She nodded and went past the gate.

Zayd's arm was hurting like hell. The blood had seeped on his sleeve, which was now stuck to his skin. He didn't want to touch it. He returned the bike to Raghu and walked leisurely back to the guest house. In his room, he took off his jacket. The leather was ruined beyond repair. He gingerly took off his shirt, looking at the threads of the torn edges that had clotted along with his blood inside the wound, which was, thankfully so, not very deep or large—just short of an inch.

Someone knocked perfunctorily and the door opened. Ashima entered carrying a box. Glaring then wincing at the sight of the bloody gash, she placed it on the table and sat beside him.

"Pooja told you? Brave girl," he said.

She opened the plastic box. "She is a stupid girl and you are a sneaky man." She lifted his arm with a feather light touch and placed a towel on his lap.

"It's nothing! My jacket saved me from the worst."

The way she delicately probed, prodded and examined the wound, made him smile.

"I think this needs stitches," she declared. "We should go to a doctor."

"Oh, come on! The blood is clotting as it is. This is nothing more than a baby scratch. I'll just clean it and bind it myself."

"*Offo*… leave it. I'll do it."

She cleaned the wound and applied lots of antiseptic lotion, binding it a little too tight for his comfort, but he didn't complain. He just sat there watching her working on him with her lower lip pressed under her teeth. She kept glancing at him from time to time, going slowly from pink to red under his gaze.

It was his turn to see red when she took out a syringe.

"What are you doing?"

"Giving you a tetanus injection."

"Injection? Are you sure you can do this? When did you learn to administer injections?"

"Great! Now I'm vindicated. There is something that you are scared of," Ashima chuckled, filling the syringe with the medicine and making a show of knocking the air out of the syringe.

"No way am I going to take this injection from you." He put both his arms behind his back and stood up.

"Why not?" She wriggled her eyebrows.

"What qualifications do you have?"

"You are not supposed to question me, remember you said that you love me."

"Yeah… but you don't love me back, so I don't trust you."

"Zayd… you don't have a choice. Sit down."

"You are enjoying this, right!" He sat again.

She smiled and shook her head, the way she did with Rishabh. "Come on, I have been giving insulin to Amma since ages. Give me your arm, the other one."

He reluctantly extended his hand and she expertly injected the vaccine.

"There, you are done. I'll send turmeric milk after dinner, just drink it without any tantrums and you will be fine by tomorrow." She put all the medicines inside the box and closed the box.

"Yes, doctor." Zayd exhaled and watched her leave, leaving him under her spell once again.

***

Ashima entered the house to find Amma in a blind rage, shouting at Pooja. She was crying, standing in one corner of her room and Rishabh was cowering and sniffling at his study table. Amma had seen Zayd's blood on Pooja's clothes and had got the whole story from her.

"This is what you get by sending girls to college. Stupid girl… could have been raped, it would have been a blessing if he had murdered you. Going with a man like that. What good time did he show you?"

Amma wheeled her chair towards Pooja, pulled her down to the floor and slapped her. "Did you have a good time? Your brother is not with us. Shouldn't you have thought about us? What would have we done if something had happened to you?" Pooja sobbed harder and Rishabh wailed louder.

Ashima rushed to Pooja, trying to shield her from Amma. "Amma what are you doing? Leave her."

Amma went on as if possessed, hitting Ashima also in the process.

"Amma control yourself. Is this the way to treat an adult daughter?"

Shankar had picked up Rishabh and tried to soothe him.

"Is this the way a responsible adult should behave? Our daughter, Rohit's sister, roaming the streets of Kasauli with a strange man, where everyone recognizes her. Have you no shame?" She started crying and slapped Pooja again on her leg.

"Amma, I didn't know…" Pooja cried. "I'm sorry Amma, I'm so sorry."

Amma wiped the tears with her saree and wheeled out of the room, muttering, "Now we have to be in debt of that criminal. I'll never ever thank him. Trying to endear us to him in every possible way. Trying to take my Rohit's place."

Ashima hid her exasperation by turning her face away.

"He wants to take Rohit's place in this household, but it will never happen… never… do you hear?" Amma kept shouting and cursing everything in sight till she was exhausted and went to sleep without having dinner.

***

Zayd's arm healed well as he changed the bandage the next day. Though he didn't voice it, he was glad to see that Abdul was back at the outhouse and the mishap didn't pull any unwanted attention.

That day while taking his regular walk through the town, he saw the buzz around the otherwise staid premises of the Gymkhana Club. On enquiring, the staff told him that they were preparing for a charity event. The 'Rhythm and Red' concert was being organized by a Delhi-based NGO for the first time in Kasauli. The photograph of Ashima in the pub flashed in his mind. An idea began to sprout. He picked up the pamphlet from the iron stand. The tickets were expensive but it would be worth the chance.

He reached the guest house after making the arrangements and found Ashima and Pooja sitting under the gazebo. Ashima was mending something and Pooja was shelling peas. Pooja saw him first and ran inside the house.

"I guess I'm not a popular person around," he said.

"No… no… she is miserable about last week's incident, and feels shy around you. Wanted to thank you but doesn't because of Amma."

Zayd nodded and told her about the concert and got the expected negative response. He didn't disclose that he had arranged for the tickets, thereby taking her approval for granted, but still heard her out. She cited all the obvious reasons, which according to Zayd could be managed, and didn't agree. After a few minutes of sitting in discorded silence, she began gathering the peas, the bowls, her sewing kit and the clothes.

"*Bhabhi*, you go. I'll look after Rishabh." Pooja stood at the entrance of the gazebo.

"Pooja, why did you run away? Today is a perfect opportunity to thank Zayd."

Pooja raised her eyes to him and muttered, "Thanks for… I don't know how I could have made that mistake. Trusting—" Her eyes started watering.

Embarrassed, Zayd waved his hand and tried to put her at ease. "Oh, it's fine. Forget about it. Like t'was a bad dream."

Pooja nodded and turned towards Ashima, but didn't meet her eyes. "*Bhabhi*, you like western music so much. You should go. You never get to have fun. Please, I'll feel better for being so… so nasty with you." She ran away again after uttering the last few words.

"Why was she nasty to you?" He frowned.

Ashima's gaze followed Pooja until she disappeared inside the house, and to his chagrin, her eyes filled up too. She swallowed and blinked before answering his question, "Nothing, something trivial."

"I don't see anything trivial in the said and unsaid conversation between the two of you. Out with it. I could never imagine Pooja being nasty with you."

Ashima looked at him. "You are like a dog with a rag-cloth."

He chuckled. "That's a new one."

She smiled.

"But I cannot be side-tracked. Spill it…"

"She was jealous of you, because I give more importance to you instead—"

"Instead?" Zayd's scowled. Rohit's presence once again invaded his time with her.

"Instead what? Instead of her, who else. What did you think?" she answered quickly.

Was she finally acknowledging his importance in her life? Could he take the liberty of thinking on those lines? Zayd dropped the far-fetched idea and picked up the pamphlet for the fest. At least she had agreed to think about it.

The next day he told her that he had bought the tickets. She nodded, but didn't say anything. The time on the ticket said 07:00 pm onwards, but she put a cap of two hours from 10:00 pm to midnight. The only person who knew she would be absconding from the house was Pooja. They agreed to meet at the gate at 9:45.

***

Ashima didn't know what had happened to her— behaving like a teenager on her first night-out. She stood in front of the almirah, thinking about what to wear. What if someone recognized her? What if she met Kanyal or someone known to their family? She had been mad about concerts and was a huge fan of pop songs. Last she had gone to such an event, she had worn a red skirt with a leather jacket. Since she was with her friends, she had had alcohol and screamed to her heart's content. That had been seven years ago, before Rohit happened. Though it felt like eons ago.

This outing might not be that exciting. She still had time to back out. But she wanted to go. What a mess!

Dismissing the lingering doubts about the wisdom of sneaking out like this, she focused on her dismal wardrobe. It was not as if she had many choices. Her collection now comprised of only salwar suits and sarees. And she needed to wrap something around her head and face, so it had to be a salwar suit. She picked up a black one, with red and white printed trimming. It would not do if someone recognized her. The event was in an open-air theatre. Zayd had told her they would sit on the far side of the large grounds and that there would be enough privacy as the high mast lights would be focused on the stage. But Ashima wanted to be safe now than sorry later. With the black dress, she could blend into the shadows easily.

At the last moment—just for a change—she put on the large, silver hoops on her ears.

She gave last minute instructions to Pooja, making sure she had Zayd's mobile number. Habitual unease seized her again as she picked up the spare set of keys and loitered in the room unnecessarily until Pooja pushed her out of the house.

Her heart in her mouth, Ashima moved towards the gate. She could make out Zayd's form, waiting for her in the shadows of the pine trees outside. He straightened as he spotted her. The gate creaked a bit, though not alarmingly as she locked it again from the inside. She gasped when Abdul appeared behind Zayd.

"Ignore him," Zayd whispered between clenched teeth at her questioning glance, and steered her by her elbow to the black Maruti 800 he had hired. Abdul followed them on a motorbike.

The concert was in full swing when they reached and everyone's attention was on the performers. The atmosphere was electrifying with the loud music and the general crowd swinging with the music. For Ashima, it was like she had entered a long forgotten world.

She couldn't take her eyes off the stage in the centre of the floor. The theatre was a recessed brick floor area with concrete steps circling the stage. The crowd was either standing beside the stage or sitting on the steps. Beyond the steps, the pine trees and the grounds were left untouched. Few people, who preferred to listen and enjoy the music, had chosen to sit on the benches under the trees.

Zayd hurried her through the gates across the uneven grounds. She stumbled and latched on to Zayd's arm as she reached out for support. Muttering an apology, he clasped her elbow and guided her towards a cluster of trees. As she found her foothold, he slid his hand along her arm to clasp her hand, and didn't let go even when she tried to free herself. They found a make-shift rickety wooden bench under a massive deodar tree and settled down. She chuckled inaudibly—all their rendezvous were associated with some bench or the other.

Casually, clutching her *dupatta* over her face, she ran a cursory gaze over the people in her periphery. Thankfully there was no one from their circle of acquaintances. Zayd was right about the privacy and the composition of the crowd—most of them were young college students or tourists. She took a deep breath and concentrated on the performance on the stage.

"Satisfied?"

Ashima didn't realize Zayd was watching her each and every reaction. She smiled and nodded pulling at her hand, but he didn't let go until he went to buy the drinks.

She couldn't concentrate on the artists or the songs as she watched him go. He wore blue jeans and the torn leather jacket, which he refused to get repaired. His excuse was that it would become a fashion after a while. Tall and confident, he stood apart from the crowd. People made way for him as he approached the temporary bar setup near the entrance gate.

She shifted her gaze to the stage when he started to return with the drinks, but all her senses were tuned to him. She pretended to be engrossed in the performance and looked at him only when he waved the Coke can in front of her face.

"Enjoying?" Zayd asked as he sat down next to her.

"Hmm…" She nodded, not risking a glance at him.

She was acutely aware of him and knew his eyes sought her out every now and then. His attention was more on her comfort and enjoyment than his own. He took a sip of his drink and took her hand again. She pretended not to notice. His thumb, caressing the back of her hand, evoked wicked sensations all over her body. They were playing something soft and slow. She didn't know the song.

"Do you need another?" He asked the moment she took the last sip of her drink.

"No, just relax and enjoy."

"I'm enjoying." He watched her.

Narrowing her eyes, she glanced at him. Their eyes met and the music faded a bit. He leaned in and placed a chaste kiss on a corner of her lips. His day's stubble grazed her chin, his scent enveloped her and her heart went on an overdrive. Nothing mattered but the sensations he invoked in her. She knew that he wanted her to make the next move. But how could she? Fighting the urge to turn her head for a full contact with his lips, she leaned back and broke the spell. He looked bereft and hurt.

"What is it that comes between us every time?" he whispered.

Struggling with her own conflicting emotions, she didn't have an answer for any of his questions. Why was she encouraging him by agreeing to his scheme of things when she had resolved to keep a distance? Was it only to defy someone? Had her loyalty to Rohit weakened in his absence? Was it possible to love two people at the same time?

She dropped her gaze to her hands on her lap. Everything had become so complicated and confusing.

"Or maybe, I should ask who."

"I want to go home," she said.

He grimaced and looked towards the stage. "Or maybe I know."

***

TWENTY-ONE

Rishabh was sleeping soundly when Ashima entered the room. She picked up Rohit's photo with the glass yet to be replaced. A shadow fell on the glossy surface. She whirled back, but could see no one. As she glanced at the photo again, Zayd's familiar shadow fell over Rohit's. Zayd's touch and presence were overwhelming her senses. She closed her eyes to picture Rohit in her mind, but she could only see Zayd's image.

Pulled in two directions, she hugged the photo frame to her chest, her heart beating wildly. Closing her eyes she tried to relive their last night together and failed to recall the pressure of Rohit's warm lips. Green-brown, smouldering eyes overshadowed her memories instead. Her eyes snapped opened.

Zayd resolutely refused to leave her subconsciousness. She remembered him threatening Kanyal. She pictured him lifting Rishabh on his shoulders and her little boy giggling, thrilled about his high perch in the air.

Ashima remembered the day when they had gone for the picnic. He had never told her how he had managed to get the wine and the glasses at such a short notice. She remembered his eyes that twinkled like emeralds and the way they softened every time he tucked her hair behind her ears and when he had admitted that he loved her.

Her heart skipped a beat again and she turned to the other side, unable to think and rationalize her own feelings for him. One part of her wanted to maintain her previous peaceful routine and another part craved for his attention, affection and… Her traitor heart thudded again. She closed her eyes to bar her mind from wandering in that direction, but the thoughts refused to leave her alone, tingling her nerves. A familiar ache touched the core of her being, making it difficult to breathe. Ashima sat up straight on the bed in panic.

She gasped as something pinched her finger. She looked at the broken frame on her lap. A shard had pierced her skin. Welcoming the pain, she pulled the shard out. Blood oozed out of the wound. The red, warm trickle began tracing the lines on her finger. Her heated body was once again under her control. She lifted the frame. One more shard came lose. Thinking it might hurt Rishabh, she placed the photo frame inside the drawer.

Sleep came, and along with it came myriad dreams warring with each other, screaming for attention, making her head pound in the morning.

***

Ashima was folding Rishabh's clothes, separating out the ones that needed ironing. She heard Amma's wheelchair creak and sensed Amma's glance at the side table.

"Where is Rohit's photograph?" Amma's voice boomed from the doorway.

The school shirt slipped from Ashima's fingers at the strict, harsh tone. Fighting her attraction with Zayd, the wave of guilt and disloyalty to Rohit weighed heavily on her mind.

Lifting the shirt from the floor, she forced herself to take a deep breath. "I have put it in the drawer."

"Why?"

"The glass broke." Ashima folded the shirt and put it on the pile for ironing.

"How?"

Ashima remained silent. What was there to say? How could she explain something which had gone beyond her own control, ethics and values? Anything she would say would not ring true and would seem like a justification for the broken photo frame. Moreover, she was not a child and was too tired to explain her actions, which would needlessly prolong the discussion.

"Who broke it? Even then… you should have thrown the glass away, what was the need of stowing away the photo in the drawer?" The tone and volume had gone up and Amma's voice trembled.

"Amma… please don't be upset." Ashima looked at her.

"Upset? What's there to be upset about?" She waved her hand with the rosary beads swinging around. "My only son is missing in the line of duty, for the country… and his supreme sacrifice is being forgotten. His things are being packed away, out of sight…" A lone tear slipped from her eyes.

Ashima sat on her haunches near Amma's feet. "Amma that's not true. Do you think I'll ever forget him? It's just so that Rishabh doesn't get hurt." She touched Amma's hand.

Amma jerked her hand away. "Don't sweeten me with empty words, Ashima. I know what's happening under my nose. Don't make me say it."

"Amma…" she whispered. "I'm a person… I feel…" Her eyes began welling, but she swallowed her tears.

"Yes… I know… I know you are living while my son is God knows in which hell. And now he no longer figures in your scheme of things." Amma's breath hitched.

Ashima sat down on the floor, her eyes flowing freely now. She made no move to wipe the tears. Rohit's smiling face floated in front of her eyes. *'I don't like you to be sad,'* his words, the ones he always told her, echoed in her ears.

"Don't think anything escapes my eyes," Amma continued her tirade, tears running down her face too. "When my son was giving his life to save this country, on the treacherous mountains, in the biting cold, that person was taking someone else's life, in a pub. And my son's wife—instead of living up to his sacrifice—is brushing aside MY son's martyrdom in a drawer and feeling for that criminal, that scum, who murdered someone over his girlfriend, under a drinking spell."

Ashima's tears fell as words tumbled out of Amma's mouth. She welcomed the ruthless, insensitive, erroneous onslaught. Ashima silently heard out the words that she had to bear and ignore, as venom came out of an ailing, grieving mother, whose every dream had been tied to her son, and who couldn't look forward to anything without her first born. Not even her grandchild.

By now Amma was sobbing and mumbling incoherently, wiping her tears with her saree, "Oh… Ricky!" Amma started repeating all of Rohit's childhood names that were fondly given by her.

"Amma, why are you crying?" Hearing the commotion, Pooja entered the room. "Look, you are upsetting Rishu."

"She has locked Rohit's photo in the drawer." Amma hiccupped.

"So?"

"So?" Amma's head snapped up. "Why are things changing? Why is my son being taken away from everywhere?"

"No… Amma." Ashima raised her hands.

"Keep quiet." Amma gave her a stern look.

"It's *bhabhi's* room. She should be free do whatever she wants to," Pooja said. "And I'm sick of grieving and crying in this house. *Bhaiya* would have never wanted this."

"Yes, of course. Alright, let her lock up everything." Amma pulled Rishabh by his hand and pushed him towards Ashima who fell on her lap. "Fine, go and lock him also in a drawer and forget about him. You will be free to live your life."

She turned the wheel chair and left the bedroom. Pooja followed her out trying to smoothen out the tension, talking to her and placating her.

Ashima hugged Rishabh to her chest and sat like a statue as the tears dried. After a while Rishabh squirmed. She looked down at his cherubic face and gave a feeble smile.

"Mom, will you lock me in dlawel an folgeth?"

She gave a shaky chuckle and pulled his nose. "No silly, how will you fit in the drawer? You are such a big boy now."

"Amma saidth?"

"She was angry."

"Why?"

"Because." She ruffled his hair and pushed him to stand. "Question-answer time over. Let's start on your homework, come on…"

It was easy to distract a small child, but not the adults. How did one explain to an emotional adult her own feelings? The loneliness, the need for human interaction, the rapport that one shared with a friend, and some affection, that was all that Ashima wanted. Her eyes fill up again. She shook her head and concentrated on the mundane routine of the day.

***

Zayd waited for her on the bench after dinner but she didn't come. He sat at the window trying to write the final scene, but deleted more than five-thousand words because nothing felt right. Finally he shut down the laptop and lay on the bed. He drifted in and out of a vague, dreamful, restless sleep.

The next day he saw the whole house come alive with frantic activity. Everyone was running around doing something or the other. The house was being washed and cleaned. Ramprasad had taken leave from his hotel and was seen wheeling the senior Mrs. Joshi. Her face was animated as she instructed everyone. Someone was arriving, may be an important relative or guest.

In the afternoon, a cavalcade of Sadhus wearing saffron clothes were welcomed inside the house and left three hours later.

In the evening someone knocked at his door. He found Mrs. Joshi at his door, with Ramprasad wheeling her chair. Had she come to know about their night at the concert? He was sure she was going to ask him something and he'll not be able to refuse.

"Ramprasad, wait outside."

"*Ji.*"

"I have come to thank you for what you did for my daughter. Please sit."

Zayd opened his mouth, but she beat him to it.

"Let me finish." She raised her hands. "I'm really grateful. You are a good man Mr. Rizvi, no doubt. You don't have any malice in your heart…" She sighed and continued. "I used to have, but now my heart is clear too. And I have a request."

His blood stopped circulating in a cold premonition of what was about to come.

"I request you to leave this town. You want to live at a hill station, there are plenty in this country. You can take your pick, but please go somewhere else." She folded her hands. "Please, I beg of you. This is a request from a tired and heartbroken, old woman."

He stood up. "Please ma'am, you don't need to do this."

"I need to… I have to. My family will fall apart. No one will marry my daughter. As soon as you can make some arrangements, please go. This is a request from a mother. God bless you." She called Ramprasad in, and he wheeled her away.

***

TWENTY-TWO

Ashima glanced at Zayd as he sat near her the next night in the back garden. She wanted to stay away but couldn't. She had missed two nights in a row. His company beckoned her like waves to the seashore. She was definitely addicted to him.

Her eyebrows went up when she spotted that he was hiding something under his jacket, but he didn't show it. She tried to read his face, but it was devoid of any emotion.

"Who was the man who came today?" he asked.

"*Panditji…* he's Amma's *guru.* They have an *ashram* in Rishikesh. Sometimes Amma calls them to honor them. He is the one who has predicted that Rohit has a long life. This current period is tough on him, on all of us, and then it will be fine." She sighed.

"She asked me to go," he said, matter-of-factly.

"She did?" Ashima frowned, trying to ignore the panicked beating of her heart. "And…?"

"I'm considering it. The book is almost finished." His tone was dry and emotionless.

The book? Oh yes! He had come here to write a story with Kasauli as the setting. A fist squeezed her heart. "I'll give your balance back, naturally."

"The balance…?" He frowned, then chuckled, shaking his head. "Oh, of course. Naturally."

"What?" If he wasn't bothered about leaving why should she show her interest in anything related to him. It was imperative to keep things formal.

"Here have this." He took out a wine bottle—a white one this time—from under his jacket and opened it. "Might as well finish this if I have to go." He held her fist, gently straightened her fingers and handed the bottle. "It'll help you relax."

She raised one eyebrow, never realizing that she was so tense, and took a sip straight from the bottle. The fiery liquid ran down her throat, warming her insides.

"I'd bought two the other day. That one was for you, this one's for me."

Ashima took another sip and exhaled. He would go soon. It was inevitable. He was just a tourist, a passer-by. It would be for the best, for both of them. Her heart protested silently. As usual, she smothered the feeling exerting her willpower over it. But this time the ache refused to subside. Her heart twisted vehemently, pressing against her lungs. She looked at the sky trying to bear and ignore.

It was a lovely starry night, the sky oblivious to the storm raging inside her.

She glanced at him as he took the bottle from her. An electrifying pulse ran though her every time his hand touched hers. Without looking at him, unobtrusively, she put some distance between them.

He never gave any indication that he was as disappointed as she was. Wasn't he even a wee bit affected about his going? He was the one who was always declaring his love, and now he just sat there calmly sipping wine and relishing the nature's silence around them.

Ashima gasped and bent forward as a sparkling cracker burst down below in the valley in one of the villages. "They are celebrating something, I guess."

"Is there a festival today?"

"No, can't think of any. Must be a wedding. Yes, that could be the reason. Aah… look at that… another one!" She caught hold of his hand. "Wow… look. Isn't it wonderful?" She glanced at him, then froze as she realized he was watching her instead of the scene below. "What—"

He placed his trembling hand over hers when she was about to release his wrist, and tightened the hold. "You look infinitely beautiful when you are animated and excited. I want this cheer and joy permanently etched on your face, never to fade."

"Zayd?" Dazed she didn't resist when he leaned in and placed his lips on her cheek. In that moment, she realized that he was as affected as she was with the prospect of leaving.

"I don't want to go. I want to remain with you forever." The last bit was whispered with a longing that touched her heart like nothing had before.

The pressure of his lips and his feather light breath against her skin melted all her resistance. She turned her head and received a fluttering kiss. She wanted to taste every inch of him. He let out a silent moan. Her breath now mingled with his. Her free hand moved towards his chest. He inhaled deeply when her hand caressed his skin above the opening of his shirt. It was encouraging to know that he was as breathless as her.

"What magic are you weaving on me, Zayd?" she whispered against his lips. "I don't have the will to resist anymore… though resist I must." Saying so she nipped at his lower lip, then pushed him away.

He let her go.

Plonk.

A fat drop of water fell on her hand.

Plonk.

Another one fell on his chest, where her hand had touched him a moment ago.

She chuckled, ignoring the sizzling at the core of her being. "Oh my, it's raining!" She stretched her hand and a couple more dropped on her outstretched palm, after which there was no stopping. It fell on them like a mischievous friend drenching them as if playing Holi.

Laughing silently, they scampered inside the back corridor and ended up in his room, which was the only place where they were safe from the slanting downpour. The electricity was cut off the next second, plunging them into a passionate, breathless darkness. She could hear her heart beating over the pitter-patter of the rain-drops.

"It always rains like this, without a warning. One moment you will be dry and the other you will drenched as if standing under a waterfall. More so in August." She knew she was blabbering, even as she wringed her wet *dupatta* to drip out the extra water. "I should be going. Do you have a torch? Or maybe—"

She gasped as Zayd took a step towards her pushing her inside the room and closed the door. He gently pried the *dupatta* from her hand and threw it on the chair.

"Zayd…"

He pulled her close to him and pushed back her wet lock as if angry with it for clinging to her without his permission. All rational thoughts went out of her mind when he showered small kisses along the line of her shoulder to the nape of her neck. Her body seemed to have developed a mind of its own. Despite all the warning bells ringing in her brain, her hands snaked up to his shoulders and wound themselves around his neck. The cautioning sounds faded away as she leaned her head on his chin.

"Oh Zayd… we shouldn't." He silenced her by taking her mouth in his own and thrusting his tongue inside.

The whiff of the wine assailed her senses and intoxicated her, pushing every logical thought to oblivion. It was just the two of them with rain pelting on the roof and the faint musky scent of the wet earth enveloping them.

It felt like a dream as she ran her hands all over his shoulders, neck and finally tangled into his thick hair, even as she pressed herself along his hard planes. A heart was beating fast, whose she didn't know. He stroked her back, waist and hips, imprinting her with his touch.

"Aashi… I love you so… you have no idea."

She sighed against his lips, completely under the spell of that monsoon night and the waves of desires his warm hands were invoking. His embrace felt so real… so right…

Her need for someone real and warm to fill the vacuum in her life penetrated the defensive walls she had built around her.

Nuzzling her neck and raining kisses all over, Zayd picked her up and moved towards the bed. Her hands moved of their own volition and tugged at his shirt when he lay her on the bed. Two buttons popped out as he yanked the shirt above his head impatiently and threw it on the floor.

"You are beautiful." Zayd stood staring at her. Their eyes were now accustomed to the faint moonlight filtering through the lace-curtained windows.

Didn't he realize that he himself was perfect in all respects? On their own accord, her hands went to his chest, caressing the hard planes. His gaze, in turn, slowly, possessively moved downwards from her face, heating her entire body.

She knew the wet pink *kurta* clung to her breasts and that he could make out the outline of her bra, but nothing mattered under his smoldering gaze. Her breath rose and fell, racing in tandem to his pulse. The wind howled and rain fell drowning the sound of blood pounding in her ears.

He sat down and leaned over her, brushing the curls off her cheek and neck. His lips followed the path from her shoulder to her neck, finally taking over her lips. His thumb caressed her cheek.

"This has been tantalizing me since the day I saw you hunting that ghost," he said kissing the mole on her cheek. Lightening crackled once, lighting the room for a second.

In that moment he, and only he, existed, murmuring sweet nothings in her ears, creating havoc with his hands and lips, shrouding her with his masculine scent, taking over all her senses. She gasped as he covered her with himself. Her arms went around his neck, pulling him to her.

Slowly, tenderly he filled all the empty voids in her world, bringing her the fulfillment she had craved for so many years.

***

It was after a long time that Ashima stirred in his arms and reached for her clothes. He sensed her withdrawal, and knew the magical hours were over. But he didn't want it to end, and so he tightened his hold on her waist and planted a kiss on her shoulder.

Wordlessly, she pried his hand off and dressed in the dark. Her fair skin glistened against the moonlight, igniting another wave of desire in him. But he knew he had to give her time to reconcile with the new reality— their reality.

Zayd sighed and ran his fingers through his hair, missing her warmth. Her faint fragrance lingered on the pillow, and he buried his face in it. Closing his eyes, he relived the last two hours—the incomparable, divine hours of his life.

She hadn't said that she loved him whenever he had confessed. In his experience, girls generally wanted love, but not Ashima. Her heart belonged to Rohit. He, Zayd, had to be satisfied with a few stolen hours.

***

TWENTY-THREE

Refusing his offer to accompany her to the front door, Ashima walked back like an automaton. Her heart had frozen, chilling her from the inside. She had gone on the path of sin, betraying her husband for a moment of ecstasy.

Entering her room, her gaze fell on Rishabh sleeping soundly. His open mouth as he slept reminded her of Rohit, more painfully. She wanted to caress his cheek, as she always did, but couldn't. If she touched him would Rohit get to know about her indiscretion?

After what felt like an eon, Ashima moved towards the bathroom. Pouring a full bucket of cold water on her head, she dropped down to the wet floor. The bucket fell from her hand and rolled towards the tap, the noise muffled by the plastic mat she had installed for Rishabh's safety. Sitting there blankly, she lost track of the time.

A sound from the bedroom alerted her. A mother's instinct forced her to push back her miseries and focus her attention on the present. She peeped from the bathroom and saw Rishabh thrashing the blanket with his legs, trying to uncover himself. Then he turned to the other side and did not stir. She quickly changed into her night gown and toweled her hair. Suppressing a sneeze, she stretched on the bed and pulled the blanket over Rishabh and herself. Bodily needs eventually took over and she fell into a restless sleep, shielded from the fog of guilt for a few hours.

***

Zayd paced the corridor in front of his room. It had been two days since their night together. He desperately wanted to speak to her. From the tit bits he had extracted from Shankar, he knew that Ashima was running a high fever. He daren't ask anyone else, and Rishabh was too young to convey the right status. The one thing he was going to gift her was a cell phone. He mentally added it to the list of things he wanted Akshat to bring whenever he came from Delhi. It would be like a parting gift, an excuse to remain in touch.

Pooja and Radha were holding fort in the kitchen, unwilling to talk beyond the monosyllabic responses to his veiled concern and questions.

'Yes, she has fever.' They told him.

'No, it's nothing.' He was informed when he asked if it was anything serious. *'Doctor says it is the seasonal cold and viral.'*

It was not as if she had been exposed for very long to the rain the other day. They had run inside the moment it had begun to drizzle and had forgotten to even switch on the fan. Everything was forgotten that night. Nothing existed except the fact that she had reciprocated his feelings. He wanted to take her in his arms again. Now that the last barrier had been crossed, he wanted her beside him all the time. He wanted to care for her. He was sure no one would be able to take care of her the way he could.

The third evening, he heard her voice in the kitchen when he was having dinner. The urge to check on her made him lose his appetite. His throat went dry, and he couldn't even swallow the bite he had in his mouth. Somehow he finished the meal and went to sit on the stone bench facing the valley, waiting for her. But she didn't come. Maybe the doctor had asked her to rest. He retired to his room by midnight, but tossed and turned the whole night.

***

Ashima had been watching Zayd sitting under the gazebo daily. From time to time, he glanced towards the front doors or whenever anyone opened them. She knew he was waiting for her. When he didn't spot her, he would go back to his laptop and stare at the screen. He must be eager to meet her again. It was natural. But she didn't have the courage to face him. One part, the emotional one, craved for him and the other, the practical one, held her back.

Guilt nibbled at her guts. Anger at losing her senses, her values, her morals, grew with each passing day. She had fallen low in her own esteem with that one night of lust. No, no it wasn't lust, Zayd had said he loved her. Yes, he loved her, she could make that out from the way he treated her, like she was someone precious, something fragile. It was evident in the little things he did for her.

But what about her? Did she reciprocate his love? If it was a night of love then what about her love for Rohit? And if it wasn't, then did pure carnal desires drove her?

She felt worthless and disgusted with herself, shamed at her lack of control. How could she behave so wantonly in Zayd's arms? What would he think now? Would he think she was reciprocating his love—the love which

242

he had declared throughout that night? What would he think if she refused to talk to him? That she believed in one night stands. That it was just an itch she wanted to scratch. That she was not in love with him. Or was she?

She dropped the curtain and closed her eyes.

Love. She let out a silent groan. What was love? Didn't she promise to love Rohit eternally? Didn't she take the vow six years back about not noticing any man other than him? Was it the first vow or the second one? She didn't remember. But she distinctly remembered the fire in the *havankund*, the red and orange glow of the warm flame. They sat side by side, promising each other many things. In these six years, he had kept his promises but she had broken hers. A sob clogged her throat.

***

Ashima gasped as Zayd caught her arm and pulled her into his room. Her heart thudded as her body came in contact with his hard planes. She had thought he was out. She had seen him going out of the gate. How did he come back without her knowledge? She had still not figured out how to tell him that that night didn't mean anything to her.

The contact of his lips over hers made her forget everything once again. She reciprocated, matching his fervor. Her hands went to his chest and his went to her waist. But when he caressed her, brushing his thumb over the bare skin, she came back to reality and stopped him. She pushed his hand away and closed her mouth not giving him access.

He lifted his head. "If I didn't know better I would have thought you are avoiding me." He caressed her face. "How are you Aashi? I was so worried about you." He lowered his mouth again.

She turned her head to one side and he ended up kissing her cheek. "Leave me, Zayd. Please."

"Come on sweetheart, no one would see us here. I was dying to talk to you after that night."

"That night is over… done with. It is broad daylight. Another day." She evaded his lips and pushed him back, but was not able budge him by even an inch.

"When you're around I can't think of anything, least of all the time. I forget myself when I see you, even when your eyes flash at me in anger and your hair falls like a curtain hiding you from me." Pulling her closer, he tried to kiss her again.

"Please Zayd. Behave yourself." Frowning, she pushed at his chest with all her strength, frantically thinking of how she could keep him at a distance.

Somehow her distant, curt attitude penetrated through the haze of romance. He loosened his hold but still held her in the circle of his arms.

"You look thin. Are you absolutely fine?" He touched her forehead with the back of his hand. "No fever or weakness?"

"Zayd, stop this and let me go. I request you to forget everything and not read too much into what happened between us."

"Not read too much…?" He frowned searching her face. "You mean our relationship?"

"There is no relationship and there is no 'our'."

"There isn't?" He raised one eyebrow.

"No. You are assuming too much from a one night stand."

"One night stand?" He left her as suddenly as he had grabbed her, his face ashen.

"Yes, it was just that, a one night stand." Her heart twisted as she noticed a shadow of doubt and pain flashing in his eyes. But it had to be done, or he wouldn't let go. There was no future for him with her.

He chuckled. "Next you would say that you have slept with all the single men who stayed in the guest house."

Unknowingly he gave her an opening. "Maybe, how do you know?" She lifted her chin.

He looked stricken for a moment, then smiled. "You are doing this on purpose, aren't you? You are trying to drive me away."

"You are going in any case… so… you know." She shrugged.

He narrowed his eyes and noticed the *mangalsutra* around her neck. He looped his fore-finger around it and pulled. "You wear this only when you want to keep me at a distance. Every time your heart beats for me, you try to bring his memories between us."

"You are disillusioned. He is not a memory, he is real," she hissed. How dare he talk like that? He reminded her of her mother.

He sighed and caressed her mole. "There's nothing wrong in feeling again, sweetheart. Your whole life is in front of you. And it's a long, lonely road. You can't just live under the cover of some unrealistic hope." He tried to hold her arms but she pushed his hands away.

"Don't go there, Zayd."

"You will have to accept the reality that he—"

"—is not dead, he is missing in action."

"Ashima, you need to reconcile with the reality. There is no news. Do you think he could have survived that altitude when his plane came down?"

"You want him dead for your own selfish reasons."

"What nonsense!" His jaw tightened. "How could you have such a low opinion about me?"

"I never promised anything to you. I craved for some attention and it went beyond control, that's all. It was just one night, and it meant nothing to me. So forget about it and let me pass."

"You are such a big liar."

"Zayd, don't make me say things that both of us may regret. I am already regretting a lot of things."

"Oh really! Do let me know what you are regretting." Stepping back, he closed the door of his room and leaned against it, crossing his arms in front of him. "Let's thrash this out and bury it once and for all."

"Don't give me that wide-eyed innocent look that you are in love with me and can't think rationally around me, when you remembered to be practical while I had totally lost it."

He frowned. "What are you talking about?"

"Who was ready with a condom that night? As if… as if you had been prepared for any eventuality."

He spread his hands in the air. "Oh, come on. I was trying to protect you."

"You had come all along thinking you'll be able to seduce me?" Then something else occurred to her that drove a green dagger deep into her. "Or was it that you were ready to sleep with anyone who was willing? And I happened to be the first fool to fall for your charm?"

"What the heck? It was nothing like that… and you know it. How can you doubt my feelings?"

"Feelings? Hah… nothing but an empty word for guys of your generation. Married women are the safest bet. Aren't they?" She clasped her hands and dug her nails in her palm.

"Guys of my generation… safe bet…" He caught hold of her arm and jerked her towards himself. She braced her hand on his chest and looked up in his angry eyes. "Don't make me angry, Aashi. If I am being gentle with you, it doesn't mean I am on the wrong." The brown specs in his eyes also changed color from honey brown to dark chocolate. This was the first time she had seen them actually changing. It was fascinating to see the riot of colors in his eyes. But she blinked and exhaled, forcing herself to remain in the present.

"Why did I never think of that? I was so much under your spell that I forgot about my morals, my husband. And you were so much in control that you were able to think about protection." She gave a forceful tug to free her arm.

He finally obliged and left her. "Fine, if that's what you want to hear. Then fine. Yes. After four years in prison, getting laid was the first thing on my mind. I'm not ashamed to admit it and was responsible enough to think about protecting me and my partner. If that's a crime, go sue me."

An invisible stone hurled itself to her guts to hear him refer to that night in such a crude way. She glared at him. She was so confused but self-preservation prevailed. "And that was what it was. You wanted something and you got it. The same is the case with me. Let's keep it like that. Let's not make it something grand, which it was not."

His eyes shuttered, masking the pain her words were inflicting on him. It was time to be brutal. Though mostly she held herself responsible for the situation going out of hand, she had to rebuff him in the worst possible way.

"One more thing. Do you think I would have associated with you, a Muslim? I could never envisage a future for my son associating with a person of your religion."

Looking at his feet, he stood there slumped against the wall and eyes on the floor, as she went past him.

***

It had been two days since that nonsensical, fiery discussion. It had hurt. A lot. But after Zayd had thought and dissected the entire conversation, one thing was crystal clear. She had tried too hard to convince him, or maybe herself, about the futility of their relationship. It didn't ring true. Time was running out.

Senior Mrs. Joshi had asked again about his date of leaving the guest house. He asked her for a week's time.

He tried a number of times to talk to Ashima, but she didn't give him any chance alone. She had stopped coming towards the guest rooms and the rear area of the house altogether. Trying for another tactic, he decided not to step out of his room, giving her the silent treatment she had been handing out to him. Shankar was his only contact with the outside world. But still, she didn't speak to him.

Three days later he saw her going to the church and followed her. She was sitting outside in the garden and didn't react when he sat beside her.

"I had one last question. Please answer it truthfully." He began.

She sighed.

"If you like a person who is from your community, will you marry him?"

"I'm already married." The answer came immediately, almost on autopilot.

He exhaled and nodded. "I wanted to tell you a story."

She closed her eyes. "Zayd, get lost."

"There was this woman who loved her husband to distraction. The husband professed to love her, but had the hots for the woman's sister. One day, the wife got to know and both of them had a major fight. The husband stopped coming to her, stopped interacting with her. The woman pined for her husband, his love, his attention. A year later, she was diagnosed with cancer and died within a year. The husband and the sister married the next month."

"*Panditji* might be right, you know. I dreamt about Rohit yesterday, and the morning ones usually come true. I have decided I'll confess, and he will forgive me."

He exhaled. "She was my mother. I've seen her pine for my father's affection and attention. She hoped if she lived her life according to him, he would love her back. This hopeless hope eats you up from inside, this yearning. In your case at least he loved you."

"I'm sorry for your mother."

"Aashi—"

"Stop tormenting me, Zayd. If you really love me as you say you do, go away and leave me alone… just go away," she whispered, covering her face with both her hands. After a minute, she left.

He sat there worrying about her future. What was at the end of this wait? Another wait. Another cycle of make believe hope. Did anyone know?

He had to do something about it.

What if Rohit was alive? Zayd would lose everything. He would cease to exist for her. But then he would have the satisfaction that he gave her the happiness no one had been able to give.

But if Rohit was not… he sighed rubbing his face with his hand. Would she accept him? Or… hate him for eternity for being the bearer of the bad news? He could get hurt, but right now her indifference hurt too.

Either ways, he wouldn't rest until it ended—this endless wait. His own feelings no longer mattered. Nothing mattered except getting her out from her dream zone—where there was only some hoping, some waiting, and some more hoping—to reality.

Baba had once said, 'For attaining catharsis, one had to go through the pain.'

***

TWENTY-FOUR

Zayd took with him the spirit of the home. The whole house had begun to look haunted. Shankar sulked and brooded. Rishabh was confused why his best friend had left. Ashima couldn't convince him he was only a guest like any other and had moved on. Pooja, mercifully, didn't ask any questions. The only person who was happier and chirpier was Amma. She wheeled herself all around instructing Radha and the maid to scrub every inch of the floor of his room. The curtains, bedcovers and towels were taken off and washed in Dettol.

The people of the town, the alleged well-wishers, had stopped sending referrals to the guest house. There was an occasional demand for food for a party, but otherwise there was no business. For the first time after inaugurating the guest house, it was devoid of a guest.

But Ashima was least bothered. She felt she had lost something precious a second time. When she had first heard about Rohit missing in action, it felt as if destiny had snatched away her security blanket. But with Zayd going, it seemed like she herself had sawed away a part of her soul. Was it even possible to love two people with the same intensity? The only consolation was that he would find someone and would move on. He would not pay the price of her weakness and waste his life.

She reveled in the pain and desolation like a masochist, losing interest in everything. Sitting all day either in the living room or her room, she stopped going out of the house at all. Every corner of the house, Raghu's dhaba, the market, the treks, as well as the church reminded her of him. Amma ignored her, glaring at her from time to time. For once, she ignored Amma too.

But when she saw Pooja crying over Rohit's photo, she realized how her state of mind was affecting Pooja and Rishabh. She pulled herself together and forced herself to take interest in the daily chores. After a couple of days, their routine began to take some semblance of normality. She even managed to fake a smile when required in front of the family. The nights were the most difficult though. Dry eyed, she would lay awake in bed and would catch a wink or two only in the wee hours of the morning when her body and mind succumbed to biological needs.

Three weeks later the daily routine coming on track was jostled with worries again.

Ashima was trying to read a magazine when a motorcycle honked at the gate. She peeked through the lace curtains and found Shankar opening the gate for Abdul. He drove on high speed, quickly parked the vehicle and barged inside the living room.

"Where is Zayd *bhai*?"

"Zayd? He left days ago."

"Where to?"

"I don't know. Why what happened?" Ashima's heart began to pound.

Abdul continued to stare outside the window.

"What happened?"

"He is missing."

"Missing?" She repeated like a parrot. Had Kanyal done something?

"He hasn't reported to any police station for the past two weeks and they are not able to find him at his regular jaunts or with his *naanijaan*." Frowning, Abdul darted his glance here and there, then began pacing the room. "*Saheb* will be here anytime. I was responsible for him and I have lost him. I have failed him a second time."

Naanijaan? *Saheb*? Lost him? He wasn't making sense. "Who is *Saheb*? And how could you be responsible?"

"*Saheb*, Zayd *bhai's* father, had asked me to follow him everywhere, then that *manhoos* incident at the pub happened and now he is not to be found anywhere. How will I show my face to him?" He stopped and looked at her with pleading eyes. "Please Mrs. Joshi, I need to know everything. Did he give any hint about where was he going?"

"No, we didn't speak for a few days before he left. He spoke to Shankar. Wait let me call Shankar. What about his cellphone?"

"He has left it in Delhi."

Shankar was unable to throw any light on Zayd's whereabouts.

Abdul left, leaving a distressed Ashima in his wake. According to Abdul, he had last met Akshat and had taken a few lakh rupees as loan. Why did he need such a large sum? Where could he go? A familiar sensation of fear churned inside her.

***

Two days later a bevy of white Ambassador cars entered the driveway and a number of people in grey safari suits with black sunglasses moved in all directions, encircling the car at the centre. And it was Abdul who opened the rear door.

Ashima stood at the door fearing the worst, as a feeling of déjà vu enveloped her. She had faced something similar four years earlier. Today the difference was that the men and the cars were not from the Air Force and were more in number. She braced herself for the worst as she waited for the visitor to get out from the car.

She was surprised to see a distinguished man in his fifties walking towards her. For a moment, he looked uncannily familiar. Realization dawned slowly and she couldn't believe that Zayd had yet again not told her the complete truth about himself—the truth that his father was a prominent and respected political figure. And she had no doubt he was Abdul's '*Saheb*' and Zayd's father. The resemblance could not be denied. But he didn't look too distressed, so that was a consolation.

With Abdul and the guards by his side, Ashima understood the extent of the clout Zayd always mentioned, and why Kanyal had ceased to bother Zayd, and by extension, her so easily.

Mr. Rizvi's regal bearing gave him a larger than life persona. Behind him, the guards converged and moved in a synchronized movement. She went forward like an automaton bound by the polite norms of the society to receive a guest with a polite smile.

"Mrs. Joshi." He folded his hands in a namaste and offered her a salaam, greeting her in both their cultures.

She reciprocated the gesture, not surprised that he knew her.

"I am Zayd's father, Zaqir Abbas Rizvi. I believe he stayed in your guest house."

"Yes." Her voice hoarse, the affirmation came out as a whisper.

"May we sit? Somewhere a little private."

"Yes, of course." She then remembered her manners and ushered him to the living room. Two of the guards checked the room and left to wait outside. Ashima instructed Radha to bring some refreshments.

"You have a lovely house."

"Thank you."

"Abdul says Zayd loved living here." Mr. Rizvi chose the single-seater sofa.

"Yes, I believe so." Ashima settled on the opposite one.

"So what happened? Why did he leave so abruptly?" He crossed his legs and directed his attention to her. His eyes were brown, unlike Zayd's.

"He must have finished his book. He said he had come here to write."

"This is not what Abdul told me."

She felt a tingle on her nape. "Well… as far as I know he didn't leave abruptly. The evening before he left, he told my staff, Shankar, that he wanted to leave and to keep his bill ready in the morning."

"Did you speak to him that day?"

"No."

"When was the last time you spoke to him?"

She frowned. "Is this an interrogation?"

He sighed. "No, Mrs. Joshi it's not. I am just worried. He was last seen in Delhi. He has disappeared without a trace from there. You have no idea about my dilemma. I can't raise a red alert to find him and I can't stop an inquiry. My whole political career is on the line here."

Her eyes widened. "Your only son is missing and you are worried about your career?" Suddenly she was angry with him.

Mr. Rizvi was stunned for a moment, then shook his head. "You have no idea."

"Why do you think he disappeared? Aren't you worried? What if something has happened to him? What if he has been abducted?"

Throwing his head back, he laughed earnestly. "Do you think someone can kidnap Zayd?" he asked.

"The question is why would he just disappear? It seems you think that he has done it on purpose!"

He narrowed his eyes, so much like Zayd, and looked at her. "You don't seem to hold a good opinion about me."

She looked at her hands and tried to check her emotions.

"What has he told you about me? That I am an ogre? Out there to get him?"

"No, he is very reluctant to talk about himself or his family."

"Is it?"

"I just know that you are pretty influential, and if he does anything worthwhile people think you were instrumental in his achievements, so much so that he has dropped the family name from his author profile."

"He told you all that and still you don't know where he could be."

"No, I don't. But clearly after leaving this town, he had met Akshat."

"Abdul must have told you… hmm… And do you also know Zayd met your mother before he disappeared?"

Her heart dived into her stomach and the blood slowly drained out of her head, leaving her cold. Why did Zayd meet her mother? How did he get her address? How could she not tell her about his visit?

"So, you didn't know." Mr. Rizvi nodded, just looking at her. "I am surprised why your mother never told you. Are you close?"

"Of course my mother and I are close, why—"

"No. I meant, how close are Zayd and you?"

She tightened her lips then spoke. "We were friends."

"Were?"

She knew she was going to be no match to Rizvi's intelligence if she continued to remain frazzled. It would be wise to remain calm and handle the conversation. She took a couple of deep breaths and answered.

"We had some falling out."

"So he left."

"Maybe. Yes, I think."

"Thank you Mrs. Joshi. If you don't mind, can you rent out your rooms to me and my officers for a few hours?"

She nodded.

He stood up. "And yes…, if you can remember any person, any conversation, information he had mentioned in passing—no matter how vague—please let me know."

"Yes, sure."

***

The first thing Ashima did was call up her mother. But her mother couldn't tell her anything. Just that Zayd was polite, cultured and well behaved. And it was nothing but a routine visit.

In the afternoon, when she was sitting with Rishabh with his homework, she remembered Zayd mentioning someone called Baba. She stepped out in the corridor and Mr. Rizvi sitting outdoors, dictating a letter to his secretary. She told him about the person in the prison. Rizvi nodded deep in thought, then dialled a number and gave the information to someone.

"I think he respected him a lot and listened to him as he would to one of his elders."

"Did he now?"

"I think so, because he sounded quite fond of him."

Mr. Rizvi gazed up at the horizon. "I don't know why, but for the first time in my life I am jealous." He chuckled. "Jealous of a criminal. What an irony!" He shook his head. "But, why am I bothering you with all this? Thank you for being such a good friend to my son." He searched his pockets and handed her a visiting card. "If you remember anything else, please call me on this number."

"Mr. Rizvi, how much do you love Zayd? Not as your successor but as your son."

"Mrs. Joshi?"

"Please call me Ashima, and I request you to hear me out with an open mind. Please. When was the last time you had treated him as your son, as your child?"

He looked at a loss for words.

"Have you ever focused on his talents, his abilities? Kids crave their parents' attention and approval for their accomplishments. Only then do they respond positively."

Rotating a pen in his hand, he sat contemplating what she had said.

She was impressed by his control with her and the liberty she had taken.

"You are a highly intelligent lady, Ashima, I'll bear in mind what you have told me. So... now I have something for you to figure out. Can you deduce something out of this? Zayd borrows money from Akshat and then approaches your mother for information about Flight Lieutenant Joshi." He noticed the flicker of her eyelashes. "Yes, casually. It was all routine, even your mother didn't think it was anything out of the ordinary. What do you make out of this? Why would he ask about the Kargil war, the details of your husband's plane crash and the search missions? And another factor to keep in mind is his—if you don't mind—affection for you."

She dropped her gaze to her feet. The color on her face must have been evident, because he added, "Please don't blame yourself. He is like that… very emotional… and impulsive. But you think about it objectively when I say he has not been kidnapped or abducted. I have my conclusions, but I want to hear yours."

Realization slowly dawned as she assimilated the information. The conclusion was far-fetched, but made sense if one kept Zayd at the centre. "Was he… was he thinking of running his own search mission?"

Rizvi smiled. "Yes, a search mission. But not the one that Mr. Ved was conducting. I am afraid the idiot has gone to the other side, to search for your husband."

"Other side? You mean…Pakistan?" Her eyes widened. "Pakistan! How is that possible? For that he would need a visa. They don't allow a visa for someone like him. He told me."

"Yes… and I'm afraid he might have gone there illegally."

***

TWENTY-FIVE

Zayd traced the pattern of the Indian Air Force badge and thought about Flight Lieutenant Rohit Joshi. For the first time he thought of him as a person, a soldier for their country, and the extent of his sacrifice. For the first time, he understood Rohit's mother and Ashima's plight, and their attachment and loyalty to him. Zayd felt it too.

For the first time, he was not envious of Rohit. How lonely it must have been? Dying amongst a bunch of strangers in a strange land, all alone and so cold.

"Parachute didn't open properly. He died the moment he crashed on the ground." The old man added, reminiscing about the war. "So many men dying… young men… *Allah khair kare*." The man raised his eyes and hands towards the sky. "Two days, no one came. The body had begun to rot, we had to burn it."

Zayd looked at the man, whose eyes, clouded with cataract, were focused on something beyond the field. A boy stood holding a leash of emaciated goats that grazed on the sparse brown paddy. This was the seventh village he had visited along the LOC in the Kargil area on the Pakistan side.

The devastation by the heavy artillery was evident even after four years. Random bullet holes adorned the walls of the houses. While they had faced bullets for the past many decades, the Kargil war had been particularly damaging. The villagers had dug bunkers to hide during the war.

With no source of income and the agricultural land rendered useless, the young had migrated to cities and towns. The future looked as bleak on this side of the line as it did on the other side.

"*Janaab*, we should leave now. The sun will go down soon." Zayd's driver-cum-guide repeated the request a second time. They had to reach the border soon.

Zayd nodded and took another photograph of the badge, maintaining his story of shooting stills for a magazine as a photographer-cum-journalist.

The journey back was also fraught with danger. The only identification he carried was a fake, faded Pakistani driving license provided by his handler on this side of the border, arranged by Baba's contacts.

Zayd sat in the run-down vehicle and prayed that crossing the border back would be as uneventful as the time he had crossed it two days back.

For once, Allah didn't disappoint him.

He was able to relax only when he sat in the bus from a village in India to Jammu, finally on the last leg of his trip. Battling the overpowering fatigue of continuously being on guard and traveling for so many days, he rested his head on the head rest of the seat and allowed his thoughts to go towards the person whose life he was going to rip apart.

He hated to be the bearer of such a devastating news. It was suicidal, but necessary. He knew the risk he was taking, knew that she would hate him for doing this to her. She might even banish him from her life. How did it matter? He was never a part of her life. The thought cut his heart in two. He swallowed the bile rising in his throat and closed his eyes.

But he wanted closure for her and wanted her to move on in life. He did not want her to be stuck in never-ending dilemma, pulled by society, morals, ethics, and restrictions. He did not want her to get old without anything to look forward to, without any human contact, living in a black hole, just waiting for destiny to intervene.

Like his mother, who first waited for his father, and then for death. Like himself, when he had waited for the court's verdict, and later for the authorities to approve his parole. In his case there was an end date in sight, he knew sometime or the other he would be free. But in her case, no one was batting for Rohit or her.

In the bigger scheme of things, he never mattered.

***

Ashima wiped the frame clean and admired Rohit's smile. The glass had been replaced and the frame restored to its position by her bedside. Now that she had made a decision to tell him about her indiscretion, she was at peace. She hoped he would understand and forgive her, but if not, she would accept the consequences.

The house bell rang loud and clear, pulling her out of her reverie. Someone opened the door, and Shankar spoke in his halting, muffled voice and ushered the visitors in the drawing room. As she placed the photo frame on her side table, a thump and the sound of a piece of furniture crashing echoed in the silent house.

She ran to the drawing room to see Amma slumped in her wheelchair, with Wing Commander Tyagi rubbing her hand and arm. The stool beside the chair was tilted at an awkward angle with one leg broken. Shankar stood on the other side wringing her hands trying unsuccessfully to hide the flow of tears from his eyes.

"What happened?" She rushed to Amma's side and sat on her haunches. Amma was drenched in sweat, the color drained from her face. "Amma, are you all right? Just breathe slowly… in—"

"Aashi… oh Aashi… have faith in God," Amma gasped, holding her head in her hands.

"God? What are you saying, Amma?" Her hands gripped the handle of the chair. Rohit! Her innards sank. The presence of Wing Commander Tyagi registered along with the premonition of the eternal black clouds gathering in front of her eyes.

It was then that she saw her parents sitting on the sofa opposite to Tyagi. Raw pain and bottomless empathy in their shimmering eyes confirmed everything that was unsaid. Her father stepped forward as she swayed on her feet, but stopped when a weeping Shankar caught hold of her hand and pushed her on the sofa.

"I'm really sorry Mrs. Joshi, but I have received this piece of information from the Pakistan embassy. They have handed enough evidence—"

Pakistan embassy? Evidence? How come the embassy was associated with Indian Air Force? Last she knew Zayd had gone to Pakistan illegally. He couldn't contact the embassy. So how had it become official?

Everything confused her, as a million bees buzzed around her head. Tyagi's soft monologue, on Rohit's badge being found by a Pakistani journalist, condolences repeated once again, merged with Amma's muted sobs.

Sitting on the floor beside her feet, Shankar was crying openly.

Life drained out of her body, leaving her cold and numb. She had just enough energy to stare at the potted money-plant peeking from the doorway. The leaves were all shades of green, laughing and swaying with the breeze. Bees were never attracted to a money-plant Ashima could see no bees around the money plant, then how was she able to hear them?

"Mamma, *dadi* crying, ish she hurthin?" Rishabh's voice entered her consciousness.

When did he come home from school? He was perched on her lap looking worried for his grandmother, unconcerned that he would never see and know his father. From four years of habit, she smiled at him and ruffled his hair, reassuring him. Why should he be concerned? She was glad he had been spared the ordeal of loving someone, then losing them. Rishabh still watched Amma but was less worried since Ashima was dry-eyed. Tears would not do, for she had to be strong for everyone. What difference would the tears make, now that he was gone? There were enough shed in the last four years.

Wing Commander Tyagi handed Rohit's metal badge, which was a little black on the edges with a tiny little dent on one corner. He was saying something about a journalist who found it in one of the villages along the LOC. The meaningless words courage, bravery, and honor, again fell into her ears.

"Mrs. Joshi, do not hesitate to call in case you need any help."

"Thank you." Ashima stood up clutching Rishabh's hand. "Shankar, the money plant has not been watered for days. Just put some water today."

Her mother stepped towards her. "Aashi...?" she whispered.

Ashima took a deep breath, nodded at her mother, then turned to the other grieving mother. "It's okay, don't worry Amma, we'll manage. Nothing has changed. I'm here." She patted her hand, lifted Rishabh in her arms and left the room.

"She's in shock..." someone said.

She wasn't in shock, she was angry. She picked up the phone and dialed a mobile number she knew by heart. He picked up in one ring.

"Zayd, I want to speak to you."

***

Hugging her knees, she was sitting on the steps of the gazebo that evening when Zayd entered the guest house. Shankar met him in the parking lot. It had been two days since Wg. Cdr. Tyagi had broken the news he had planted with the help of his infamous friends.

The last rites for Flight Lieutenant Joshi were completed the day before. She hadn't shed a single tear and had barely eaten, as he was informed by a despondent Shankar.

Watching the way she sat slumped on the steps, Zayd swallowed a lump and berated himself for bringing this on her. He wanted to take her into his arms and make the pain go away. He had never envisioned this scenario when he had decided to go to Pakistan. The news would be painful, he knew, but the torture in Ashima's bearing tore at his heart bit by bit.

If she sensed him approaching, she didn't show a sign and sat motionless in the same position, facing the green expanse of the valley. He stepped forward and sat one step below her.

She glanced at him, then again rested her chin on her arms. He spotted the Indian Air Force badge in her hand. They sat there in silence, watching the butterflies play hide and seek. The breeze, as usual, ruffled everything, from the tree-leaves to their hair.

"Why did you do this, Zayd?" Her voice drifted towards him, hoarse and dry. "Why? I never thought you would take revenge on me."

"Don't Aashi! How can you be so blind where I'm concerned?"

"Tell me everything about that place, that village… what did that villager say, what did they see?"

"What do you mean?" He had never thought she would piece everything together so fast.

"Don't take me for an imbecile. I know this is your doing. You spoke to my mother. I know it. Your father had come here. You went to Pakistan. Somehow you handed the photographs and the badge to someone there and they got back to us."

Zayd remained silent.

"Tell me everything about that place, Zayd. Please."

"It'll be of no use. Why do you want to know? Why do you want to torture yourself?"

"I owe that to him Zayd. You have loved and lost someone, and I think you will understand."

He sighed. "His parachute wasn't open when the villagers saw him. It must have malfunctioned or he must have been severely injured and couldn't open it. He fell down the hilly terrain. You know how it is. They said he died on the spot, that it wasn't painful."

"How do you know? How do they know? Why didn't they return… … him?" Her breath hitched.

He knew she couldn't bring herself to utter the word 'body' for Rohit. He took her cold hand between his and caressed it, trying to provide some support, trying to ease the pain in her eyes. "They didn't have any communication mechanism and waited for the army to take some action. But no one came for two days, so they cremated him." He made it sound honorable, hiding the fact that it was done using some wood and kerosene.

"And the ashes? What did they do with the ashes?" A tear sneaked out.

"They were extremely poor people with nothing to look forward to. They didn't tell me and I didn't ask. There is no point torturing yourself—"

"And the badge? How did you get the badge?" She glanced at him when he didn't speak and pulled her hand away.

"I didn't get it. It was with the head of the village. I guess the authorities must have taken it from them after the journalist wrote to them."

"Was he your friend? That Pakistani journalist?"

"No. The information was passed through unknown channels."

She fell silent gazing faraway.

"He must have been in so much pain…" she whispered after a long time, fingering the badge. "… must have been so lonely… in a strange land… amongst strange people, must have suffered so much in those last hours. He must have thought about me… us… when his plane was shot…"

It was not a statement or a question. She was grieving for Rohit and maybe it was for the best, and it was her way of accepting the situation. He couldn't tell her that most of his bones had broken due to the fall.

"Would he have thought that he would never see us again? And now he will never know his son. Never know that he exists. His flesh and blood…" A sob escaped her. The next instant she hid her face in the crook of her arm and shook with barely audible sobs that tore at his heart and bought tears to his own eyes. He moved near her and hugged her.

Zayd was relieved that the dam of grief that she had held inside for years together had broken finally. The doctors and elders were getting worried about her mechanical handling of chores since the time she had heard the news.

"He had named his plane *Jugnu*. Said it was like a firefly in the sky. He would be so emotional… reverential about his flying, for his plane. And that made me so jealous that he began calling me *Jugnu* too. He used to tease me that he loved both equally—the plane and me. I retaliated by saying I loved *Jugnu* too. By and by we ended up calling each other by the same name." She chuckled, her voice hoarse with clogged tears.

She hiccupped and sat straight. Wiping her tears on her shawl, she pushed his arm and shifted away from him.

Zayd didn't know whether the temperature had dropped or she was freezing him away.

"Why did you do this Zayd? Why did you take away our only hope to live? I would have lived my entire life in the prospect that one day he would come and we'll be happy. One day he would meet Rishabh, would see the wonder we had created together."

"It would have been a long and lonely life Aashi."

"I don't care. How could you?" She caught hold of his jacket and shook him. "Why did you do this to me… to us… why? Just because I refused to sleep with you? Refused to f—, oh God, oh God…" She left him and began crying again, hiding her face in her hands.

His hands, about to pull her back in his arms, halted mid-way at her voice. Her knife-like words plunged into his heart. Nothing would heal the wounds that she had inflicted on him.

"You know when we were young, kids used to say that we should never trust people with light eyes. They always turn out to be backstabbers," she said, twisting the knife a little more.

He sat there frozen with pain, unable to think or move. People had a bad opinion about him, but this topped everything. He had expected this, but nothing had prepared him for the agony caused by her words.

Wiping the last of her tears, Ashima turned towards him. "Why are you still here? I don't want you in my house. I request you to leave immediately. I don't want to see your face. Ever." She threw the scathing words at him, inflicting lifelong wounds, and turned from him, still clutching the badge to her chest.

He swallowed the unshed tears clogging the back of his eyes and left.

***

Through the hazy curtain of her tears, Ashima watched him go out of her life. She saw the vehicle driving away, but she was past caring. He had made her a widow and Rishabh an orphan and could never have a place in her heart. The cold in her heart that had thawed in the past few months began spreading its tentacles once again.

Ashima moved when she saw Pooja holding Rishabh in her arms at the threshold of the living room. Her legs protested as she put her weight on them. She moved like an old woman with only the weight of responsibilities on her shoulders and a bleak horizon stretching ahead of her.

Ashima halted on her way to the kitchen for dinner when she saw Amma motionless, doubled up in the wheelchair, clutching her left arm.

"Amma!" she gasped and shouted, "Shankar, Radha..." then ran to Amma's side.

Instructing Pooja to call the doctor, she supported Amma and rubbed her arm. Later both Shankar and she were able to settle her on the bed, but Amma kept gasping for breath and complaining about chest pain.

It was after long, agonizing hours that Amma slept, though her breathing was still erratic. Pooja was beside herself with worry and couldn't stop crying. After much cajoling from Ashima, she ate one roti and cried herself to sleep.

By morning, Amma lost the battle between life and death. Her will to live was hinged on the hope that her son would return one day. That hope was gone, taking Amma along with it.

***

TWENTY-SIX

As their grief of losing Rohit and Amma found closure, everyone settled into a routine. The house felt haunted once Pooja and Rishabh went to college and school. Ashima decided to close the guest house. Rohit's pension was good enough for their monthly expenses. Besides, there were no search missions to fund. The house was huge, so she thought to convert the back rooms into one single apartment and rent it.

Kanyal's land had been sold off. Who bought it she didn't know. He shifted his base to Chandigarh and visited Kasauli occasionally.

Later on they came to know that someone was building a bungalow for the new owner, a lady. Shankar brought the news that some royal lady had bought it and was planning to make it her summer retreat.

Contrary to Ashima's expectations, they built a small house with no more than three rooms and an outhouse near the entrance. The rest of the grounds were converted into a terrace garden in the front and a kids' playground at the back. The construction went on at a break neck speed and in no time, the neat house was finished.

The owners never came though. A caretaker moved in with his family, but they did not interact much with anyone in the town.

Once, Pooja mentioned Zayd, but one look at Ashima's face, and the discussion did not go any further. Rishabh forgot him, by and by. Shankar sometimes mentioned him with a wistful note in his voice. After Ashima, he missed him the most.

Yes, she missed him.

And yet, she couldn't blame anyone. She was the one who had driven him away. Angry and helpless in the hands of destiny, she had taken out her anger on him. In her grief, she had lashed out at him. Viciously. And he never called again. Why would he? Any self-respecting individual would never come back after the way she had insulted him.

Ashima couldn't help herself, and kept tabs on him through the news over the internet. There wasn't much, reclusive as he was. But she knew that he had made Delhi as his base. His book, the one he wrote in the summers, had become an instant hit. Rumors were that this one would be picked up to be adapted into a movie.

Then one day she saw his photo with a girl, clicked as they were coming out of a posh building hand-in-hand. The picture was hazy, like they were trying to avoid the camera, but it was him. She could recognize him anywhere, anytime. That day she stopped browsing the internet and reading his books. She packed them in polybags and stowed them in the store.

When did she fall for him? Perhaps when he had planned the picnic or when he had arranged the tickets for the music fest. Ashima cried herself to sleep for a few days after seeing the photograph. Then those tears also dried off, as the others had, and were replaced by a dull, constant ache all around her heart, which refused to leave her. She was unable to sleep and had lost her appetite.

She had once again lost her love. Yes, she was in love with him. A corner of her heart had twisted in agony when she had seen him drive away. But unlike Rohit, at least she knew he was alive and doing well. Maybe someday, years later, she would go and meet him and laugh over their August… what should she call it? Romance? Fling? She didn't know. Every word seemed too shallow for the depth of emotions she felt for him.

A month later, a package from Akshat came as a harsh surprise. Judging from the size, it seemed there were books inside it. She sat with the package, not finding the courage to open it. When Pooja asked about the package a second time, she tore open one side and peeked inside. They were indeed books… written by Z. Abbas. She slid them back into the envelope and tossed them on the upper slab of the store room.

***

Six months later

Someone rang the bell mid-afternoon when Ashima was about to sit with Rishabh for his homework. Cursing under her breath, she opened the door to find a grim Akshat towering over her.

"I want to talk to you," he growled.

Ushering him inside the living room, she asked him if he wanted some refreshments.

"Do you think this is a social visit?" he snarled.

Ashima looked at him glaring at her, and frowned.

"I want to understand how could you treat him the way you did." He began pacing the room. "After what he had done for you… the risk he had taken… all on his own."

His presence reminded her of the loss once again, and the familiar ache returned. "What do you want me to do?" she whispered.

"You are asking this… even after reading the books I had sent you? Didn't his anguish and pain touch you at all? How could you be so hard hearted? I expected at least a call."

"Books, what books?" She blinked.

"Didn't you get the books? I had couriered them myself?"

A memory clicked in place and she remembered Shankar handing her a parcel, which she had thrown along with his other books in the store. She could feel Akshat's keen eyes watching her every facial tick.

"You never read them! Oh, God." He threw his hands in the air and began pacing the length of the room. "Has he ever meant anything to you, Ashima? Do you even know he had to go to the prison again for one year?"

"Prison? Again? But why?"

"Because of you."

Confused and worried, she stared at him.

"He missed his periodic attendance at the police station when he had gone you-know-where, so his parole was cancelled. Do you know he suffers from PTSD? Do you even know the horrors he had faced in the prison? Thankfully we have been able to get him out on parole again, and only one year of the sentence is left."

He paused for a second, rubbed his face and began pacing again. "He was getting better here. Was able to sleep better without those persistent nightmares. He had told me. But he is back to the same condition."

Ashima looked down unable to bear.

"I had thought that… I had hoped… but all my intuition, with respect to your feelings for him, has gone haywire, Ashima. You didn't even open his books? Even when you are the only one with whom he has bared his soul, ever."

"I'd never asked him to do anything for me," she whispered.

"Yet he did. And he did it because he loves you to distraction. He cared and was afraid for you. He didn't want you to waste your life like his mother did for his father." He sighed and lowered his voice. "Anyway… only two copies of that poetry book exist. He wanted to keep it private, just between you and him. But when you didn't respond I read a couple last week and couldn't stop myself… He doesn't know that I have read them or that I'm here." He continued to speak as she opened her mouth. "And I think, it's your turn to reciprocate. And don't tell me you don't love him. Never thought your archaic morals, prejudices and ego will be more important than honest emotions and him."

He stormed out of the room, leaving her alone—conflicted and confused.

***

Ashima ignored Shankar's beaming, questioning eyes when he saw Akshat driving away, and ran to the store room, searching frantically for the packet. She couldn't find it anywhere. She couldn't recall the shelf she had thrown it on. The boxes were thrown aside, the bags and the rags strewn all over and there it was—the yellow envelope with Akshat Mehra's name as the sender. She grabbed it and ran to her room.

Rishabh had come back from school and had changed his clothes. Her mind on the packet on the side table, she asked about the school day. Luckily he was not in a chatty mood and declared he would eat lunch on his own. She silently thanked his new independent streak, and gave him a peck on the cheek. Rishabh ran to the kitchen, calling out for Shankar.

Ashima opened the packet and found the books. One was the thriller he had been writing when he was here and the other was a thin poetry book. With trembling hands, she turned the cover, and tears welled in her eyes. It was the dedication page, which read…

For Ashima

For Ever

The book contained poems, along with pencil sketches, about the conversations they had had last year—the night on the bench, the day at the church, the picnic and the concert, the first night they had spent in each other's arms, and even one for the day when she had been so cruel to him. And in the last poem, he had bared his heart to her, his loneliness at being away from her. Tears ran down her cheeks as she read each one of them.

She opened the second one, the novel, and smiled. Even this was dedicated to her, but not by her name. He had dedicated it to 'The Barefoot Ghost Hunter'.

She laughed silently. What should she do? Was Akshat right? Was her ego holding her back from contacting him? Was Zayd waiting for her? Did he still want her? Then who was that girl in the photo? Maybe just a friend, or an acquaintance.

She finished the novel sitting up till the wee hours of the night and then read the poems again. She cried again. They made her feel guilty all the more. She had hurt him a lot. He had hidden the rejection and pain behind that stoic façade, but she had noticed that momentary flicker of his eyes when they had veiled the pain. Maybe he waited for her to make the next move. Obviously, since she had asked him not to show his face again.

She had to see him!

The wish germinated fast urging her to take action immediately. Involuntarily she sat up on the bed. The yellow envelope on the side table slid down and something fell out—a card. She picked it up and the envelope. It was Akshat's visiting card. Now that the decision had been made, she couldn't wait for the morning. She picked up the phone and dialed Akshat's number.

***

TWENTY-SEVEN

The cottage was at a walking distance from where the bus had dropped Ashima in Solan, around 40 kilometers from Kasauli. It was a little unnerving to find him living so near. Akshat's directions were so accurate that the road and the mud path seemed incredibly familiar.

It was a steep climb and Ashima was a little winded by the time she reached the small clearing. The pine trees gave way to a small green patch surrounding the small single storey cottage with a sloppy red-tiled roof, as was the norms in the hills. The wind was a bit strong, indicating that it might rain in a few hours.

She raised her hand to knock on the iron-mesh front door, but the door swung open quietly the moment her hand came in contact with it. She pushed it all the way.

No one could be seen in the spartan room as she entered and looked around.

The term cottage was a mockery. It was a shabby studio apartment, with a single wooden bed with a thin mattress on the right and a slab for the kitchen on the left.

Across the room, there was another door that opened to a wooden deck outside. She could see Zayd perched on an easy chair, with his laptop on his knees. Unshed tears threatened to make their appearance the moment she saw him. Their last meeting replayed like a broken record, reminding her of her insensitive tirade and his silent anguish.

The chair was placed at an angle that allowed her to see his profile without him noticing her. But he did.

His fingers froze on the keyboard.

She quickly blinked back her tears and had swallowed them down by the time he turned and laid eyes on her. She couldn't help but watch him hungrily, taking in the jeans and the leather jacket, and… those eyes. He was indeed looking thin with the black shadows back on his face, worse than the first time she had met him.

His eyes latched on to her face, scanning and scrutinizing each and every feature. It felt so achingly familiar. Then, to her utter surprise, he shook his head and continued with his work. She frowned.

What the heck?

She also decided to play the game and instead looked around the room that had been his home for the past few months. There was a mini fridge, but it was empty. The ice-box, though, did have an open pack of Corona. A few had been consumed. There were a couple of packets of Maggi noodles and some choco-chip biscuits too. How did he manage without proper food?

Something crashed in the back yard. Ashima spun around to find Zayd standing with his notebook lying on the floor. It seemed that she had spoken her thoughts aloud and startled him.

"Oh my… did you break it?"

Zayd stood rooted to the spot, least bothered about his laptop lying on the floor, apparently unharmed.

Relaxing, she turned towards him with a slight—as she had practiced it—casual smile on her face. "Hi… there."

"Aashi?" His voice a hoarse whisper as if he hadn't spoken for days, and her name worded as a question as if he was having trouble believing his eyes.

"What? Have you forgotten me? So soon?" She chuckled trying to lighten the emotional atmosphere—emotional, at least for her—for she didn't want to cry. She was done crying, so she swallowed the lump in her throat and took a step towards him.

"Zayd…?"

"I thought my imagination had conjured you. You have been haunting me day and night," he said without any emotion.

She chuckled, a phony short laugh. "You have always had an outlandish imagination. I hope your laptop is not damaged."

"You've lost weight."

She heard a hint of the old concern in his tone. She smiled, masking the tight-fisted ache in her heart. "Is that the only thing you can say after such a long time?"

"I'm scared to say anything."

Her breath hitched at his words and the way he uttered them—cautiously. She desperately wanted to erase that lost look from his face. She stepped on the patio, and took the last step towards him.

"How do you sense my presence every time?" she asked the question that had been lurking in her mind for a long time.

"You tell me." His voice reached her in a hushed whisper traveling on the wings of the breeze. Everything faded into oblivion except his eyes that had turned dark green. "Your eyes change colors." She knew she was stalling.

He still stood at the same spot, waiting.

"I'm sorry," she finally spoke, looking into his bottomless, shimmering eyes, finding it surprisingly easy to say the words, to apologize. She swallowed. "I have come to apologize. I've hurt you a lot. I hope you'll forgive me… one day."

She didn't know what else to do or say when he showed no reaction. A moment later he pushed his hands in his pockets. His lips tightened a bit. She hadn't expected much, but she had never imagined this kind of an uninterested response. The photograph of that girl with him floated in front of her eyes.

That's it. It was over. She had killed anything he felt for her. Akshat was wrong. Zayd wasn't waiting here for her. It was better to remove herself from the scene before she embarrassed herself by breaking down in front of him.

She stepped back. "Okay, I think I'd better be on my way. Rishabh—"

"That's it?"

The harsh, incredulous tone stopped her in her tracks.

"You have taken the pain to come here just to apologize?" His teeth gritted as he uttered the words.

"I… um… I…"

"You left Rishabh and Pooja all alone and took a two hours' bus ride to say just those few sentences?" Now his lips curled into a vicious sneer.

"What do—?"

"You could have called me and appeased your conscience, as far as I'm concerned."

In a flash, Ashima understood the contradiction between his harsh words and the moist anguish in his eyes. She understood the shallowness of her apology. Their relationship was past mere words. He needed more from her.

"You have—"

She closed the distance between them in two quick strides, clutched the lapels of his jacket and kissed him, stopping his tirade. "I love you, Zayd," she said against his lips, putting her hands around his neck and pressing her body against his unresponsive one. "Zayd, I'm sorr—"

The next second, with a muffled groan, he crushed her to him. "Thank God, Aashi… Oh thank God…"

She forgot everything. A traitorous tear ran down her cheek. He murmured something about loving her to distraction. She burrowed her face in his chest and broke down. Tears flowed shamelessly, untamed and unhindered. With each sob, he tightened his embrace around her, assuring her that everything was okay.

"Please Aashi, don't." Zayd hugged her, and caressed her hair. "Don't." He rubbed her back and stroked her hair, murmuring soothing words.

"Aashi?"

A hiccup shook her, and she couldn't stop.

"Aashi, enough. There's no need to cry so much now that we are together." He tried to lift up her chin.

But she was still sobbing and sniveling.

"Come, I'll show you the gardens." He tried to distract her and turned towards the steps. But he couldn't. He touched her wet cheek, then caressed the mole. His thumb moved over her lips.

She gripped his wrist and closed her eyes and mumbled. "I don't want to see the bloody gardens." Clutching his jacket she lay her face on his chest again, and cried some more.

"Are you wiping snot on my shirt?"

She sputtered. "It would serve you right, for writing poems for me, but going out with that girl."

"Which girl? Aah… so you saw that. Normally I'd asked the PR staff to take off all my photographs, but I decided to leave that one. That was before I'd even met you. I hoped you would see it, get jealous, and call me."

"Me, jealous? Never."

"Liar." He lifted her chin and placed his lips on hers.

She sighed. Her hands sneaked up his shoulder and her fingers threaded through his hair to pull him to her.

Zayd had pictured this scene so many times in the past months, but reality was infinitely better than his fantasies. He kissed her temple, unable to believe she was there with him. His lips devoured hers and his hands caressed her familiar curves. She had lost weight, lots of it, and he could span her waist with his hands.

She caressed his shoulder and neck and cupped his face. "I still can't believe that I'm looking at you. I had lost all hope that I'll ever meet you again, given that I had driven you away." Tears fell from her eyes again.

He flicked at them and kissed her temple, her eyes, her nose and finally her mouth, showing his desperations, baring his soul.

She chuckled and spoke against his lips. "I didn't even know how to get you back."

He grinned and planted another kiss.

"Akshat said I'm heartless and have an ego."

"You met him?" He raised his head.

"Hmm… he came to Kasauli and gave me a long lecture."

"He's nuts, but don't tell him that."

She laughed. "He is a gem of a friend. The poems are beautiful Zayd. When did you write them?"

"I don't want to talk about the poems. You have not been eating properly."

"Neither have you. Now that you are with me, we can take care of each other." She went on her toes and hugged him, and felt him shudder. She couldn't get enough of him. He sighed and pulled her close to him, so close that she was standing on his toes. They stood there unmoving, taking strength from each other and acknowledging the deep bond between them. Spent after the emotional outburst, he rested his head on hers.

"I love—"

She put her finger on his lips. "Sh… sh… sh, don't say anything." She traced his jawline with her lips. "Just love me Zayd… and let me show you how much I love you…"

Another tear escaped her eye, and he caught it on his finger. Lifting her in his arms, he moved towards the bed.

***

In the aftermath of a hurried, desperate union, they lay on the bed sated and content. After a few minutes of silence, Ashima sighed and turned on her stomach to find him watching her. "I thought you'd gone to sleep."

Zayd chuckled. "I'll be a first class fool to go off to sleep on such a beautiful day of my life and, not to mention, inflict insult to your charms." He made round circles on her waist with his thumb.

"Why did you take such a risk? What would have I done if something had happened to you?"

"You wouldn't have known. And no one would have been affected."

"You are wrong. I would have known. And your father? He loves you. I saw it in his eyes the other day. He was worried about you."

He smirked.

"Zayd, from a child's perspective whatever he has done may seem wrong to you, but I think he deserves a chance. Didn't he take care of Kanyal when he threatened you?"

"I'll think about it. Don't spoil this day. Come and show me again. Your score is quite low as far as our love is concerned."

She smiled, leaned on her elbows and kissed him again. He responded with the same ardor as he had the first time, and tried to pull her on top, but she put her hand on his chest.

"I have to go, Zayd. Can't leave Rishabh and Pooja alone for the night."

"I know, but just a few more minutes. I'll come with you." One hand caressed her cheek and the other caressed the smooth skin at the small of her back. "I still have not explored everything about you."

She sighed. "The poems were… are wonderful."

"Aah… the poems! I'm gonna frame them and put them in front of me everywhere. And I will make them my screensaver too." He nuzzled her neck.

She laughed, then pushed him away. "I have to go now."

He released her, not saying anything. He put his hands behind his head and just lay there watching her dress, making her fumble. She leaned and put a hand on his eyes. "Don't watch."

"I like watching you. And anyway the sun is setting, so I can't see much."

"Just close your eyes, okay?"

He didn't say anything, but smiled. After a couple of minutes, the rustling of clothes stopped and she touched his cheek. He opened his eyes.

"I'm sorry, for everything, Zayd," she whispered.

"I won't mind even if you kill me."

She stood, and smiled down at him. "Is this a thriller writer or a poet speaking? And why will I kill you? Do I look like a killer?"

"It's the poet. In our poetic world, anyone can kill. There are various ways of killing. You can kill me by chucking me out of your house, or not meeting me again, or simply by your eyes when you turn all cold towards me, with that one look."

"Will you be able to forgive me anytime soon?" she muttered.

Overwhelmed, he hugged her close, feeling complete after many years. Autumn had ended. He could smell the spring in the horizon…

***

EPILOGUE

Two weeks later…

"**Aashi**, how could you agree to his proposal?"

"Mamma, you wanted me to marry again and live my life."Ashima smiled, relishing her mother's discomfort.

They were sitting in her room and she was showing her the gifts from Zayd's *Naanijaan* that she had given Ashima on the eve of their engagement the day before. They had had a quiet ceremony with only immediate family members present, in his part of the property that was adjacent to hers. Yes, the Kanyal plot was bought by his maternal grandmother, who gifted it to Zayd.

"Yes, but not with a Muslim and that too a criminal…"

"You never thought that when you gave him all the information—behind my back—about Rohit and the search missions. What if he was caught? Did you ever think about that?"

"I didn't know that he would go there, across the border I mean. He tricked me too. Anyway isn't his father a hotshot? And Zayd should have known if he was in any danger."

"Well, he knew and he still took the risk. And you were a part of that heist. If he had been caught, his father would have been called a traitor or, worse, a terrorist. Both their lives would have been ruined."

"Okay, I get that. But shouldn't you wait to marry? He is still on parole!"

"Mamma please, I have decided. And you know when I decide, no one can budge me from my decision."

For once Ashima was thankful to Rishabh who chose to interrupt as Mamma opened her mouth to voice some other lame opinion to oppose her marriage to Zayd.

"Granny… look…" Rishabh came running with a big, colorful plastic box.

"What is this, Rishu, and who gave it to you?" It was an expensive kids' toy laptop, which could be used to play various musical tones and simple video games.

"Big man and Aayd, my friend," he said referring to Zayd and his father. His speech was improving, but he could still not pronounce 'z'. He punched the buttons randomly, making the toy play the rhymes and various other sounds.

"So you remember him now. Did you say thank you?"

"Yes… yes… yes…" He danced with the music.

She looked at the books, the toy, her son dancing with happiness and she knew it was the right decision.

***

Ashima stood before the mirror in her bathrobe. She was running terribly late. Zayd had been very patient about everything, but she had never left Rishabh with a stranger. She had to get used to it. Her boy was growing up. Moreover Zayd and her relationship demanded that she made time for them—exclusive, uninterrupted time.

The resort was very prestigious and the baby-sitter was charming. It didn't take long for Rishabh to switch loyalty to the girl. Ashima watched him say good night to her with a pang. So enamored he was with the nineteen year old that he didn't even look at her when she left his bedroom. How silly of her to get jealous!

Brushing away the idiotic thoughts, she concentrated on Zayd's gifts. He wanted her to wear his choice of clothing on their first official and private evening… oops 'date'. He had made it a point to correct her throughout the flight from Delhi.

She unwrapped the package and gasped. Nestled inside the tissue was an amethyst-colored, georgette-chiffon dress. With great care, Ashima lifted the delicate garment. It was a halter neck dress with the tight bodice sewn with white seed-pearl and sequins and the skirt falling in a straight line one-inch above her knees. The next box made her gasp. In the box was a pair of silver stilettos. She hadn't walked in high heels in ages. God forbid, if she fell down taking him along with her, how would he react? She giggled at the picture, and took off her bathrobe. There was no time to spare.

Zayd stood at the far end of the villa's balcony overlooking the swimming pool, waiting for her. Someone was taking energetic laps. It would be fun to teach Rishabh to swim.

They had an early dinner, and now a chilled bottle of champagne waited in the silver ice-bucket along with some hors d'oeuvres for their date. He glanced at the setting. The playlist with slow, sensuous music was ready on his laptop. His plan was to dance, finish the champagne and then think of something else.

He had been starved for her exclusive company from the day he had announced to his family that he wanted to marry her until yesterday at the airport. Always surrounded by their extended family, they never had decent courtship time.

Finally away from the crowd, they were in Maldives on their honeymoon, sponsored by his father. Abbu's wedding gift to them. He didn't know what magic Ashima had woven over his father. Abbu hung on to every word she uttered. He had even begun to agree with Zayd sometimes, not mentioning politics or his party even once.

The man finished swimming and left the pool.

The moon cast silver shadows on the now still, shimmering water and the palm trees. The leaves glistened making various patterns as they swung with the breeze. Her absence intensified by the crude humming of crickets and the whistling of the air, but suddenly everything became musical. He turned around and found her standing at the doorway, looking radiant and sexy. The layered haircut made her hair curl around her face, enhancing her beauty. He was so in love with her. It seemed surreal that she would always be by his side now—for all his life.

"I just spoke to Pooja. She is enjoying the Delhi winters with *naanijaan*," she said, walking toward him.

"That's great. Rishabh settled?"

"Yes… I think he is in love with his babysitter."

He chuckled. "That's good, now I'll have the complete attention of his mother."

"Hmm… as if…" She pouted. "Well, at least someone's happy."

"Why? Aren't you?"

"I feel a wee bit jealous."

He laughed and extended his hand. She stepped forward and walked into his arms.

"You look divine." He buried his face in her hair and inhaled her scent.

"Thanks for the dress. You have marvelous taste." Standing on her toes, she lifted her head to thank him.

It was supposed to be just a peck, as a thank you for the dress, but he crushed her to him, reluctant to leave her. He just couldn't stay apart when he found her alone, given that the opportunity had become rarer this past one week since they got married.

The marriage was a simple affair in the court followed by an extravagant dinner thrown by his Abbu, inviting the who's who of the country. But it was his large family who kept her engaged from morning till the wee hours of the night. They wanted to meet the idiot who married the black sheep of the family. His *naanijaan* had prepared her to expect something like that and Ashima had taken everything with a pinch of good humor, praising Zayd whenever she could.

It was hilarious as well as poignant to see her batting for him. Watching her get frustrated when she couldn't convince them. Remembering all that, he gave her another tender kiss, then loosened the hold.

"First things first! I have a gift for you."

"Another one? Why? You have already given me so many things!"

"It's not from me." He handed her a box that was lying on the table. It was a double strand of diamonds studded in gold, with matching earrings.

She gasped. "Zayd, from where did you get that? They must be so expensive."

"They belonged to Ammi, she would have given them to you." He turned her around and fastened the necklace. "She would have been so happy."

They looked up at the stars, twinkling like fireflies.

Her eyes watered. "Maybe she is."

"I think he would be happy too," Zayd said and mentally sent a solemn promise to Rohit that he'd look after his *Jugnu* all their life.

"Yes," she whispered as a lone tear sneaked from her eye.

*** **END** ***

OTHER BOOKS BY RUCHI SINGH

Bewitched

The eternal dance of attraction, lust and love has been going on since time immemorial.

The divine apsara Menaka descends to Earth at Indra's behest to distract the sage Vishwamitra from the penance that would bring him unimaginable powers. Menaka succeeds in bewitching Vishwamitra, but her actions are destined to have dire consequences for both.

Eons later, their story is set to repeat itself.

Poorva has always played by society's rules and ideas of decorum. But what happens when her own loved ones betray her in the worst way imaginable? Does she still have to remain bound by their rules?

Rudra plays with power and people like they are pieces on a chessboard. He has no qualms about indulging his desires, be it money or women, but is determined not to be bound by either.

What happens when these two diametrically opposite souls are brought together by fate?

In the game of power, lust, greed and betrayal, some win and some lose. But are there any winners or losers in the game of love?

Like Menaka and Vishwamitra, are Poorva and Rudra too destined to see their story end in tragedy? Or will the divine power prevail?

www.ingramcontent.com/pod-product-compliance
Lightning Source LLC
Chambersburg PA
CBHW061334160726
47995CB00001B/26